## Bolan knocked Aguire to the floor in a flying tackle

The Cuban spluttered beneath him, cursing, but his voice was drowned by heavy metal thunder as the windows shattered under a blast of automatic fire.

The door crashed open and two men surged across the threshold, submachine guns blazing. Bolan raised his pistol and squeezed off a 3-round burst that pinned one gunner to the wall and sent his comrade staggering for cover. The warrior hauled an Uzi clear of the duffel bag and moved forward to engage the rest of the attack force.

Firing the Uzi, Bolan unclipped a frag grenade from his web belt, pulled the pin and lobbed the orb overhand. Microseconds later detonation tore the night apart.

Aguire made his move without thought. Gathering his legs beneath him, he lunged for the duffel bag, intent on securing a weapon.

The Executioner intercepted him, resting the smoking muzzle of the machine pistol against the Cuban's chest.

"Don't even think about it, guy."

# MACK BOLAN®

## The Executioner®

# DON PENDLETON'S
# THE EXECUTIONER®
## FEATURING MACK BOLAN®
# BLOOD RUN

## A GOLD EAGLE BOOK FROM
# WORLDWIDE.

TORONTO • NEW YORK • LONDON • PARIS
AMSTERDAM • STOCKHOLM • HAMBURG
ATHENS • MILAN • TOKYO • SYDNEY

First edition January 1990

ISBN 0-373-61133-1

Special thanks and acknowledgment to
Mike Newton for his contribution to this work.

Without duty, life is soft and boneless.
It cannot hold itself together.

—Joseph Joubert

Duty is the sublimest word in our language.
You cannot do more. You should not wish to do less.

—Robert E. Lee

I've seen my duty, and I'm carrying it out
as best I can. Some people say the odds are
stacked against me. But I knew that from the start.

—Mack Bolan

To the men and women of the FBI's
Violent Criminal Apprehension Program—VICAP.
God keep.

# PROLOGUE

Ernesto Vos was never comfortable when he had to travel far from home. It wasn't simply parting from the luxuries he had accumulated at his fortress home in Bogotá that bothered him. A child of poverty, he could make do with simple pleasures if the need arose. As he examined his reflection in the windowpane, Vos silently admitted to himself that what he felt was fear.

It wouldn't do for any of Vos's soldiers to imagine their boss afraid. His reputation had been built on his sheer ferocity, a taste for blood and combat that had christened him "El Tigre" on the streets of Medellín, before he weeded out the competition in a string of dirty little wars to stand alone at the pinnacle of his profession. Fear was alien to Vos in those days, when a younger man had everything to gain and nothing in the world to lose. His life had seemed a minor thing to risk in the pursuit of gold and power. He had watched the other dealers, yearned to emulate their lifestyle with the flashy cars and women who could break your heart by simply entering a room. Vos knew that if he died in the attempt to seize that prize, it would be worth the effort. Nothing mattered short of victory.

But now the victory was his, and he had built an empire of his own. He had a harem at his beck and call, a troop of soldiers ready to annihilate his enemies on cue, if any could be found. He dined with politicians, judges, headline entertainers, making friends and contacts to perpetuate his empire. From the gutters, he had risen to achieve his every secret fantasy.

Times change. Perspectives change. The boy with nerves of tempered steel was now a man with everything to lose if he allowed himself one small mistake, a single careless step. His enemies were still alive and well, but they had changed their faces and their tactics over time. Instead of stalking him in alleys, they brandished warrants and injunctions, writs of search and seizure, fat subpoenas ordering him to appear for this or that investigation where he would be pilloried and made to look a fool.

The Yankees were such hypocrites at heart. Vos filled a need, provided services for which they paid him very handsomely indeed, and still they would insist on going through the motions of resistance, passing laws that only served to make his work more difficult—and therefore more expensive.

In the sanctuary of his fortress, Vos was frequently amused to hear the politicians calling for a wider, tougher war on drugs. How many of the soapbox preachers had themselves indulged in his cocaine from time to time? How many had accepted campaign contributions from his front men, channeled through the several civic groups and labor unions he controlled? How many took the time to notice that their children had been snorting drugs for years, supporting Vos's empire even as the politicians tried halfheartedly to bring him down?

He sometimes wondered what would happen if the traffic in cocaine was wiped out overnight. Could Wall Street function? Would the entertainment industry bog down without its daily flurries of imported snow? How many million-dollar athletes would begin to drag their heels in practice? Where would lawmen turn to supplement their meager pay?

It might be interesting, he thought, to interrupt the flow for several days and watch the righteous maggots squirm. A shortage would be good for business, boosting prices on the street, and it might also be instructive for his enemies. A squeeze play, as it were. He could deprive the fat cats of their payoffs, leaving them to deal with several million of his hungry customers. A week should do the trick, while Vos sat back and played his private games in Bogotá.

He smiled, the mirror image ghostly, lacking any trace of human warmth. It was a tantalizing thought, but he wasn't about to interrupt the stateside flow of powder on a whim. He understood the rules of play and knew that politicians were required to make these noises for the public, wooing votes from sheep who more than likely used his drugs themselves. If everyone who talked about the evils of cocaine would simply cease to buy it, Vos would have to find himself another line of work. But he wasn't concerned about that farfetched possibility.

He *was* concerned about arrest.

The periodic visits to America were risky, now that he'd been indicted on a list of federal charges longer than the U.S. Constitution. Safe at home, he could dismiss the charges as a mere charade, more window dressing in the phony war on crime. It would be different once he stepped onto American soil. He'd be subject to arrest and prosecution—he might even be convicted, if a witness could be found to testify against him.

They'd have a problem there, of course. His insulation from the daily traffic was superb, with buffer layers of middlemen assigned to handle every routine task from harvesting the coca leaves to peddling grams and kilos on the street. If there was killing to be done, Vos pushed a button, made a call, and someone else arranged the details. Only half a dozen people in the world could link his name with the narcotics trade and make it stick. In the event of his arrest on U.S. soil, they'd be rounded up and killed to break the chain of evidence.

Vos had designed the system himself, anticipating treachery, the urge of weaker men to save themselves when pressure was applied. He thought his safeguards would be adequate, but they hadn't been tested under fire. A measure of uncertainty remained, and so he felt himself at risk each time he left Colombia. At home he could control the law. Abroad...

The seaplane had been flying low, evading radar, and the sparkling water now looked close enough to touch. A string of shaggy islands broke the surface, short on beach and long on tangled undergrowth. The Keys had always been a smuggler's paradise, concealing pirates, rummies, covert agents of the CIA at war with Cuba. Vos regarded it as perfectly appropriate for him to carry out his business here. He was continuing a grand American tradition.

Still, the meeting was unorthodox to say the least. Aguire had been cryptic on the telephone, despite the scrambler, mentioning his contact with a customer who was prepared to purchase seven thousand kilos each and every month, year round. No name were mentioned, but a suitcase filled with earnest money had been handed to Aguire in Fort Lauderdale, a small down payment on the income they would earn from this account alone.

If Vos could cinch the deal.

The customer insisted on a face-to-face with his supplier. It was totally unorthodox, and Vos had nearly scrubbed the deal. But he was captivated by the thought of moving almost ninety thousand kilos yearly to a single buyer. Calculating on the standard wholesale rate, that came to something like two *billion* dollars in a single year.

A businessman was forced to weigh his risks against returns, and Vos had first suggested that the buyer come to Bogotá. They could discuss the deal in private, Vos could entertain his guest like royalty, and their mercenary friendship would be sealed. He was disturbed by the rejection of his offer, unimpressed by arguments that Mr. X was anxious to protect his image by avoiding any hint of impropriety. And yet, two billion dollars made allowances for certain eccentricities.

The meeting would be brief—an hour at the most—and he would be away before the FBI or DEA was aware of his presence in the Keys. When they inevitably heard the rumor, days or weeks from now, it would be one more victory for Vos against his enemies. He'd have shown them, once again, that writs and warrants weren't worth the paper they were printed on.

The seaplane circled once, and Vos could see Aguire on the beach below, two other men beside him, one more in the launch offshore. The trio on the beach was standing guard on the three-piece matching luggage. Vos allowed himself a smile, imagining the weight of so much currency, the things that it could buy.

The drugs weren't on board, of course. He never traveled with a shipment under any circumstances, knowing that a gram of powder in his pocket would eliminate the need for witnesses, destroy his years of careful preparation for defense in court. If he was caught with drugs, his life was over, finished.

It had been seven months since he'd seen Aguire, one of six who could connect him positively to narcotics traffic in North America. His territory was the Gulf, from Florida to Texas, and he'd grown wealthy in Ernesto's service, funneling the powder inland, dealing with distributors in bulk who passed their product on from half a dozen major staging areas to dealers in a block of twelve southeastern states. Aguire's counterparts were stationed in New York, Chicago, Southern California, San Francisco and Toronto, covering the major markets and their various subsidiaries.

They were all expendable.

The pilot made a perfect touchdown, and Vos's troops were on their feet before he stirred. He never traveled anywhere without security, and flying visits to the Keys meant four guns minimum. For this trip, he'd laid on five and slipped a pistol in the waistband of his tailored slacks for personal insurance.

Vos allowed his men to pick their places in the launch. It gave the boat stability, and they could shield him with their bodies if an ambush had been laid on shore. It was preposterous, of course, and yet...Vos didn't like the way that trees and undergrowth marched almost to the water's edge. The beach was nothing but a sandy sliver wedged between a mass of jungle and the sea.

More reason to complete his business swiftly and be gone. He'd observe the normal courtesies, express his honest pleasure at the prospect of a fat two-billion-dollar windfall, but he wouldn't linger where he was wanted by the law. It would be foolish, flirting with disaster.

Aguire's two companions had dressed casually, in keeping with the climate, but their craggy faces didn't fit the tourist image. Vos was mildly curious about their background and connections, but his mind was focused chiefly on their luggage and the bags of money that would come his way in future months.

The sand was firm beneath his feet. Vos shook Aguire's hand and waited while the introductions were completed. On his left was Michael Wix; his comrade, narrower of face and build, was Ansel Crane. They'd be pseudonyms, Vos realized, but what was in a name?

"Good trip?" Wix asked without a trace of interest.

"Uneventful." Crane was studying Vos's bodyguards, eyes shifting toward the seaplane, like a gambler calculating odds. "We have important business to discuss."

"No bullshit, huh? I like that. Problem is, there's been a little change of plans."

"What sort of change?"

Before Vos finished speaking, he was conscious of another sound intruding on his consciousness, approaching rapidly from somewhere out to sea. Without a backward glance, he recognized the sound of helicopter engines.

"Fact is, you're busted," Wix announced, as men in camouflage fatigue erupted from the jungle, automatic rifles covering Vos's men. "You have the right—"

He never had a chance to finish. One of the drug lord's soldiers broke in the direction of the launch, another opened fire on reflex, and the beach exploded with a clap of sudden thunder. Vos went down and hugged the sand, his first cold rush of fear supplanted by lethal rage against the traitor who had sold him out.

Aguire.

Someone tripped across his legs, went down, and stopped a bullet as he tried to rise. Vos felt the automatic pressed against his ribs, glanced up in time to see Aguire racing for the trees. He shifted, slipped one hand inside his ruined jacket—freezing as the muzzle of a weapon prodded him behind one ear.

"I wouldn't," Crane advised him.

It was over in another moment: three men dead, five others wounded and the seaplane grounded by machine-gun fire directed from the helicopter. Vos allowed himself to be disarmed and handcuffed, knowing it was useless—suicidal—to resist.

"Where were we?" Wix was smiling now. "Oh, yeah. You have the right to remain silent. Anything you say can—and will—be used against you in a court of law. You have the right to speak with an attorney. If you can't afford one, what the hell, we'll throw one in for nothing. Do you understand these rights that I've explained to you?"

Vos fixed his eyes upon Aguire, who was cringing in the shadow of the trees.

"I understand my options perfectly," he said. And smiled.

1

Mack Bolan made a drive-by on his target, circling once around the block before he found a spot to park his car downrange. The vehicle was a Mercedes, rented with the neighborhood in mind, and Bolan didn't think that any night owls on the block would call for Denver's finest if they chanced to look outside and see it standing at the curb.

If they should see the driver, though, all bets were off.

The Merc had been for show, but Bolan's garb was strictly functional. He wore an inexpensive overcoat to hide his blacksuit and the military harness with its guns, ammo magazines, grenades and Ka-bar fighting knife. An Uzi submachine gun was suspended from its shoulder strap beneath one arm. The coat concealed everything except a small telltale bulge. His face and hands were smeared with war paint, and the combination of his camo makeup with the overcoat gave Bolan the appearance of a flasher who'd gone too long without a bath.

The streetlights here were few and far between, providing islands of illumination that were easily avoided. Bolan recognized old money in the homes around him, and he knew old money would resist the civic urge to plow up streets and sidewalks, planting vapor lamps at intervals of twenty feet. Old money could install security devices that made streetlights obsolete, and Bolan kept that thought in mind as he struck off across a broad expanse of manicured lawn.

New money was his target for the night. Specifically the kind of money earned by peddling poison on the streets. His target was a stranger, but he knew the guy by reputation, from a summary of information in his files at Justice. Jaime

Santana was a modern success story for all the wrong reasons. A product of the 1980 Mariel boat-lift, he'd come to the United States complete with a criminal record of burglary, rape, narcotics trading and attempted murder. The attempt was documented through conviction, while a dozen more successful homicides had never been charged against him. After brief detention in a holding pen outside Atlanta, Santana had managed to persuade a judge that his offenses were "political," a patriot's campaign against the Communist regime of Cuba, and he was released to prey upon American society.

Narcotics was the game, but on a larger scale than Santana had ever dared to dream of in his native Cuba. Denver was his chosen base of operations. The competition had been fierce in larger cities such as New York, Chicago and Los Angeles, while markets flourished in the neighborhood of Boulder, Vail and Aspen. Santana dealt any kind of drugs available, but cocaine was his specialty. He kept it snowing all year long in Denver, treating customers to Cuba's version of a Rocky Mountain high.

While Bolan thought of Santana as a deserving target, he hadn't picked the mark himself. A call from Hal Brognola had been instrumental in delivering the Executioner to Denver. Justice had devoted eighteen months to planting someone in the Cuban's syndicate, an agent starting on the streets and moving upward through the ranks on sheer initiative, with an occasional assist from Washington. He'd been close to pay dirt when he disappeared, and nine days later, hikers found his body in the mountains south of town. It took forensic experts two more days to verify ID from dental charts, and they could only say the agent was a long time dying under skillful hands.

It was an action that demanded some response, and with the case in flames, the men of Justice had begun to search for alternate solutions to the problem posed by Jaime Santana. Brognola's call had set the wheels in motion. If it all worked out, their problem would be solved tonight. Forever.

Bolan stood in shadow, scanning Casa Santana. TV cameras had been tucked beneath the eaves to cover street and driveway. Bolan drifted to the side and shed his overcoat to scale a wooden fence that had clearly predated Santana's arrival. Older money valued privacy in Denver, but it rarely gave a second thought to physical security. The new arrival had refrained from startling his neighbors by erecting defensive walls, and Bolan meant to take advantage of the lapse.

He spent a moment perched on the fence to verify that there were no attack dogs in the yard, then dropped into a combat crouch. A porch light burned in back, but otherwise the yard was dark, as floodlights would have drawn unwelcome notice from the neighbors. Bolan held the Uzi ready as he moved around the house and found a vantage point beneath the corner-mounting camera that was set to scan the yard.

A sentry stood beside the pool, his back to Bolan, his gaze directed toward the starry night. A plume of cigarette smoke fluttered overhead and was disperseed by the prevailing mountain breeze. Secure from prying eyes, the lookout didn't try to hide the automatic shotgun tucked beneath his arm.

The guy would have to be taken care of before an entry to the house could be effected. Bolan watched the camera make its arc from left to right and back again, not quite a half circle. Stepping out just long enough to glance along the back of the house, he saw no other video equipment, nothing in the way of overt backup systems.

He timed the camera, calculating that he'd have thirteen seconds to eliminate the guard without an audience. It would require precision timing and a fair amount of luck, but it would be his only chance.

He left the Uzi on its sling and drew the sleek Beretta 93-R from its shoulder harness, thumbing back the hammer as he took his stance and aimed. The weapon's special silencer was Bolan's own design, maintaining point-blank accuracy up to thirty yards, or roughly twice the present range. With any luck at all . . .

He started counting down the numbers as the camera made its sweep. Downrange his target shifted, turning to present a profile, edging closer to the pool as if on cue.

Ten seconds now.

And five.

He stroked the trigger, riding out the recoil as the parabellum mangler drilled his target through the ear and punched him through an awkward pirouette. The gunner lost his footing, tumbled backward, splashing down before the TV camera motored back to scan the spot where he kept his fingers mentally crossed in hopes that anyone assigned to watch the monitors would miss the floating body.

The camera kept on tracking to the left and Bolan made his move, the numbers running as he sprinted thirty feet to reach the nearest door. He had a maximum of thirty seconds left before the camera doubled back and caught him on the doorstep, but he meant to be inside by then.

The door was locked.

He knelt and brought the lock picks into play, a sheen of perspiration adding luster to his camo war paint. Fifteen seconds. Ten, and he was thinking that a bullet might do cleaner work, when something clicked inside the mechanism and he was through, the door pressed shut behind him.

He moved through the darkened rooms until he reached a staircase, dim lights burning on the landing overhead. The climb was tense but uneventful, leading Bolan to a hallway where a single door stood open, spilling light across the deep shag carpet. Stepping closer, the Beretta in his hand, he risked a glance around the doorjamb.

Television monitors were mounted in the wall directly opposite, their views of front and back devoid of life. It scarcely mattered, since the guard on duty had his full attention focused on a *Penthouse* centerfold, turning it this way and that, as if rotation of the magazine could add some new dimension to the photograph. At seven feet, the soldier didn't even have to aim. His bullet drilled the sentry's skull from back to front.

He backtracked, climbed another flight of stairs to reach the master bedroom, pausing just outside the door to listen briefly. Breathless whispers told him Santana had company, but there was no time left to lose.

He kicked the door open and stepped across the threshold, crouched, the Beretta leading. Santana lay stretched out on the bed, a nude young woman straddling his hips and working overtime while pornographic fantasies unfolded on a large-screen television set nearby. The lovers missed his entrance, lost within themselves, and Bolan punched a bullet through the VCR to capture their attention. Uttering a world-class scream, the luscious lady sprang away from Santana, her hasty exit leaving him without a secret in the world.

The Cuban gaped at Bolan, making no attempt to cover himself with the rumpled sheets. His eyes were on the gun, and modesty meant nothing to him at the moment.

"Hey, man, this isn't necessary. We can talk about it."

"Wrong."

The first round snapped the dealer's two front teeth off at the gum line, drilling through to clip his spine. The second opened a keyhole in the Cuban's forehead as he toppled backward, leaking onto satin sheets.

Retreating, Bolan met two gunners on the stairs who were responding to the woman's scream. He let his Uzi do the talking, with a burst that blew them both away before they had a chance to reach their holstered weapons. Bolan stepped over their bodies and made his way outside. He took the time to stow his gear as lights began to wink on across the street, a sleeper's slow response to muffled gunfire.

Thirty minutes to the west, in Lakewood, Bolan locked himself inside a truck stop rest room to change clothes and wash off his war paint. In the parking lot, he found a pay phone, fed it coins and counted down four rings before a man's voice answered on the other end.

"Hello?"

He recognized the voice, but there were still procedures to observe.

"I need to speak with Leonard Justice."

"What's your number?"

Bolan read it off the dial and listened while it was repeated back for confirmation.

"Give me five, ten tops," the other voice instructed.

"That's affirmative."

Six minutes later he was waiting when the pay phone rang. Leo Turrin's voice seemed clear, though in truth he hadn't left his desk. The time lag had been used to route his call through a scrambler, thus securing the line.

"How goes it, guy?"

The warrior let himself relax a bit. "It goes. In fact it's gone. I'm finished here."

"Okay." There was an unaccustomed hesitancy in the other voice. "You going anywhere right now? I mean, have you got anything on-line?"

"I'd thought about some sleep."

"Well, you could do that on the plane, I guess."

"I guess. What's up?"

"We've got a situation here in Wonderland that has to be handled by someone who's discreet." Justice paused. "Actually it's a two-man job, and the security of both men has to be beyond reproach."

Bolan remained silent.

"Striker, is there a chance that your brother, Johnny, would be able to ride shotgun for you on this one? The departments involved are so full of leaks we can't take a chance on anyone else. This mission is priority one."

Mack Bolan closed his eyes and waited for the first instinctive rush of anger to subside. When Leo spoke again, his voice was cautious.

"I recall you've worked together several times."

"Reluctantly."

"We're on the spot with this one."

"Why should this be any different?"

"Right. Okay. But if you find it in your heart to make a call . . ."

"I can't make any promises," Bolan said at last. "I'll ask. That's all."

"That's plenty. Hey, I guess I ought to tell you where the meet's supposed to be."

The Executioner memorized the name and address of a Jacksonville motel, hung up without goodbyes and waited in the darkness while he put his thoughts in order. One more call to make, a question to be asked. He was dreading it because he knew the answer in advance.

The kid would never turn him down.

Even if it meant his life.

IT WAS AN HOUR EARLIER in San Diego, and "the kid"—known to his friends as Johnny Gray—was thinking that it might be time for bed. He made the rounds, examining the doors and windows, checking the security devices that had been installed to stack the odds against surprise attack, and made his way upstairs.

The house had been remodeled after Johnny acquired the property, a renovation process that had been completed over six months' time, with emphasis upon defensibility. Long-range communications gear has been installed, along with sweepers to detect the presence of a bug or wiretap. In the soundproof basement, weapons could be modified and tested on an indoor shooting range. Surveillance cameras and alarms secured the house against intruders, giving occupants a first-shot capability in the event of an assault.

The job had cost a bundle, over and above the basic price of house and land, but Johnny had covered the expenses from a war chest held in common with his brother. What the neighbors didn't know would never hurt them, and they had no idea that Johnny Gray had once been known as Johnny *Bolan.*

"Gray" was now his legal name, a consequence of family changes wrought by circumstance and brother Mack's unending war against the Mafia. Adopted by a sympathetic federal agent and his wife, the sole surviving relative of Mack Bolan, the Executioner, had been able to complete his education and enter military service without drawing any of the media—or syndicate—attention that his given name would doubtless have attracted. Decorated for his service in Grenada, Johnny had been proud to help his brother with several of his stateside missions during recent months, and he maintained the San Diego strongbase as a combination refuge, arsenal and clearing house for vital information, seeing less of his brother than he preferred, but following his struggle from a distance.

The telephone's insistent trilling quickened Johnny's pulse. Each line produced a different tone, eliminating any vestige of confusion as he reached for the receiver. One was "open" and reserved for daily business, fitted with an answering machine to screen the nuisance calls from telemarketing. Another was for business, with the number known to half a dozen clients and the members of the storefront law firm where he spent most weekdays in a suit and tie. The third line, strictly private, routed calls through several cutouts prior to making the connections at his home, and only one man living had the number.

His brother, Mack.

He lifted the receiver on the second ring. "How are you?"

"Hanging in. You clean?"

He punched a button and the sweeper flashed its green light for the go-ahead.

"Affirmative."

"I had a talk with Justice."

"Oh?"

"He invited me to Jacksonville to talk about a job."

"Okay."

"A two-man job."

The young man's pulse immediately quickened, and he swallowed hard to clear his throat before he answered.

"What's the deal?"

"I haven't got a clue. It's strictly face-to-face."

"You think it's straight."

"I trust the source," Bolan replied. "I'm just not sure I like the terms."

"Who's riding shotgun?"

"That's the thing. It's up to me."

"I'll pack a bag."

"It's not supposed to work this way."

Johnny read his brother's concern and frowned. "If things worked out the way they were supposed to, you'd be dropping off your kids with Mom and Dad on weekends. I'd be Uncle Johnny, and we'd all sit down to dinner at Thanksgiving. Things don't work, we fix them up the best we can."

"I told the man I'd ask. I'm hoping that you'll turn me down."

"Why's that? You worried I can't cut it?"

"Hell, I don't know what 'it' is."

"So let's find out. Could be we'll both say no."

"Could be." The warrior didn't sound convinced.

"I'll try to make the next flight out."

"You've got some time. They're not expecting us until tomorrow evening, sixish."

"Right. That's Jacksonville International?"

"The same. I'll meet you, if you leave the time and flight on tape."

"Sounds good. I'll see you then."

"Stay frosty, little brother."

"Is there any other way?"

The line went dead, and Johnny cradled the receiver. Several dozen questions came to mind, but none were answerable at the moment. He would pursue the answers with his brother when they met in Jacksonville. Meanwhile there were arrangements to be made.

Suppressing the excitement that he felt inside, he turned back to the telephone and started punching numbers.

2

"You think they'll come?"

"*He*'ll come," Brognola answered testily. "I can't begin to speak for anybody else."

"It's still a two-man job, you know?"

"If Striker says he'll ask someone," another voice replied, "it means he'll ask."

The second testy voice belonged to Leo Turrin. He seemed about to graduate from testy into full-blown anger. The third man in the room, one Felix Pratt, held up both hands to signal for a truce.

"All right already. I just thought I'd ask."

"You ask a lot," Brognola snapped. "The DEA's supposed to have its own safehouses, transport teams, the whole nine yards."

"We do," Pratt replied. "Hell, we use them all the time, but this is different."

"Right."

"You know the score on Vos. You've seen his jacket. He's got contacts everywhere—and I mean everywhere. We could be looking at a major foul-up if we use our normal teams and routes on this one."

"Brief translation—you don't trust your own damned men."

Pratt glared at Turrin. "That's a crock. I'd trust them with my life."

"But not your case?"

"We can't afford to blow this, dig it? Vos has been a major source of coke in the United States since 1982. He's been The Source, hands down, for eighteen months. We put this bum away—"

"And one of his lieutenants has the business back on track before you're done selecting jurors," Turrin finished for him.

"So, you're saying that it isn't worth the effort?" Felix Pratt apparently couldn't believe his ears.

Brognola intervened, uncomfortable in the role of referee, appearing to support a plan that he'd hated from the start. "He's saying each department has priorities. We've worked with the DEA before, as you well know. We've finished more than one job you guys fumbled on the five-yard line."

A flush of color tinged Pratt's sallow cheeks. "So what's your point?"

"My point is that you're not the only one concerned about this case. I've got no beef with prosecuting Vos. I think it's great. Assuming that you couldn't blow his ass away at the arrest, he needs to rot in jail. But now I've got my people on the line to cover someone else's action, and that makes me nervous. You understand nervous?"

"I live with nervous."

"Then we understand each other."

"Fair enough. I'm wondering how well you understand your boy."

Brognola caught himself about to check his watch, and scowled. "He's got an hour yet. Nobody told him that he had to be here early."

"I'm just nervous, like you said."

"Well, don't be," Turrin offered. "If there's one thing you can still depend on in this whole damned mess, it's Striker showing up on schedule."

"Sure. Okay."

Brognola spent a moment studying the reproduction prints that decorated the dingy motel walls. Their meeting place got more depressing by the moment, and he fought the urge to light up a cigar. The air was close and stale enough already.

Leo seemed to read his mind and grinned as he addressed himself to Pratt. "You fellows always travel in this kind of luxury?"

"We play the game by any rules that win. This place was nearly empty—hell, it's always nearly empty—and the owner's on our hook. A couple of my people caught him dealing kilo weight last year and rolled him over."

Turrin made a sour face. "You're telling me the manager's connected? We've got people breaking cover for a face-to-face, and now, for all I know, some whipdick with connections may be sitting in his office with a Polaroid and snapping everyone who comes and goes. For Christ's sake, Pratt, did anybody in your shop consider looking up the definition of 'security'?"

"That's funny. You're a riot, Leo. This bum's looking at a stretch of twenty-five to life if I suspect he's thinking of a sellout. He tries crossing me, and he won't have a dick to whip."

"Well, I'm convinced," the man from Justice quipped sarcastically. "He sold me, Hal. You sold?"

"I'm sick and tired of bickering, that's what I am." Brognola had been up and out at five o'clock that morning, and every minute of the past twelve hours was written on his face. "They've still got time. They'll be here when they can. Until Pratt tells his story and we get an answer, the complaint department's closed."

Pratt shrugged and Leo grimaced, but they both fell silent, drifting off to neutral corners like a pair of weary fighters. Brognola tried the television, found a Bronson movie he'd seen a dozen times, and turned it off again before the actor started kicking ass. The big Fed had no patience for the world of make-believe annihilation at the moment. There was plenty on the street to go around.

MACK BOLAN LEFT HIS SIDE ARM and its shoulder rigging in the car when he went to meet his brother at Arrivals and Departures. He wasn't defenseless, even so—the airport scanners missed a plastic knife he carried in a Velcro ankle sheath, as well as the two-inch buckle dagger on his belt—but if it came to distance work he'd be helpless. There was little chance of being recognized in Jacksonville, Bolan reasoned, but you never knew precisely when your path would cross a friend's—or enemy's—and he'd be relieved when they were on the road again.

He checked the video display and found that Johnny's flight from San Diego, with a forty-minute stop in Dallas, was expected to arrive on time. That gave him half an hour, and he drifted past the shops that offered alligator boots and snakeskin products, scowling at a "nature" layout that included two stuffed bear cubs and their mother. Bolan understood the hunter's urge, and he had done some hunting in his youth, on summer trips outside of Pittsfield, but the world had turned since then, and he'd seen too much of killing to consider it a sport.

He put the shop behind him, killed some time examining the titles in a smallish bookstore. Vietnam was "in" these days, from all appearances, and while a few nonfiction volumes still bemoaned the "tragedy" of U.S. policy in Asia, most seemed more objective in their treatment of the war. In fiction, the heroic cover art bore small resemblance to the jungles he remembered from another life.

He drifted on, obtained a candy sample from a smiling teenage girl at one shop and washed it down with soda from another. When twenty minutes had passed, Bolan picked up his pace as he headed for the numbered gate where Johnny would arrive.

Their time together had been sparse, as always, during recent months. He tried to phone the San Diego base at weekly intervals, but visits were another thing entirely. Months slid by without a glimpse of Johnny, and despite the fact that he had grown accustomed to their distance over time, it never ceased to rankle Bolan that his sole surviving relative was out of reach, effectively off-limits. When they met, necessity demanded that he keep it brief—a few short hours now and then, perhaps an overnight on special holidays if neither was committed to another cause.

It rankled, sure, but Bolan had been conscious of the terms before he signed the contract, picking out a life-style that would separate him from the world of friends and family, perhaps forever. There had been a time when Johnny was completely out of touch, the sketchy details of his life relayed by Hal or Leo Turrin, secondhand. The warrior understood and gave his blessing to a scheme that changed the family name, providing Johnny with the chance to live a normal life.

The last thing on his mind in those days had been using brother Johnny as backup on the kind of missions that were recognized as Bolan's specialty. It had happened more than once, and John had saved his life in Texas—once again in Arizona—but he couldn't grow accustomed to the feeling. It seemed wrong, somehow, to gamble with his brother's life, no matter if "the kid" freely volunteered to play the game.

A disembodied voice announced the flight's arrival, and he moved to stand before the giant windows, watching as a Boeing 727 taxied into its approach. A member of the ground crew, dressed in yellow coveralls and waving flags that looked like Ping-Pong paddles, led the airship to her berth and waited while the loading bridge was locked into position. Bolan felt anticipation mounting as the engines died, and rumpled passengers began to make their way along the tunnel.

Johnny was the twenty-second face in line, and Bolan met him at the gate, a handshake standing in for the embrace both might have favored in less public circumstances.

"Decent flight?"

"No problems."

"Baggage?"

Johnny cracked a smile and raised a fat Adidas tote bag. "What you see is what I've got."

"You travel light."

"I couldn't think of any way to check the hardware through."

They moved along the concourse at a steady pace, bypassed the escalator leading to the baggage carousels and exited into sunshine.

"Still no inkling on the gig?" Johnny asked as they approached the car.

The warrior shook his head.

"A two-man job is all I've heard. Right now, you know as much as I do."

"That's a comfort."

"Right. You ever get the feeling you're a mushroom?"

"You mean where everybody keeps me in the dark and feeds me bullshit?"

"That's the one."

"I feel that way from time to time."

"I almost didn't call you."

"There's a vote of confidence."

"I almost didn't come myself."

"Who's feeding who?"

"Okay, but I don't have to like it."

"We don't have to *do* it, bro'. The problem is, they've got me curious."

Relief. No doubt about it.

"Yeah," the soldier said. "Me, too."

THE TROPICAL MOTEL HAD BEEN a local showplace once upon a time, but something like a quarter century had passed since it was anything but drab and ordinary. Neon palm trees advertised the place out front, but they looked cheap and lifeless in the daylight. Johnny had a feeling they would look the same by night.

"Some kind of super meeting place they've got here," he remarked.

"At least it's quiet."

"Dead would sum it up, I think."

Two cars beside their own were standing in the parking lot. An aging station wagon sat outside the office, faded Nixon stickers peeling on the bumper, rust beginning to devour paint and chrome around the wheel wells. Bolan pulled in and parked beside a standard "unmarked" government sedan, its paint job, license plate and whip antenna readily identifying it for anyone with eyes to see.

"We late?"

Bolan shook his head. "You're early."

They didn't have a chance to knock before the door swung open. Hal Brognola filled the portel, putting on a cautious smile and quickly stepping back to let them pass.

"I'm glad you both could make it."

Johnny nodded in response. The man from Washington had changed since their first meeting, in San Louis, during

Bolan's one-man campaign against the Mafia. A teenager in those days, Johnny had seen Brognola several times since then—most recently when the Executioner had gone on trial in Texas—but there hadn't been a sit-down conversation in a long, long time.

Two other faces waited on the sidelines, and Brognola made the introductions, careful to rely on code names where appropriate. While Johnny was familiar with the name of Leo Turrin, they'd never met before. He shook the federal agent's hand and read a faint suggestion of uneasiness—perhaps anxiety—in Leo's smile.

"I've heard a lot about you," Johnny said.

"That goes both ways. It's good to have you on the team."

"Not yet," Bolan interjected. "First we have to hear the game plan."

"That's where I come in."

The voice of number three was laced with gravel. Johnny thought it matched his face, a weathered oval lined by too much bitterness, a sandy crew cut bristling on top.

"Felix Pratt, with the DEA," Brognola offered, fading back to snag himself a chair. "It's his production. He can fill you in on all the details."

"Right. We might as well get comfortable." They were seated while he opened up a briefcase and retrieved a fat manila folder. "I assume you're both familiar with Ernesto Vos?"

"Colombia," Bolan replied. "A major mover in the coke trade."

"That's our boy." Pratt's smile was brittle plastic. "We've had warrants on the bastard for a year, but they're no good in Bogatá. He used to travel stateside five, six times a year, but since we filed indictments, he's been hanging close to home."

"I'm not surprised."

"To make a long rap short, we got ourselves a handle on his main man out of Dade. A dealer called Aguire, first name Carlos. Caught him with his pants down on a smuggling operation that was strictly off the record with his boss. He got three choices: thirty years hard time, a word to Vos that he was selling out the side, or one day's work for Uncle Sam.''

"He bit?''

"Like *Jaws*. He figures he can find someplace to hide and burrow in before Vos puts an army on his track.''

"You don't?''

"Who cares? He staged a phony meet that put Vos in the bag on Friday, and we'll keep him healthy long enough to testify. From there, he's on his own.''

"You're beautiful,'' Brognola said. "A sweetheart.''

"I'm a realist,'' Pratt answered, shrugging off the criticism. "Hell, Aguire knew the risks before he started selling coke to kids in junior high school. Fuck him.''

"This is fascinating,'' Johnny interrupted, "but we could have caught it on the evening news. You want to spell out your problem?''

"That's why I'm here. We couldn't spring the trap without Vos knowing that Aguire set him up. Our boy can put Vos in Atlanta through the next millenium, but he's a sitting duck right now. I need him breathing for the trial.''

Bolan frowned. "The last I heard, you had a few safehouses stashed around.''

"There's no such thing as 'safe' with Vos involved.''

"The DEA can't guard one man?''

"We're taking steps, of course, but we've had...problems in the recent past.''

"What kind of problems?''

"Leaks, primarily. We stage a raid and come up empty, or we set an undercover buy with some of Vos's people and the rats don't show. I'm working on it, but we don't have time to work the bugs out in the next four days.''

"Who set the deadline?''

"The judicial system. Justice won a change of venue to Los Angeles, on grounds of possible corruption locally, and pretrial action starts on Thursday. If Aguire isn't there on time, we're down the tube.''

"So, what's the problem?'' Johnny asked. "Why don't you stick him on an airplane?''

"There's a question of security.'' The man from the DEA put on a sour face and swallowed bitter medicine. "Can I be frank? The plain truth is, I don't know who to trust around the office. Hell, with this much riding on the line I don't trust anybody. There, I've said it. I'm prepared to eat crow all day long if it will help."

"Help *how*?"

"We're flying Vos out Wednesday afternoon," Pratt said. "No problem there. He'll play along because he's counting on Aguïre to be dead before the gavel falls on Thursday. What I need is someone clean, above suspicion—and outside the agency—to make delivery on time."

"May I assume you've got a plan in mind?" Bolan asked.

"The overland express. A three-day drive from Jacksonville to La-La Land. You navigate. We'll ante up the wheels and hardware if you like. No one outside this room will know your route or ETA. It should be simple."

"Should be."

"Well..."

"Diversions?"

Pratt examined Johnny's youthful face with something closer to appreciation.

"They're already in the works," he answered. "Once we're set on a departure time, I activate Plan B. We've got a halfway double for Aguïre under wraps, and he'll be flying west about the time you leave. With any luck, the shooters ought to follow him, and you can make your crossing while they chase their tails around L.A."

"Sounds simple," Johnny said.

"I won't pretend it's foolproof, but I think we've minimized the risk."

"You're not obliged to take this on," Brognola cautioned from the sidelines. "It's an option, nothing more."

"We choose the route," Bolan said.

"Affirmative."

"And if we should encounter opposition on the way?"

"You take whatever steps are necessary to assure delivery," Pratt said.

"How many local agencies are in the picture?"

"None at all. If I have doubts about my owned damned stuff, I'm not about to trust some sheriff's deputy in Hicksville."

"So, they won't be standing by to lend a hand in case of trouble."

"You'll be on your own," Pratt told them both. "I make no bones about it. It's the only way to play this hand."

Bolan turned to his brother, as their eyes met, something passed between them. Johnny understood his brother's reservations, and he shared those doubts across the board, but he wasn't prepared to walk away because of the risks involved. After another moment he nodded, smiling.

"Right," the Executioner told Felix Pratt. "We're in."

AN HOUR LATER, once the details had been covered, the brothers found a restaurant two miles away from the Tropical Motel. They took a booth in back and ordered steak with all the trimmings, knowing that they might not have another chance to eat a decent meal before they reached Los Angeles.

Assuming they both lived that long.

"You buy Pratt's story?" Johnny asked.

The warrior thought about it for a moment, frowning. "For the moment. It's safe to say he's playing down the trouble in his own backyard. The DEA's as jealous of its territory as the Bureau for the Company. For Pratt to ask Hal in at all, he must be looking at a major hassle."

"And if things are that bad—"

"There's no telling what we might run into on the road. You guessed it, little brother."

Johnny smiled indulgently. "You turned in quite a shopping list back there. Expecting heavy opposition?"

"Every day. I thought we'd better pack the bare essentials, just in case."

"I'm not complaining, mind you. I just like to know what's going down."

"We won't know that until we're on the road. I have a nasty feeling."

"Yeah. I know the one."

"You know, there's still no need for you to come along on this. We've built in rest stops, and I don't imagine that

Aguire will be anxious to go thumbing on his own with every gun on Vos's payroll itching for a shot. No reason why you shouldn't go back home and hold the fort."

"Well, I can think of one."

The soldier waited while their steaks were laid before them and the waitress moved away. "I'm listening."

"You want me out. That means you think I might be needed. I appreciate the thought, but if it's all the same, I'll stick around."

"Goddammit, Johnny—"

"Hey, don't thank me, bro'. My treat."

"I hope it's not your funeral."

"Well, if it is, I ought to be there, don't you think?"

"What makes you so damned stubborn, anyway?"

"I think it's in my blood."

The Bolan blood, he thought, and cut himself a slice of steak in lieu of further comment. Once Johnny made up his mind, an argument was futile. And he was correct in his assessment of the problem. Bolan feared his brother would be needed on the road, which meant he wished the young man to be anywhere other than the expected free-fire zone.

Something had been missing from Felix Pratt's story, and while he couldn't put his finger on the missing item, Bolan had a sneaking hunch it might be critical to their survival once they took delivery of their prisoner and started west. Three days could be a lifetime, and he wasn't anxious for his brother to assume the role of human sacrifice.

The kid—the *man*—had been through so damned much already, that in Bolan's mind he shouldn't have been called upon to go the extra mile for strangers. Johnny had paid his dues, from the explosive carnage that had claimed the other members of their family, leaving teenaged Johnny Bolan wounded, to the new life he'd built as Johnny Gray. It seemed unfair to ask for more.

The choice, however, wasn't Bolan's . . . and it might not be his brother's, either. Sometimes, the Executioner knew, the Universe reached out and chose warriors independently of human hopes and dreams. Sometimes a fighting man got drafted, and he went along regardless of the cost because he simply had no choice.

Sometimes.

Like now.

**3**

The county jail in Jacksonville is geared to handle many different types of prisoners, from common drunks to psychopaths in need of constant physical restraint. The easy in-and-out brigade of alcoholic vagrants, drifters, petty thieves and other misdemeanants are confined in holding pens—called tanks—where they can mingle freely in their misery while sleeping off a drunk or waiting for the bondsman to arrive. When juveniles are taken into custody, they are secured within another wing and segregated racially theoretically to protect them from the threat of rape by older prisoners, gang violence and assorted other dangers that persist inside the walls. There is a medical facility for walking wounded at the jail, a psychiatric wing with padded cells and orderlies on standby, plus an isolation tier for prisoners who turn state's evidence against their one-time friends. On top of everything, perched in the architectural equivalent of the penthouse, there is a block of maximum-security cells known collectively to guards and prisoners alike as High Power.

High Power is reserved for the worst of the lot, the *crème de la crime*. Inmates are selected for the block on various criteria, but all are ranked as dangerous and unpredictable, explosive, capable of any violent act. Suspected serial killers are confined in High Power, provided their crimes have been brutal and numerous enough to qualify for special handling. The other High Power alumni include child-killers, violent serial rapists, habitual escape artists and the odd mafioso.

In High Power, prisoners shave with locked safety razors, and guards carry electronic stun guns in addition to their riot batons. Food trays are delivered and retrieved through locking "mail slots" in the doors of individual cells, and inmates are subjected to twenty-four hour surveillance against the triple threat of suicide, escape and outside attack. There is no such thing as an exercise period in High Power, but inmates who behave themselves are granted weekly shower privileges. If they begin to smell betweentimes, body odor is regarded as a minor price to pay for personal security.

From the beginning, there had been no real debate about Ernesto Vos's qualification for High Power. Suspected in an estimated fifty stateside murders—including two of federal drug enforcement agents—Vos was rated both as a primary escape risk and a probable target of assassination attempts by his competitors in the narcotics trade. From High Power, it was suggested, Vos could neither reach outside the walls nor could he be reached. It was a brave attempt, but every system must, inevitably, have a flaw. In this case, it would be the sixth amendment to the Constitution.

Nathan Trask had been defending criminals in court for twenty-seven years. He viewed it as an avocation, something thrust upon him by his destiny. The fact that serving criminals had also made him filthy rich was secondary in the lawyer's mind. His clients paid no more than he was worth, and for their money they acquired the services of an outstanding legal mind. They also purchased access to his contacts in the courts, the legislative branch of government, in law enforcement and the media. By hiring Nathan Trask, they hired an army.

Most suspected felons wound up pleading poverty and working with a public defender fresh out of law school, happy to see burglary or rape charges bargained down to larceny and simple assault in the interest of clearing a court calendar. The vast majority of criminals couldn't afford to speak with one of Trask's junior partners, let alone retain the man himself and see him take their cases into court. The legal eagle's time was valuable and he charged accordingly.

In Nathan Trask's opinion, no crime was too vile, abhorrent or repulsive to deserve a strong defense...provided that the vile, abhorrent and repulsive criminal could pay his way. At three hundred dollars an hour, that narrowed the field of competition considerably. But Trask was never short of clients.

Ernesto Vos had been Trask's client for the better part of eighteen months, since agents of the FBI, the DEA and IRS had launched a wave of harassing attacks against the drug lord's stateside empire. With indictments in the wind, Vos couldn't visit the United States and cope with legal problems on his own, but he respected talent and he was determined to employ the best. In Nathan Trask he found a topflight legal mind with friends across the board in government, prepared at any time of day or night to challenge warrants, file restraining orders or injunctions, and obstruct the seizure of assorted autos, airplanes, boats and houses.

On the side, Trask also carried certain messages—and sometimes payoffs—to the kind of people Vos could never reach in person, even if he had been free to travel stateside: judges, legislators, candidates for office who required a quick financial boost in their campaign, a prosecutor faced with crippling expenses after doctors diagnosed his only child as suffering from cancer. Some would never know that they were speaking indirectly to the man from Bogatá; a few wouldn't have cared in any case. When they were called upon to pay their debts, they would respond on cue, or they would face the certainty of swift and final punishment.

This afternoon, Trask made his way through half a dozen checkpoints en route to the High Power "penthouse," allowing himself to be searched and scrutinized, his briefcase opened in a search for weapons. He followed arrows painted on the floor and walls, spent time in steel-barred sally ports and smiled for the surveillance cameras. He had an escort for the elevator ride to High Power, another hulking deputy met him there when the doors hissed open. The man led Trask along a beige corridor, through more barred gates to the tier's single visiting room.

The furniture, consisting of a table and two chairs, was bolted to the floor. Trask sat with his attaché case before him while the guard went off to fetch his client. Several minutes passed before the deputy came back with four companions who surrounded Vos as if expecting him to make a break to nowhere. They seated him across from Trask, fastening his left wrist and both ankles to the chair with chains.

Trask frowned. "Is that entirely necessary?"

"Yes, sir."

Silently the squad of deputies retreated and the door was closed. One man remained just outside, his moon face plastered to the wire-mesh window, watching every move Trask made.

"Are you all right?" he asked his client.

Vos responded with an easy smile. "I've been in jail before. Some of them were not as civilized as others. How goes the case?"

Trask cleared his throat, his briefcase still unopened on the table. He wouldn't need notes to tell him there had been no progress in his bids for bail.

"It's still no go on any kind of bond," he said. "I'm filing an appeal, of course, but in the circumstances, I see no reason for optimism. You're considered an escape risk at the very least, and no one wants to take responsibility for opening those gates."

"A campaign contribution?" Vos suggested.

"Federal judges aren't elected. They're appointed for a term of life, and none I know of are prepared to risk impeachment and disgrace on your behalf. A grant of bail at this point would be suicide for anyone who signed the paperwork."

"Then I must win release by other means."

"From where I sit, that has to mean dismissal of the charges. With Aguire in the prosecutor's bag, we haven't got a prayer in that direction."

"Then we must remove Aguire from the bag."

Trask frowned, his eyes averted. "That's no easy job."

"If it was easy," Vos replied, "I could not find it in my heart to pay a million dollars cash for his removal."

Trask glanced up at Vos, concluding that his client was entirely serious. "A million cash?"

"Upon completion of the job. When our amigo has been dealt with and the charges are dismissed for lack of evidence."

"It may not be that simple. DEA will have his affidavits filed and introduced as evidence. His death won't mean a thing with all that paperwork, the videocassettes and tape recordings."

Vos dismissed the problem with a gesture of his one free hand. "Confessions and cassettes do not concern me. Evidence has disappeared before. It will again."

"Have you got something in the works?"

"A fool allows his fate to be controlled by circumstances. I am not a fool."

"Of course not, but—"

"I wish for you to make arrangements, Nathan. Carlos must be silenced by the time we face the judge in California. He must not appear in court."

"I understand, Ernesto, but I don't know how—"

"I do," Vos countered. "There is one man you can trust to make arrangements. Call him when you leave. Immediately. We have no time left to waste."

"His name?"

Vos whispered it, delighted by Trask's obvious surprise. From memory the dealer cited home and office numbers of his contact, repeating them while Trask dug out pen and notepad. Jotting down the numbers in reverse order in case the piece of paper was lost, Trask didn't note the contact's name. His memory was excellent, and shock would help him keep the name in mind.

"Will he cooperate to that extent?" the lawyer asked.

"I have no doubts."

"In that case, I believe we're finished for the moment. I'll be back tomorrow with a full report of his response, if you can think of anything you need . . ."

"My freedom. It is in your hands."

"I'll do my best."

"I know that, Nathan." Vos was smiling now. "You love this life too much to fail."

Trask signaled to the deputy that he was finished, clinging to his seat as Vos was led away. He hoped the deputy didn't observe his trembling as he rose and trailed his escort toward the elevator. This time, as the steel-barred gates swung shut behind him, Trask imagined they were locking him inside, and sudden claustrophobia produced a sheen of perspiration on his forehead.

He had just agreed to the solicitation of a felony—or several felonies, including murder and a string of lesser crimes such as bribery, obstructing justice and destroying federal evidence. The latter risks were nothing new to Trask, and he had learned to deal with tension by experience, but farming out a contract—and a million-dollar contract in the bargain—was a first.

He wondered if he had the nerve to pull it off.

And passing through the checkpoints on his way to freedom, Trask was well aware he had no choice.


"I WANT PROTECTION."

Felix Pratt leaned back in his chair and spread his hands. "You have protection, Carlos."

"This is not protection." There was anger in Aguire's voice as he surveyed the small apartment, curtains drawn against the threat of daylight.

"We're moving you tomorrow. Never fear. I've got it covered."

"Vos will find me, hunt me down and have me killed."

"No way. I've got a decoy on the launchpad, and by the time his shooters realize they've fucked it up, we'll have you in L.A., tucked up in maximum security."

"How many escorts will I have?"

"I'm pulling in two experts."

*"Two?"* Aguire felt a sinking sensation in his stomach, coupled with a sudden throbbing pain behind one eye. "Two men? Vos has an army on the street. Are you insane?"

Pratt's smile was strained. "I think we can agree it doesn't pay to advertise. If I stick you in armored car with black-and-whites for escorts, I'd be telling Vos exactly where you are."

"He doesn't need your help. He'll find me anyway."

"I'm betting that he won't."

"You're betting with my life."

"And my career. I can't afford to fuck this up, no way, no how. The company you keep, right now I'd say your life means more to me than it has ever meant to you."

Aguire scowled. "Two men. Where did you find them?"

"Never fear. I went outside the shop. These guys are specialists in hit-and-run, evasion, counterterrorist techniques . . . you name it. If I had to make the trip myself, I'd want them riding shotgun."

"Fine. *You* make the trip."

"Now, Carlos, we've been through all that. There's no way I can make it any safer for you. Hell, the change of venue to L.A. was your idea, remember? You said Vos has too many connections here in Florida."

"He has connections everywhere."

"Agreed, but no one knows the route you're taking. Three nights on the road, and then you're in Los Angeles, safe and sound. I've got it covered."

"And the others?"

Pratt frowned. "We're looking."

"Vos has dealt with them already."

"You don't know that. There's a decent chance that Cruz is hiding in Toronto. We've got people looking for him, but they have to go through channels, working with the RCMP. And Chicago thinks they have a line on Sanchez. Maldonado left a message he was going on vacation. We've got feelers out with NYPD and the Bureau, but they haven't traced him yet."

"They never will, unless they trace him to a grave."

Pratt didn't bother to comment. "Barbosa's place was empty when the Frisco team went calling. I'm inclined to think he got a tip and saw them coming. I believe he'll surface, given time."

"Enriquez?"

"He went out to get some smokes last night, and that's the last his wife has seen of him. She says. I'm betting that he's found himself a hole and pulled it in behind him, waiting for the smoke to clear."

"A hole. I would not be surprised."

"There's no way Vos could tag them all that fast. He's only human."

"There were six men who could link him with the business. Vos knows I betrayed him. He cannot afford to take a chance on others bolting while he sits in jail. I know the way his mind works, Pratt. Those men are dead."

The DEA man shrugged. "Okay. Let's say you're right. So what? You ought to thank your lucky stars Enriquez has been taken care of in L.A. He would have been the one assigned to take you out before the trial."

"If I survive that long."

"You ever hear of looking on the bright side, Carlos? I've never seen a guy so set on giving up."

"I have not given up," Aguire protested. "I face reality."

"Face this. The surest way to boost your life expectancy from this point on is by convicting Vos and putting him away forever."

"He will be replaced before the prison gates swing shut."

"What's that to you? The new kid on the throne won't give a flying fuck who put him there. If anything, he'll figure you're some kind of hero, setting up his rise to fame and fortune. Any way you stack it, he'll be too damned busy counting out his cash to waste time paying Ernie's IOUs."

"Vos still has many friends."

"We'll see how long they stick around when he pulls life plus ninety-nine. You ever hear of Al Capone?"

"Chicago?"

"That's the one. The tax boss nailed him for eleven years in 1933, and there were stories in the press about how Scarface Al was pulling strings from Alcatraz, deciding every little thing about what happened on his old home turf. Fact is the Nitti crowd took over everything in sight and cut it up among themselves. They put Al on a pension, like some kind of secretary who's retired. The day he got paroled, he headed straight for Florida and next thing anybody knew, the bum was dead."

"I see your point, but—"

"Hey, no buts. The Nitti crowd were gentleman compared to Vos's playmates. And when Ernie takes the fall, he won't be coming back. You follow? Bye-bye birdie."

"No parole?"

"Oh, he'll be eligible, sure. But first he'll have to serve the standard first half of his sentence. Life plus ninety-nine would make that sixty-five years, minimum. How old you say he was right now?"

"Ernesto Vos is thirty-five years old."

"Well, there you are. You think he's going to make the hundred-year mark in a cell? And if he does, do you plan on being here to greet him? Carlos, sweetheart, all we have to do is see you through the trial, and you're home free."

"I wish I had your confidence."

Pratt grinned. "I'll lend you some."

"Two men," Carlos said again, unable to suppress a tone of disbelief.

"Two soldiers. Stone-cold killers. Hell, if these guys can't protect you, no one can."

"That is precisely my concern."

"I'm tired of dancing with you, Carlos. When we popped you running grass from Mexico, you had a choice to make. I could have hung you out to dry on that, or let you walk and try to make Vos understand why you were dealing with the Castro brothers on your free time. You decided it was easier to sing. *You* made that choice. If you'd prefer to change your mind, I'm easy. We've still got the bulk-weight important charge, and Vos will walk without your testimony. Shall I guess what he'll be doing after thirty seconds on the street?"

"You need me, Pratt. Remember that."

"It's on my mind around the clock."

"When do I meet these supermen?"

"They'll pick you up tomorrow morning. Think of it as a vacation, all expenses paid. You'll have a chance to see America, up close and personal."

"Tomorrow morning."

"Right. You ought to try to get some sleep."

"Goodbye, Pratt."

"Not goodbye, amigo. Just so long."

Pratt spent a moment with the guards before he left, reminding them to stay alert and watch for any signals that Aguire was prepared to bolt. He wasn't prepared to let his only living witness slip away, while the appointed sentries filled their time with cards and stories that were mainly sex. If Aguire went, he'd be going out feet first, and there had damn well better be some DEA men stretched out on the ground beside him.

Carlos had been right, of course, about the other five— Barbosa, Sanchez, Maldonado, Cruz and Enriquez, the five men who could theoretically connect Ernesto Vos with cocaine traffic spanning North America. Within a day of his arrest, Vos had reached out for each in turn, and they were gone. If any of them surfaced, Pratt would be surprised. If any of them turned up breathing, it would be a goddamned miracle.

No matter. None of them had any motive for betraying Vos, and if they weren't on his side, Pratt much preferred to have them dead. It was a simple, economical solution, and it left the outfit theoretically deprived of leadership while Vos was under lock and key. All things considered, Pratt was pleased with how the operation had worked out so far.

The snag, from that point on, would be Brognola's people. Never mind their hotshot reputations or their past performance. Pratt hadn't been privileged to inspect their files, and he had no idea what kind of show it took to please Brognola. If the new boys fumbled...

Moving toward his car, Pratt lighted a thin cigar and let the smoke trail out behind him. He'd been compelled to go outside the department for help, and Hal Brognola's shop had been the only game in town. The man from the DEA would have to keep his fingers crossed and pray that everything went down on schedule. If anything went wrong, it would be his ass on the line. He'd be all dressed up with nowhere left to go.

And nowhere was a lonely place to be.

**4**

"Here she is." Pratt waved a hand in the direction of the chosen vehicle. "If you see anything you want to change, sing out. We've got a little time to spare."

"I'll let you know," Mack Bolan told him as he began his inspection.

At Johnny's urging, they had opted for a General Motors Jimmy with the standard four-wheel drive and something extra underneath the hood. The engine had been modified to yield an extra forty miles per hour at the high end of the scale, and the Police Pak theoretically enabled them to pace a speeding squad car, if they had to.

"Off-road tires," Pratt pointed out. "We had them puncture-proof, but this is what you asked for, right?"

"Affirmative."

"The puncture-proofs still have their weak spots," Johnny added, "and they're worthless if we have to lose the highway for a while."

"You traveling cross-country, guys?"

"We're keeping all our options open."

The driver's door was open, and the Executioner climbed in to get the Jimmy's feel. The rear seat could be folded down to make a bed if they were forced to camp, and the windows to the rear were tinted, foiling any attempt to see inside the vehicle.

"The glass is bulletproof," Pratt stated. "For what it's worth. I won't pretend it's perfect, but it lets you have an edge. Sometimes that's all you need."

"I've heard that."

Bolan found a CB radio beneath the dashboard, and a stack of highway maps he had requested in the glove compartment. There was nothing in the console set between the two front seats, but he would see to that himself before they hit the road.

Brognola had been pacing on the sidelines, and he chimed in now. "What kind of armor does she have?"

"It was a trade-off," Pratt replied. "Your basic quarter inch. I could have given you a tank, but what you lose in weight, you gain in speed. I figure you'll be gassing up this monster every couple hundred miles, regardless, but there's no such thing as skinny armor."

"Bumpers?" Bolan asked him.

"Reinforced for ramming, front and back. Your grille is likewise tougher than the standard model, but it's not invincible. Don't get me wrong on this. You start in butting heads with semis and you're bound to lose."

Bolan popped the hood, and Johnny moved around to check the power plant. On Johnny's cue, he turned the engine over, then let it idle, revving several times to let his brother hear the mill unwind. When Johnny was satisfied, he killed it and the hood was lowered into place once more.

Stepping down, he made a final circuit of the Jimmy, noting that the plates were Florida civilian-issue, as he had requested. Otherwise the vehicle looked slightly used, and Bolan knew that it was last year's model. He'd been concerned about the idea of driving anything too new, too perfect, that would make them objects of attention on the road. The creamy neutral paint job helped to make the Jimmy inconspicuous despite its size, and once they got some road dust on the vehicle, colors would be difficult to judge with any accuracy from a distance.

"Satisfied?" he asked his brother.

Johnny shrugged. "She ought to do the job."

"We'll take it," Bolan said to Pratt.

"Will that be cash, or charge?"

The joke fell flat, but Pratt forced a chuckle as he moved in the direction of the tailgate.

"It was pushing things to get those extras that you wanted, but I think we ran down everything you noted on your shopping list. I'm on the hook for these myself, so try to bring back anything you can."

"With any luck, they won't be needed," Bolan said.

"Whatever. Better safe than sorry, right?"

Pratt took the keys from Bolan, opened up another latch and dropped the tailgate. Turning back toward Bolan he looked smug, self-satisfied.

"Gentlemen, choose your weapons."

There were plenty to choose from, Johnny thought, as he joined his brother to survey their arsenal. Spread across the rear deck of the Jimmy were several items, starting with the pair of M-1 assault rifles. One was the carbine model with a shortened barrel and telescopic butt stock, while the full-sized version had a 40 mm M-203 grenade launcher mounted under the barrel. Next, a matching set of Uzi submachine guns, full-size and mini, the former featuring a folding metal stock. Beside the SMGs, he saw a pair of handguns, including the Israeli-made .44 Magnum Desert Eagle that his brother had requested and a sleek Beretta 92-S for himself.

Four canvas satchels took up the rest of the space in back, and Johnny checked each in turn. The first contained a dozen extra magazines and cleaning gear to serve the M-16s. The second held a similar supply of ammunition and equipment for the Uzis, while the third was packed with magazines, loose rounds and cleaning gear for both the handguns, including a custom silencer for the Beretta. The fourth and heaviest bag contained six frag grenades and a dozen 40 mm shells to fill the M-203 launcher.

"You've got enough stuff there to stop an army," Pratt observed. "Or slow it down some, anyway. I'm hoping we can keep this little expedition on the quiet side."

"My thoughts, exactly," Bolan replied. "But since you haven't found a way to guarantee safe passage...."

"Better safe than sorry. Yeah, I know."

Johnny reached out and picked up the carbine as his brother chose the full-sized M-16.

"What's going on?" Pratt asked.

"A little checkup," Johnny told him. "Nothing personal, but if these pieces break down in a crunch, there won't be time to send them back for factory repairs."

"By all means, be my guest." Pratt smiled, but it was strained, as if his personal integrity had been insulted.

No tools were necessary for fieldstripping the M-16. Johnny cleared the weapon, removing its magazine and checking for live rounds in the chamber before he slid the bolt forward, pressed out the rear pin and opened the rifle. With swift, practiced movements, he stripped the firing pin assembly, the extractor, the buffer assembly and drive spring, carefully studying each component in turn. When he was satisfied, he reassembled the rifle, snapped its magazine into the receiver and set the weapon back in its place.

The Uzis were next, and Johnny took the full-sized model, pulling its 32-round magazine before he pressed the catch in front of the rear sight, lifting the cover away from the receiver. He raised the bolt, disengaging its forward end and lifting it clear, along with the SMG's recoil spring. The extractor was next, followed by removal and inspection of the stubby barrel and the trigger mechanism. Finding everything in order, Johnny reassembled the weapon, fed its magazine into the pistol grip and replaced it on the deck.

His examination of the Beretta barely took a moment, with removal of the slide and an inspection of the firing mechanism. Johnny tried the silencer, unscrewed it and returned it to the satchel, loading up and chambering a round before he stowed the side arm in its custom shoulder rigging. Bolan had checked his 93-R through in luggage on the eastbound flight, but he was studying the Desert Eagle with an eye for detail, nodding when he felt that there was nothing more to see.

"Okay, we're on."

Pratt grinned. "You guys don't want to try them out? Blow up a house or something?"

One more dud, and he retreated into silence.

"Are we ready?" Hal Brognola asked.

Johnny caught his brother with a sideways glance and smiled.

"As ready as we'll ever be," the Executioner replied.

CARLOS AGUIRE STUBBED OUT his cigarette and checked his Rolex watch for the third time in sixty seconds. He was nervous, but it didn't pay to let your feelings show in situations where your life was riding on the line. Experience had taught Aguire that his enemies would seize on any show of weakness and destroy him if they could. Where strength was unavailable, its mere illusion sometimes did the trick.

"Should be here any minute," one of Pratt's associates informed him, drifting toward the window for a peek through venetian blinds. The agent wore a 9 mm Smith & Wesson combat ASP on his hip, and Carlos flexed his fingers, picturing how easy it would be to take the weapon, turn it on his guards and make his way to freedom.

Fantasy.

Aguire had no place to go, no refuge where he would be safe from Vos's hunters. They would sniff him out like hunting dogs no matter where he tried to hide. If he didn't dispose of Vos, as Pratt had said, there'd be no place in the world that he could call his own.

And after Vos was put away? Then what?

Aguire lacked the federal agent's confidence that all would be forgotten and forgiven. Those who followed Vos might not be interested in settling his debts, but they would need a show of strength to launch their reign. What better testament to their power than a blow against the federal government itself? A strike against the same "protected" witness who had cleared the throne for their ascension in the first place.

In retrospect, Aguire almost wished that he'd decided to do the time for smuggling grass and blown Pratt off about the witness gig. His chances of appeasing Vos were better on an outside deal than turning stoolie for the Feds, but he had panicked, thinking of Ernesto's reputation for exacting cruel revenge. The slightest hint of a defection was enough to spark a killing frenzy, and the DEA had played upon his fears to put the wheels in motion. Now he had no choice but to continue with the game and pray that he was still alive at its conclusion.

He wasn't impressed with the arrangements Pratt had made for transportation to Los Angeles. Two men, regardless of their backgrounds, hardly qualified to stand against the army Vos would field against them. Half a dozen men might have done it, but Carlos understood Pratt's point about remaining inconspicuous. A fighting squad in transit drew attention.

Aguire figured he was creamed.

Los Angeles was roughly two thousand miles away, and while Aguire took no honors in geography, he knew that they'd have to cross eight states to reach their destination. Much of that, from northern Florida to eastern Texas, was his own damned territory, and he knew the kind of lethal talent Vos could marshal with a phone call. If the price was right—and Vos would make it right this time—they could be facing anything from Cubans and the Ku Klux Klan to outlaw bikers and the Mafia before they reached L.A. Vos's friends were everywhere, and even certain enemies might help him out on principle, to keep their own potential rats in line.

A car pulled up out front, immediately followed by two more. Pratt's men were at the windows, weapons in their hands, relaxing when they recognized their boss outside.

"It's showtime, Carlos."

Aguire snared his tailored jacket and slipped into it before he reached the door, waiting while his escorts led the way. If snipers lay in wait, he'd let the DEA men earn their paltry paychecks.

"Clear," one of them told him. Aguire donned his aviator shades before he stepped outside. Despite the mirrored lenses, brilliant sunlight made him squint as he emerged from the confinement of his room.

Five men had joined the guards outside. Aguire let his eyes skim over Pratt, the man from Justice, then settled on the two who had been chosen for the run to California. Both were roughly six feet tall, one younger than the other, both athletic in appearance, obviously fit. They studied Carlos with the same intensity that he applied to them, recording every detail of his face and form, apparently deciding he wasn't a threat. As they approached, Aguire noted that they moved with the economy of warriors, confident and yet aware of their surroundings.

The older man was introduced as Michael Blanski, his companion Johnny Green. Aguire knew the names were false, but it meant nothing to him. After Thursday—if he lived that long—he wouldn't see these men again.

Pratt handed him an imitation leather bag. "You'll find some shaving gear in there," the agent said. "A tooth-brush, all the basics. Plus a couple shirts and whatnot, if you get the urge to change along the way."

Aguire mustered up a smile. "How generous."

"Don't mention it."

The witness turned to face his escorts. "I believe that's everything," he told them. "Shall we go?"

"YOU THINK they'll make it?" Leo Turrin asked as the Jimmy turned a corner, and disappeared from their view.

"They'd better," Pratt replied. "We've got a year and something like two million bucks invested in this opera-tion. If they fuck it up and lose Aguire, all that work goes down the crapper."

Hal Brognola scowled at Pratt, remembering precisely why he didn't like the man. "No sweat," he growled. "They haven't blown one yet."

"I'm glad to hear it, but you know, this is the big time."

Leo was about to answer that one, but Brognola stopped him with a glare. "Let's go."

"You're leaving?" Pratt seemed genuinely disappointed. "Hey, I thought that we could have a couple drinks to cel-ebrate."

"I'll do my celebrating when they're home and dry."

"Your call." Pratt didn't seem hurt by the rejection. "If there's anything I need—"

"Dial information," Brognola retorted as he walked away, Leo trailing as he moved in the direction of their car.

When they were rolling, Turrin risked a repetition of his question. "Think they'll make it?"

"I wish I knew. Pratt's too damned smug about his de-coy. If the DEA is leaking like he says, there's no way he can keep a phony transfer secret."

"Striker chose the route. That's something."

"Yeah, but I'd feel better if he'd kept it to himself."

"There's only so much you can cover on a deal like this."

"Don't rub it in."

"They *are* the best. That wasn't bullshit, Hal."

"It's relative. At some point, quantity inevitably cancels quality."

"I'll put my money on the Bolans, all the same."

"We shouldn't have to make that bet. I don't like picking up the pieces after someone else has fumbled."

"Well, at least Pratt had the balls to 'fess up on the leak."

"For what it's worth. We still don't have a handle on the problem, and from what I've seen, he's nowhere to a solution."

They fell silent on the drive back to the airport. Both had packed their bags before they left the cheap motel where they were staying, courtesy of DEA, and there was time to spare before their flight departed for Washington. They could have stopped for drinks, perhaps a sandwich, but Brognola had a sudden urge to put the town behind him, as if flight would magically erase his doubts and fears.

Above all else, he hated putting Bolan and his brother at risk for something that was out of his control, an operation planned and executed by the DEA with knowledge of their in-house problems. Pratt had obviously known about the leak—or leaks—before he turned Aguire, but the plan had gone ahead on schedule, Pratt and his superiors assuming they could count on someone else to do their dirty work if things got hairy. Now Brognola had his best damned agent on the line, together with the guy's kid brother, and he couldn't even say for certain whether they'd been sold out.

The big Fed made a silent promise to himself. If anything went wrong in transit, if the brothers didn't make it for whatever reason, he'd find a way to even things with Pratt. It might take time, but somehow, someday, he'd hang the grinning bastard out to dry.

Brognola owed the Executioner that much.

And come to think of it, he owed it to himself.

"I need a drink," Brognola said.

"I hear you, guy."

"Who's buying?"

"Flip you for it." Leo dug a quarter from his pocket. "Call."

"I'm heads."

The coin flashed briefly, spinning. Leo caught it, opened up his hand and frowned.

"Let's say two out of three."


"WHAT'S IN THE BAG?" Johnny asked when they were rolling west on Highway 10 near Riverside.

The soldier smiled and fished Brognola's parcel out from underneath his seat. "Pull over, and I'll show you."

Keeping pace with traffic, Johnny pointed out a bankrupt drive-in restaurant ahead. "This good enough?"

"It should be. Swing around in back, so we can have some privacy."

When they were parked, he produced a set of Georgia license plates from the bag.

"We're switching?"

"Better safe than sorry," Bolan answered. "Pratt's already told us that he has a leak. No point in taking chances when we don't know what's been leaking."

"Roger that."

Outside he scanned the empty lot and highway shoulder prior to crouching with a small screwdriver in his hand to change the plates. He hadn't asked Brognola where they came from, and it didn't matter. If there was a leak at the DEA, the information passed along about their license number would be obsolete. A description of their vehicle might still put gunners on their track, but there was nothing he could do about that paint job at the moment. They'd have to play the cards as they were dealt.

When Bolan had finished switching plates in front and back, he dropped the old ones in a rusty trash bin, crawling back inside the cab.

"Pratt might have wanted those," Johnny said.

"No sweat. I'll let him know where he can pick them up."

"About our schedule—"

"It's a washout," Bolan told his brother. "I don't like Big Brother knowing where we plan to spend the night. We'll take it as it comes."

"Outstanding."

They had covered close to fifteen miles before the warrior turned to face Aguire, seated in the back. "If you can think of anything we ought to know about this trip, feel free to jump right in."

The man's smile was weary, strained.

"I know that Vos will try to kill me—all of us—before we reach Los Angeles. Beyond that, I can only speculate."

"I'm listening."

"In Florida he works with Cubans on the distribution end, and they provide the muscle when he has a war to fight. In Georgia, Alabama, Mississippi and Louisiana, there are other factions—'patriotic' groups and local syndicates— who deal with Vos for their supplies. In Texas he does business with Chicanos and the cycle gangs."

"We're still a few states short," the Executioner reminded him.

"My territory covered only Gulf states and the South," Aguire said. "There will be other groups, of course . . . but who they are, I cannot say."

"You know the men in charge out west?"

"I did, but they are dead. Vos has not wasted any time."

"Insurance?"

"Burning bridges. He will reason that if one friend has betrayed him, others may be leaning in the same direction. It is better to eliminate the innocent and save himself than risk disaster."

"So," Johnny said, "it must be getting lonely where you live."

"I am accustomed to the loneliness," Aguire answered. "It is death that troubles me."

"Let's concentrate on living for a while," the Executioner suggested. "I'm assuming that you want to reach L.A., but if you start to change you mind en route, remember that we've got a job to do. It's just a little late for you to change your mind and plan a new itinerary."

"I have nowhere else to go."

"We're straight on that, then."

"Straight," the passenger agreed. "If I could have a weapon . . ."

"Negative. I realize you're playing on the home team now, but you're an unknown quantity to us. If things go sour along the way, we need to know our enemies are all outside. You follow?''

"Perfectly." Aguire's smile was humorless. "And if we are attacked?''

"We deal with that one when it happens," Bolan told him. "In the meantime, I suggest you kick back and enjoy the scenery."

"Of course. I might not have another chance."

The smile was positively morbid now, and Bolan turned away before it could affect him. If their passenger was counting on an early funeral, Bolan meant to disappoint him. He'd been retained to see Aguire safely through the killing grounds, and he would do so if he could. And failing that, he was prepared to lay his life down in the effort. It wasn't a battle of his choosing, but he had agreed to stand and fight it all the same. Once battle had been joined, the soldier knew only one way to play the game.

With everything he had, and damn the cost.

## 5

The public phone was on its fourth shrill ring when Nathan Trask shoved past a pimply faced punk rocker and grabbed the receiver.

"Yes?"

"Are you the lawyer?"

"Yes."

"Where were you, counselor?"

"I had to find a parking space," Trask answered, knowing that it sounded lame. His heart was pounding in his chest, and he could feel a flush of color rising in his cheeks.

"This ain't some kind of fucking game. Leave early next time, Nathan."

Trask felt his heart lurch once against his ribs.

"No names!" he hissed.

"Relax. You think they're tapping every public phone in Jacksonville? Let's not be paranoid."

From where he stood, the syndicate attorney felt exposed to prying eyes, and anything seemed possible. A wiretap, bugs, directional microphones—nothing could automatically be ruled out. His present mission lay outside the sheltered realm of the attorney-client privileges, treading on the quicksand of criminal conspiracy.

Trask had been cautious when he dialed the number Vos had given him, delivering the coded message and receiving his instructions for a callback time, instructing Trask that he'd let the telephone ring five times prior to hang up. If no one answered—or if someone else should answer—all bets were off, and Trask could try out his half-baked explanations on Vos next time he visited his client in the lockup. As it was, Trask knew that he'd nearly blown it, and he wondered if he had the nerve to see his mission through.

"What progress have you made?"

The disembodied voice was smug. "We're tracking, counselor. They've changed the scheduled route."

"So much for planning."

"Hey, it's not a problem. I'm on top of it. They haven't got a chance of showing up in court."

"You say."

"That's right. I say."

Trask mustered all the nerve that he had left. "I don't mind talking to a voice without a face or name, but let's get one thing straight. My client won't have any trouble reaching out for you if things go wrong. I daresay he'd make it a priority. Are we communicating?"

For the first time, Trask detected a note of uneasiness behind the other voice. "I hear you, counselor. And there's no need for all this heavy rap. We're tracking, like I told you. They're not going anywhere that we don't know about."

"How long?"

"Get real. I can't pin down an hour, just like that. We'll wait until they go to ground this evening. Safer all around, you follow? Sitting ducks make easy targets."

"They'll be armed."

"No shit? I thought the Feds would hire some Quakers for the escort team."

Trask felt the anger rising, bitter in his throat. "I don't have time for this," he snapped. "If you have something to report—"

"Just call your office?"

Swallowing the mockery, he muttered, "No."

"I didn't think so, counselor. Before you get all high and mighty, listen up and I'll explain what happens next. Tomorrow at eight o'clock—I don't mean seven fifty-nine or eight O-one—you call me back. Another phone booth, anywhere but that one. I'll have news. You're late, I take it to the man myself."

"I understand."

"Be talking to you, counselor."

The line went dead, and Trask retreated to his car. Another day before he could expect results for Vos. More waiting, and potentially in vain. Trask told himself it wasn't worth the risk, the aggravation, but it made no difference now. The game had been his own selection. He had no choice but to play the hand as it was dealt and pray that he didn't wind up losing everything.

THE ORIGINAL ROUTE had been simplicity itself, calling for a smooth cross-country run on Interstate 10, from Jacksonville all the way to Los Angeles. Bolan had chosen the course from a cursory glance at a triple-A map, but he had no intention of following through. If there were leaks at the DEA, he meant to keep them guessing, and the surest way to throw the enemy a curve—aside from switching cars—would be to change the travel route.

They abandoned the 1-10 near Lake City, Florida, following Interstate 75 north into Georgia. From Valdosta they veered west on Highway 84, across the southwestern corner of the state, stopping for food in a Seminole County diner that advertised Good Eats. The patrons showed a marked preference for pickup trucks and baseball caps with advertising slogans printed on the front. Denim overalls and checkered flannel shirts were the uniform of the day.

They ordered the specialty of the house, which turned out to be overdone burgers and underdone french fries, with suspicious-looking cole slaw on the side. They ate in silence for the most part, carefully avoiding small talk. Bolan kept one eye on the parking lot and studied new customers as they arrived. There were no vehicles outside with license plates from Florida, but that meant nothing. Vos would have connections all along their route, and if the network failed, there'd be free-lance hunters anxious to improve themselves by picking up the bounty placed on Aguire's head.

The DEA connection, Pratt, had estimated that the price might top a million dollars by the time they reached Los Angeles. Considering the danger that Aguire represented to a multibillion-dollar empire, Bolan thought it was conservative. But all those zeroes would provide great motivation for the hungry guns who prowled the fringes of the underworld, desirous of promotion, lacking the contacts necessary for a straight shot at the big time.

Knocking off Aguire would be doubly beneficial to an up-and-coming gunner. With a million dollars in his pocket, he could start to live his fantasies, and at the same time he would score some major points with Vos, a man in need of new commanders for his network. Anyone who tagged Aguire would be sitting pretty when the dealer walked, and gratitude alone could mean a cushy job in distribution, well removed from the persistent dangers of the street. With some initiative and brains, a new kid on the block might carve himself a niche in Vos's empire that would make a million dollars look like chump change.

Some incentive.

He finished off the burger, picturing a million dollars cash. The Executioner had walked away with many times that figure in his one-man war against the syndicate, obtaining his "donations" from assorted numbers of banks, casinos, shooting galleries and bagmen. Never interested in money for its own sake, he had ironically allowed the Mob to fund its own destruction, funneling his profits into weapons, vehicles, surveillance gear. On rare occasions, he made lump-sum payments to the families of victims, knowing cash alone could never heal their wounds, but powerless to help in any other way.

Mack Bolan understood the lure of easy money, and he knew that it was seldom easy. Throwing off the nine-to-five routine, in many cases, meant a life of running scams around the clock, eternally pursuing payoffs that were just around the corner. There was money to be made through drugs, pornography and sex, but wealth was concentrated in a few strong hands, as land and power had been concentrated during feudal times. How many hookers kept a quarter of their earnings when the night was over? Where were all the superstars who planned to conquer Hollywood through hard-core films and videocassettes? How many pushers on the street would stop a slug or serve hard time in lieu of cashing in on twisted dreams?

The Executioner had seen it all before, so he knew that there would be no end of hopefuls, yearning for a shot at Vos's enemy. A moment in the spotlight, one play that could make or break their lives. It would be Bolan's job to prevent some cocky youngster—or some seasoned pro—from canceling Aguire's ticket and collecting on the contract Vos had issued. If and when they surfaced, they would have to die.

He pushed his plate back, noticed that the others had already finished. Bolan paid the bill and left a tip proportionate to the amount and quality of service. He was glad to reach the parking lot, where honest gasoline and diesel fumes replaced the smells of lard and Lysol that were trapped inside.

Their Jimmy stood between a rusting pickup and a 1967 Chevrolet. Bolan circled the vehicle once, inspecting it, although it had been visible from where they sat throughout the meal. When he was satisfied he turned to his brother, reaching for the keys.

"I'll drive."

THEY FOLLOWED Highway 84 across the border into Alabama. A few miles west of Evergreen, they picked up Interstate 65 for the southwestern run to Mobile and the Gulf. Riding shotgun, Johnny divided his time between scanning the scenery and checking the wing mirror, watching their back.

"It's amazing," he said to the silence.

"What's that?" his brother inquired.

"Well, I pictured the South as one humongous swamp, like the 'Glades or the places we trained at Fort Benning. A bus stop or two, a few honky-tonk bars where the rednecks kill time, and a chain gang out working the highway. From what I see here, all the pine trees and hills, we might just as well be in New England."

His brother was smiling. "I'd say that you need to get out more."

"You might have a point." Johnny let his smile fade. "Getting tired?"

"Not so much. We can trade in Mobile if you like."

"I can drive."

Johnny turned to Aguire, surprised by his offer.

"No, thanks," the Executioner responded. "This trip's on the house. If we run into trouble, we won't have the time to change drivers."

"Of course. As you wish."

The Colombian fell silent again, staring out at the trees, and Johnny turned back to examine the highway, wondering idly what was going on inside Aguire's mind. How did it feel to be a hunted man, more valuable dead than he would ever be alive?

The question startled Johnny, and he spent another moment studying his brother's profile. Mack had spent a lifetime with a price tag on his head, and he seemed none the worse for wear. He had acquired new scars along the way, and sometimes there appeared to be a trace of weariness around his eyes, a hint of sadness, but he still had all the moves. If something had been lost along the way, it didn't show.

Perhaps, Johnny thought, that was because he also played the role of hunter in the game that he had chosen for himself. Whenever possible, he turned the tables on the predators and let them know precisely how it felt to be pursued. In Texas, facing trial on manufactured murder charges, and again in Arizona—when he'd been wounded, run to ground—Mack had been able to turn the tide and beat the stalkers at their own damned game. He had a knack for sitting through defeat and finding victory.

The younger Bolan had been helpful to his brother, both in Texas and in Arizona, but he rarely had the chance to work with Mack from the beginning of a job. The other gigs had blown up out of nowhere, taking Johnny by complete surprise and forcing him into a situation where the game was strictly do-or-die. It was a different situation altogether, rolling overland with a specific deadline and objective, knowing that the enemy might strike at any time, from any quarter.

Johnny thought about his legal work in San Diego, how he split his time between helping the poor and working for state or federal prosecutors. It produced a strange dichotomy, defending and accusing, sometimes playing both roles in a single day. At times it made him wish for something simpler, more direct, and then his mind was drawn to Mack, the everlasting war where good and evil could be recognized, addressed as black and white.

He realized his brother had a freedom few men ever knew—the opportunity to choose his enemies and act against them forcefully, the chance to make a concrete, lasting difference in a world where compromise too often won the day. But freedom carried a responsibility as well: a duty to perform regardless of the risks involved. Regardless of the danger.

Johnny put the morbid train of thought away and concentrated on the countryside, examining the hills and trees as if the answer to their problem might be hidden there. And finding none.

AT THIRTY THOUSAND FEET, the Lear jet's pilot killed the seat belt sign and cheerfully addressed his passengers over the intercom. "We've reached our cruising altitude, and we're on schedule for the first leg into Dallas. Smoke 'em if you've got 'em."

Peering through the tiny oval window at a field of clouds, Paul Feder wished that he was back in Florida, conducting business as usual. Two days earlier, as "Michael Wix," he'd been bringing down Ernesto Vos, and now the DEA was wasting his experience on escort duty, playing decoy while their witness took another route to reach Los Angeles.

"This sucks."

Beside him, Agent Alex Coleman—lately known in southern Florida as Ansel Crane—put on a sympathetic smile.

"Forget it," Coleman advised. "It's like vacation time, with pay."

"It's like a swift kick in the ass is what it's like. If they want someone guarded, why the hell aren't we on Vos? Or on Aguire? Anyone can run this scam, for Christ's sake."

"It's supposed to fool the bad guys," Coleman offered, "so they use the best."

"You got a shovel, Al? It's getting pretty deep in here."

"So what's the beef? You worried someone else is going to get the credit for our collar?"

Feder thought about it, scowling. "No, not really. I just hate the feel of being pushed aside, you know? We put this deal together, and Pratt knows it. We've got better coming than a round-trip to L.A."

"Don't knock it. I've got friends out there. They'll fix us up in no time. You'll be glad you came, believe me."

"Bullshit."

Feder had no quarrel with the idea of getting laid: it was the thought of getting robbed that turned his stomach. Busting Vos had been the big one, and he should have been in line for a promotion. Granted, there hadn't been time for Pratt to process all the paperwork—such things took weeks in a bureaucracy like the DEA—but Feder had expected something more up front than simple "attaboys."

Like some respect, for instance.

Glancing back across his shoulder, Feder noticed that their pigeon seemed to be asleep. Pratt said he was an actor—no, a would-be actor, as the face wasn't familiar from the movies or TV. He bore a fair resemblance to Aguire, heightened by a change of hairstyle and the mirrored shades that hid his eyes, a flashy suit that must have put a major strain on petty cash. He had the swagger down, and probably would pass for Carlos at a distance, even through a sniper scope. But now, relaxed and sleeping, Feder thought that the guy left much to be desired.

And who, for Christ's sake, gave a damn?

In Dallas they were staying on the plane while it refueled. At LAX, they'd be waiting on the runway for a caravan of black-and-whites to make the pickup, whisking What's-His-Name away to county jail, where he would be residing incommunicado for the next few days. It had to be an eerie feeling for the actor, playing to an audience of none, but he was being paid, so what the hell?

If there was any action, Feder calculated it would come in Jacksonville before they put Vos on the plane. By this time, old Ernesto had to figure he was in the shit, and it wouldn't be out of character for him to try a jail break. Hell, it would be out of character if he didn't. In Colombia his word was law, and when he told a judge or prosecutor it was time to jump, they asked how high. Supreme court justices had been assassinated on his whim, and Feder knew that Vos wasn't about to take a term of life plus ninety-nine without a fight.

No way at all.

Nor would he be deceived so easily by Pratt's diversionary tactics. It made sense to help Aguire out by running decoys, but it only shaved the odds; it didn't guarantee that he was free and clear. Before he reached Los Angeles, the state's key witness stood to face a ton of heavy shit. And Feder would have given damn near anything he had to be there, standing toe-to-toe with Vos's gunners when it all went down.

But he was going out to California. On a milk run. Wasted.

"Bladder break," he grumbled, rising from his seat and edging past Coleman, standing for a moment in the aisle to get his balance. He was halfway to the restroom when something shook the jet, causing him to stumble.

"What the hell?"

He turned toward Coleman, glimpsed his partner's face, and recognized the truth, too late.

"Aw, shit."

The jet disintegrated in midair, its wings sheared off by the explosion. Fragments of the fuselage were hurled in all directions. With the momentum from the blast, the cockpit and its occupants flew on for several hundred feet, a comet trailing smoke and flame, before it slowly, gracefully, began to fall.

THE HUNTERS FOUND Aguire and his escort west of Orange Grove, Mississippi, making decent time along the I-10. The license plate was wrong, but there was no mistake. The driver hung well back, while his companion used the radio.

"We've got 'em, Central."

"Are you sure?"

"No doubt about it. Different plates, but it's your pigeon."

"What's your twenty?"

"Westbound, Highway 10. Let's call it fifteen minutes out of Bay Saint Louis."

"Don't nobody spook him, now."

"He'll never know we're here."

"All right, you stay in touch. They stop somewhere, you call in double-quick, and I'll have people out to help you."

"Roger that."

"We're sitting pretty if we don't mess up."

"I know just how to do it."

"Don't go trying anything without a backup, now, you hear?"

"I read you, Central. Out."

The shotgun rider hung the microphone on its hook and slipped a hand inside his leather jacket, drawing reassurance from the Army-issue .45 he carried in a shoulder sling. It would be easy, he imagined, just to overtake the Jimmy, pump a couple live ones through the driver's window, then see what they could see.

"You want to take them?" the driver asked.

"Hell, no. I only thought—"

"Don't think, all right? You're driving. Let's not push our luck."

The wheelman frowned. "A million dollars, Arnie. Free and clear."

"This ain't about the money, Claude."

"Oh, no? Well, what, then?"

"Shows how much you know about the business. What we're doing here is moving up, *comprende*? Paying dues and making friends that can't be beat."

"You mean we don't get paid?"

"The money's secondary." Arnie loved to dazzle Claude with his vocabulary, trotting out the big words anytime he had the chance. "We'll get our cut, all right, but I want something better."

"Shit, what's better than a million bucks?"

"Respect. Authority. We're moving in a different circle, here. If you can't see that, you're nowhere."

"I see a fortune on the hoof, that's what I see. If we call all kinds of backup in, they're going to shave that bounty down so fine it won't pay next month's rent."

"How much you figure we'll be earning if we go against our orders, Claude? You reckon everyone will be so happy they'll just let us keep the whole damned payoff for ourselves?"

"They might."

"Sometimes I truly wonder, Claude. You give me cause."

"We do the work, we ought to get the cash."

"And if we fuck it up?"

"Say what?"

"Who's in that Jimmy, Claude?"

"Some kind of stoolie."

"And who else?"

"A couple escorts."

"Are they cops by any chance?"

"I figure so."

"You figure they've got any guns at all?"

"Well, natcherly they got—" Claude stopped and glanced at Arnie frowning. "Oh. I get it."

"Hallelujah," Arnie sneered. "Now, let's suppose we try to jump them on our own, and they should manage to escape."

"We're in the shit."

"Which is exactly where I do not plan to be. I hope we're clear on that."

"Okay, we wait for backup."

"And we make damned sure that we get credit for the kill," he added. "Backup means exactly what it says. They cover us and follow my directions."

"Our directions."

"Right, Claude. Our directions."

"When you put it that way, Arnie, it makes sense."

"I'm glad you think so."

"I'll tell you something. I was getting worried for a minute, there. It looked like we were getting shuffled out."

"We're in, Claude. All the way."

"A piece of cake," the driver replied.

His shotgun rider grinned. "Like falling into a grave."

## 6

Ernesto Vos wore an exaggerated smile when hulking deputies arrived to lead him from his cell. He would have liked to strangle them bare-handed, then eviscerate their bodies, but instead he feigned compliance with their rules and regulations, posing as a model prisoner. The dealer knew that he was vulnerable here, despite the trappings of security. He understood from personal experience the way jails worked. If he offended any of his keepers by an overt act, they'd find ways to punish him. His life might even be at risk.

Vos knew that he wasn't safe within the prison walls. He had murdered men in prison—had them murdered, rather—and knew that there were always ways to breach security. Where business was concerned, with profits in the millions every week, competitors and enemies became ingenious planners, spinning webs of treachery to bring him down. Carlos Aguire had schemed behind his back to place Vos in a prison cell, and others would be swift to take advantage of his absence from the scene in Bogotá. Inevitably they would start to nibble at the fringes of his territory, but the odds were fair that they would seek his permanent removal prior to making any drastic moves.

The government of the United States might help them there, if Vos went to trial, but a conviction, life in prison, might not satisfy the vultures of Columbia. His competition understood that prison doors swung both ways, and they wouldn't—shouldn't—feel secure until he was exterminated.

Nathan Trask was seated in the waiting room when Vos arrived, and the attorney kept his eyes downcast while Vos was seated and tethered to his chair. His right arm was left free, presumably in case his signature was required on legal documents. He waited silently until the door closed tight behind him and he was alone with his attorney.

"What news?"

Trask frowned. "I'm told that everything should be wrapped up tonight."

Vos raised an eyebrow. "You have doubts?"

"I don't know who I'm dealing with. This cowboy on the phone sounds cocky, overconfident. I'm not convinced he'll do us any good."

"If he can't, no one can. Relax. It's not as if your freedom were in jeopardy."

Trask blushed. "That isn't fair, Ernesto. Dammit—"

"Fair or not, it is the truth. When we are finished here, you will be free to leave. Unless Aguire dies, my future looks like this." He waved his hand to indicate the jail around him. "I must trust your contact, Nathan. Whether you believe in him or not is totally irrelevant."

"Of course."

"Were you successful in alerting all my colleagues."

"That's a problem." Trask looked worried as he spoke. "I tried to call all five, as you requested—and I'll keep on trying if you like—but I believe they've all gone underground to ride this out."

"Perhaps it's for the best," Vos said, and smiled. The calls had been a simple way of checking up on whether his instructions had been carried out. If none of his lieutenants could be reached by Nathan Trask, it meant the killer teams had done their work efficiently. "We'll leave them to their own devices."

"As you wish."

"I wish to be at home in Bogatá," Vos said, the feigned good humor disappearing from his voice. "I need my freedom, Nathan."

"I've done everything you asked."

"Of course you have. And I am grateful for your loyalty."

"Not at all."

"Don't worry if your contact seems a bit ... impetuous. He knows his business, and he knows how I reward my faithful friends."

"If I had some idea of who he was ..."

"An ally, Nathan. That is all you need to know. Now, quick, before my keepers come again, I must hear anything he told you."

Settling back, Vos heard the counselor's report and smiled. The hare had deviated from his course, but even now the hounds were closing, making preparations for the kill. Tonight it would be finished. Several days to go, while Trask tied up the government with legal sleight-of-hand and evidence was made to disappear. Vos reckoned he should be back home in Bogotá within two weeks.

The U.S. Constitution would protect his rights to life, liberty and the pursuit of happiness.

Vos loved democracy with all his heart.

BROGNOLA TOOK THE CALL from Felix Pratt without enthusiasm, scowling as he raised the telephone receiver to his ear.

"We've got a little problem," Pratt informed him.

"Spell it out."

"Okay, no frills. Our decoy bit the big one. He was flying west and something happened. Midair flame-out. We've got people from the FAA in Tallahassee working on the site, but I already know what happened."

"Vos."

"Who else?"

Brognola felt the anger rising in his chest, a corresponding pressure building in his skull, and he made every effort to control himself.

"What happened to security?" he asked when he could trust himself to speak.

"I'm looking into it. We knew there was a risk from the beginning. I prefer to take this as a hopeful sign."

"How's that?"

"Vos has the decoy killed. That means he didn't know it *was* a decoy. Now, we string him on for a couple days, pretending that Aguire's dead, and by the time he finds out his mistake, our pigeon's in L.A. Case closed.''

"How many dead?" Brognola asked.

"Dead where?" Pratt seemed confused. "You mean the plane?"

"That's right."

"Let's see, two pilots, um, that would be five."

"You closing their case, too?"

"I wouldn't be surprised." The DEA man's voice came back with just a trace of righteous indignation. "Once we've got Vos on ice for smuggling, I can put the wheels in motion for a murder charge. He'll never fry this side of hell, but I can make damned sure he's off the streets forever. I know how to play this game."

"That's all it is to you? A game?"

"I see. You're waiting for the hearts and flowers, right? Don't hold your breath. I've lost too many men in the past twelve years, in ways you can't imagine. I made friends with some of them before I learned it doesn't pay, but I miss all of them the same. If you're about to say that I don't care about my people, mister, then I say you're full of shit."

Brognola let it slide and changed his tack. "Your plumbers on the job?"

"They're working overtime," Pratt answered, calming. "Nothing solid, yet, but if our leak had top-flight access, nothing would have happened to the decoy."

That made sense, but Brognola couldn't suppress a nagging apprehension. Striker and the kid were out there, riding with a time bomb in their laps, and he could draw no consolation from the fact that five men had been murdered by mistake.

"Is there some way to hold Vos incommunicado for the next few days?"

"I wish." Pratt sounded weary. "We've got him on a short leash as it is. Nobody sees him but his lawyer."

"Nathan Trask?" Brognola made a sour face. "You might as well let half the goddamned syndicate drop by for coffee."

"Sure, I hear you, but you know the law. Defendants have a right to meet with their attorney. What they talk about is strictly confidential. We're on shaky ground already, limiting the time they spend together, but we haven't had a beef from Trask, so far.''

"Have you got people on him?"

"Trask? You kidding? I recall the last time people from the FBI began to check him out. He had their asses in court so fast it made them dizzy. If I go after Nate today, you'll see me going after unemployment checks this time next week.''

Brognola knew it was the truth, but knowing didn't make it any easier to take. There had to be a way...

"I thought you ought to know," Pratt said, "that your people changed the route."

Brognola smiled. "Who says?"

"I put a couple spotters out to see them safely on their way. For all I know, they're up in smoke.''

"That's show biz."

"Yeah. I don't suppose you have a clue...''

"They don't confide in me," Brognola answered honestly. "If I could put my finger on them now, I'd have a Bureau SWAT team standing by.''

"I guess it's just as well. If we can't find them, how can Vos?''

"I hope you're right."

"No sweat. I'll try to get a Polaroid of Ernie's face when Carlos turns up on the witness stand. It ought to be hysterical.''

"No doubt. I hate to cut this short, but I've got several things to wrap up here before I pack it in.''

"Yeah, right. Same here. If I catch any whispers—''

"Let me know, of course."

"You got it. 'Bye."

Brognola spent a moment staring at the telephone. Five men he had never met were dead; three others—two of whom he loved like sons or brothers—might be added to the list at any moment. There was nothing he could do to help within the law. And yet...

He lifted the receiver, punching up the number of an office on another floor. A strong voice answered on the second ring.

"What's shaking, Leo?"

"Killing time. You got some word?"

The big Fed briefed him on the subject of Pratt's call, producing worried noises on the other end.

"There should be something we can do."

Brognola took a chance. "It's funny you should say that..."

PRATT TIPPED THE BOTTLE of Excedrin, palming four fat tablets, and reached for the can of 7-Up. Four tabs was twice the recommended dosage, but his head was hammering with twice the normal pain, and jawing with Brognola hadn't helped his situation any.

Pratt could understand the man from Justice being testy, sure. He had two people on the line, and now it looked as if things were getting rough out there. Pratt sympathized, but things were rough all over, all the time. Brognola should have known that going in.

It was disturbing that Aguire's escorts had seen fit to deviate from their established route. It left Pratt in an awkward situation when the brass inquired about his project status, and he didn't like the sound of "five men dead, three missing." It implied a certain lack of expertise, and Felix Pratt had built his reputation in the DEA by acting as a slick professional.

So many of the people in the DEA were burned out on their job these days, disgusted with the obvious futility of battling against the tide. The so-called "war on drugs" was going nowhere fast, with foreign aid continuing to Third World strongmen while they shipped their poison stateside by the ton. Administrations came and went in Washington, but dope flowed on forever.

Pratt resisted disillusionment by thinking of his mission as a challenge. No one else had any luck at breaking up the Bogatá connection, but that didn't mean the link couldn't be broken. Ingenuity was called for, a strategic breakthrough, and the long-awaited victory could still be his.

But was it worth the effort? Were citizens of the United States pissed off enough to call a halt and make it stick?

Would they give up their nightly snort to rid America of what the White House called a "creeping cancer"?

Pratt considered taking more Excedrin, changed his mind and slipped the bottle back inside his top desk drawer. No point in working up a sour stomach in addition to the headache. Work would serve him better as an analgesic, and he dragged the stack of fat manila folders closer, noting that Aguire's lay on top.

Aguire.

Opening the file, Pratt made eye contact with a glossy photograph. Aguire had been smiling when they snapped the picture, unaware that he was being captured for posterity. The smile was confident, a mirror of the man's conviction that his money and connections made the world go 'round.

Pratt didn't see that smile much, anymore. It had been good to wipe the smug self-satisfaction from Aguire's face and watch him as reality hit home. Pratt had presented him with simple choices—simple, as opposed to easy—and the dealer had been forced to play a different kind of game. If nothing else, Pratt gained a sense of satisfaction from the minor victory.

And now Aguire had been taken off his hands. The men from Justice were responsible for safe delivery in California, an arrangement that had secretly delighted Pratt's superiors. If anything went wrong, Brognola and his people would absorb the heat. The DEA was free and clear.

It was too bad about the decoy, but you couldn't fight a war without some friendly casualties. Feder and Coleman were—correction, had been—decent agents, and their work toward busting Vos would doubtless be remembered. This time, though, the commendations would be posthumous.

So be it.

Pratt had other fish to fry, and he'd given up on living in the past. His statement to Brognola had been accurate: too many friends and comrades had been lost along the way for him to stop and grieve each time another bought the farm. If you got bogged down in the grief, the odds were good that you would never make it out the other side. Regret was like a patch of quicksand, eating hopes and dreams along with flesh and blood.

If Pratt felt like regretting anything, he never had to look beyond himself: two broken marriages, a son he never saw, because the bitch who took him for a one-way ride on alimony liked the sun in California better than Miami Beach, a job with minimal advancement opportunities that took him to the sewer every day like clockwork. If the need arose, Pratt reckoned he could generate self-pity like a goddamned pro, but there appeared to be no point.

A savvy fighter didn't waste time dwelling on the blows that left him cut and bleeding. He moved on in search of new opponents, working out to keep himself in shape for one more round, perhaps a title shot. And if the referee should be distracted for a moment, what the hell, he threw a punch below the belt to even up the score.

Despite the throbbing pain inside his skull, Pratt thought that he had never been in better shape. He couldn't wait to hear the bell.

DECELERATION WOKE Aguire from a fitful sleep. His neck was stiff, and he experienced a moment's panic as the Jimmy slowed, but he could see no signs of ambush up ahead.

"This look all right to you?" the Executioner asked.

"I guess."

The Cajun Cottage Motor Inn resembled several hundred other small motels that they'd passed since leaving Jacksonville. It seemed as though they'd been on the road forever, though Aguire knew his sense of timing was disoriented by his frequent lapses into sleep. Despite his apprehension, travel had a stupefying impact. He'd dozed sporadically as they crossed southern Mississippi, following Interstate 10 and the curve of the Gulf, catching Interstate 12 in Louisiana for the northbound run to Baton Rouge.

"Where are we?"

Johnny half turned to face him. "South of Shreveport. If our route got leaked 'by accident,' they should be looking for us somewhere in between Lake Charles and Baton Rouge right now."

"And if there was no leak?"

"We're still on schedule," Bolan told him. "Better safe than slaughtered."

"Yes."

Johnny slipped a hand inside his jacket, making sure his weapon was within reach. "I'll check us in. Two rooms?"

"Good thinking."

"Why two rooms?" Aguire asked when the younger Bolan had disappeared inside the office.

"Just a safety measure. It should split the opposition if they don't know where we are."

"What opposition?"

"Theoretically." The soldier's eyes regarded him from the rearview mirror. "I'm still hoping that we've given them the slip."

"And if you're wrong?"

"We take it as it comes."

Aguire shifted in his seat and scanned the parking lot. The Cajun Cottage Motor Inn reminded him uncomfortably of Jacksonville and his confinement at the Tropical Motel. This time, however, there were other guests in evidence. He counted seven cars in addition to their own, which suggested that the place still had approximately half its rooms available.

"Who's the local mover?" Bolan asked.

"Vos doesn't deal in Shreveport. He has people in New Orleans, but I don't know if they've got connections this far north."

"Who would he use for muscle, in a pinch?"

Aguire shrugged. "It varies. Sometimes the Italians, sometimes not. When the Vietnamese gangs started cutting into business on the Gulf last year, he made arrangements with the Klan."

"As in the KKK?"

"Why not? They hate the Asians anyway, and they need money worse than ever now, with all the damage suits and legal fees. Vos pays them well, and they forget about his accent for a while. It's business."

"Right."

Aguire recognized the big man's attitude. He saw the world in terms of black and white, where good and evil never overlap. It was an antiquated notion, but the prisoner wasn't in a position for debate. Survival was the issue now, and that *was* absolute. Aguire couldn't find a way to compromise with death.

Johnny emerged from the motel office, scanning left and right before he joined them once again. "We're booked in number six and lucky number thirteen. Take your pick."

Bolan checked both rooms from where he sat. "Let's dummy number six," he said at last. "Thirteen has fewer neighbors."

"And it's closer to the Coke machine," his brother added.

"Right. That, too."

"You superstitious, Carlos?"

"No."

"I'm glad to hear it, man. The last thing we need now would be a hex."

Aguire forced a smile, but he could find no respite from anxiety in small talk. Sudden death was trailing close behind him, like a shadow he couldn't shake, and any moment now he feared that it would smother him in darkness.

There was no escape, but every moment he survived beneath that shadow counted as another victory, a blow against his enemies. If he could somehow reach Los Angeles alive and testify, his life—and death—might count for something.

At the very least, Aguire knew that he would be remembered.

And the thought gave him no comfort whatsoever.

## 7

The room was decorated in a style that Johnny Bolan thought of as Motel Traditional: beige walls that needed scrubbing or a fresh coat of pain; a nubby carpet that hadn't been cleaned since installation; K-Mart reproductions of some famous paintings on the walls, offset by one of Jesus that appeared to be clipped out of a religious magazine. The garish flowered bedspreads clashed with everything in sight, and charcoal worms, produced by unattended cigarettes, had scarred the genuine synthetic hardwood furniture. A Gideon Bible shared one of the nightstands with an ashtray advertising Michelob. Inside the tiny bathroom, Johnny had found the plastic glasses wrapped in crinkly cellophane and the toilet that was banded with a strip of paper proclaiming that the bowl was Sanitized for Your Protection.

"Home, sweet home," he told the empty room and set to work.

His brother and Aguire were in room thirteen, where all three would spend the night. Johnny had been sent to make room six look "lived in," banking on the Executioner's hunch that any hostile visitors would have to split their forces, checking out both rooms to guarantee a sweep. It made good sense, but the young man was hoping they could pass the night without a confrontation. They'd traveled some four hundred and twenty miles that day, and he was ready for a good night's sleep.

Fat chance.

There would be sentry duty, off and on throughout the night. But first, with any luck, there would be food. His stomach growled, reminding him that they had eaten nothing since the stop in Georgia, hours earlier.

He stripped the covers back on matching double beds and formed the pillows into shapes that would—he hoped—approximate human forms in semidarkness, when the caller had no time to pick and choose his targets. Johnny turned the television on, its volume low but audible to someone standing just outside the door. The curtains had been drawn, and Johnny crossed to the bathroom in semidarkness. He turned on the overhead light and left the door ajar. It would, he thought, provide an extra touch of realism for a midnight caller, forcing the guy to hurry if he thought one of his targets was up and about.

Johnny checked the room once more, left the key on the dresser and closed the self-locking door behind him. If they passed the night without an incident, the maid could use her passkey in the morning. He'd let her puzzle out the placement of the pillows and the television playing to an empty room. She would discuss it with the manager, no doubt, and by the time they put their heads together on the problem, Johnny and his fellow travelers would be miles away.

First, however, they'd have to make it through the night.

The sky was darkening from dusk to night as Johnny made his way back toward thirteen. He scanned the motel parking lot and found a new addition, parked outside of number nine. The pickup had a custom tarp across its bed, an empty gun rack in the window and it carried Louisiana plates. A decal in the lower left-hand corner of the windshield proclaimed the driver's membership in something called the Second Amendment Foundation. A whip antenna mounted on the bumper told Johnny there'd be a CB radio inside the truck.

He knocked at number thirteen, slipped inside and let his brother close the door behind him.

"Finished?"

Johnny nodded. "It won't rate a cover story in *House Beautiful* but it should do the job."

"We have a new arrival."

"Number nine? I saw."

"Two men," the warrior told him. "Thirties. Light on luggage, one a little shorter than the other."

"Any flickers?"

"Not a one. If they're on us, they've had at least one acting lesson."

"I could check it out," Johnny suggested. "A little blade work on their tires, and I can drop in like a helpful neighbor, scope their room for hardware."

"Never mind. If they're with us, we've seen it coming. Otherwise, I'd like to minimize our contact with civilians."

"Fair enough, but we'll need contact with a restaurant before much longer. There's a couple places up the highway selling chicken and ribs."

"In a minute." Bolan moved toward the door. "I need to make a phone call."

"Fair enough." Johnny checked his watch. "Ten minutes do it?"

"I think so."

"Right. I'll see you in eleven, one way or another."

"Negative. Our passenger's the top priority. He doesn't leave the room tonight, and we don't leave him on his own."

"If you run into trouble—"

"I can handle it."

"Okay."

No doubt on that score, Johnny thought. Whatever happened, brother Mack could handle it.


IN NUMBER NINE, the lookouts lay on separate beds, a six-pack split between them. The portable TV was tuned to *Wheel of Fortune*, with the sound turned off.

"I still think we could take them by ourselves."

"No good," Arnie Norris replied. "They split their forces. That means splitting ours, and I'll remind you that there's only two of us."

"There's only three of them," Claude countered stubbornly.

"I know that, Claude. But any way you slice it, one of us is going to be facing two men—"

"I'm not scared of—"

"And the other will be standing there without a stitch of cover when their two men finish with our one."

"If we surprise them . . ."

"Claude, I'm telling you that we've got people on the way. We're under orders. Someone isn't going to be happy if they get here and we've fucked things up."

He didn't have to spell out who the "someone" was. Claude scowled and took another hit of beer, swallowing any further protests. Norris set his beer aside and took his Colt Commander form the nightstand. He pulled the magazine then replaced it after double-checking the weapon's load.

"What kind of heat you think they're packing, Arnie?"

"I don't know. The normal cop stuff, I suppose."

"You figure .38s and shotguns?"

"I imagine so."

"Suppose they got a couple Ingrams in there, Arnie?"

"Don't you worry. With our backup coming, we'll have all the shit we need. The dragon's sending down eight men, and I don't reckon they'll be coming empty-handed."

"Who's in charge?" Claude asked.

It hadn't come up on the phone, and Arnie frowned. "We did the groundwork. Any credit for the operator, seems to me we've got the main share in the bag."

"Those other boys might not agree."

"They ought to know that this is business, Claude."

"Damn right."

Pat Sajak filled the TV screen, lips moving silently, and Norris raised the .45 to draw a bead between his eyes. "So sorry, Pat," he said, grinning, "you've just been canceled."

"Arnie?"

"Yeah?"

"You figure those two boys are FBI?"

"I wouldn't mind."

"That's heat, for damn sure, if they are."

"A million dollars helps to cool things off."

"I guess."

"You getting nervous, Claude?"

"Just thinking."

"That's your first mistake."

"So funny I forgot to laugh."

"I mean it. You can think a job to death before you ever make a move. Start worrying about all kinds of shit, and then, first thing you know, you've got yourself convinced you shouldn't do the job at all."

"It's not like that."

"I hope not, Claude. Because the dragon will be mighty disappointed if you let him down."

"Don't worry. I'll be right there with you when it hits the fan."

"I know that, Claude. We have to stick together. We're a team."

For now, Norris thought, but he kept the postscript to himself. When they were finished with the evening's work and he was paid, when he had earned his brownie points with men who mattered, Arnie meant to chart himself a new direction, find himself a new horizon. Beating on the drum for white supremacy was one thing, and he liked his work, but it was time for him to grow, make something of himself. He needed room to breathe, and it was getting rather claustrophobic in the Klan. The outside jobs, commissioned by their dragon, had provided Arnie with a new perspective on the world, and he was looking forward to the break.

Soon, now.

The screen was taken over by commercials, and he aimed his pistol at a Jewish-looking housewife selling laundry soap.

"So sorry."

BROGNOLA'S SECRETARY caught him on the threshold, hat in hand.

"Line one, sir."

Doubling back, the big Fed closed the office door behind him, crossed to his desk and lifted the receiver. "Yes?"

"I'm on an open line. You clear?"

"Should be, but keep your twenty quiet, just in case."

"We changed the route."

"I heard. It was a good idea."

"Anything at your end?"

"Someone bagged the decoy."

"Damn!"

"Roger that."

"What happened?"

"FAA's still picking up the pieces, but it looks like plastique, set to blow at thirty thousand feet."

There was a moment's silence on the other end, and Brognola could picture Bolan turning over options in his mind, deciding whether the attack increased Aguire's danger or diminished it.

"Will they believe they tagged their pigeon?"

"For a while, I hope. That's guesswork, mind you. Mr. DEA still doesn't know how bad he's leaking, or from where."

"What kind of shop's he running over there?"

"The best he can, all things considered."

"I don't buy it, Hal. It shouldn't take an army to protect one man."

"Have there been any problems?"

"Not yet. It's early, but I'm hoping we can pull it off."

"If you agree. I'll mobilize a team and have them meet you. This fiasco with the decoy changes things."

"Not really. I'm convinced we have a better chance without the fanfare. Anyway, if DEA has leaks on this one..."

Bolan didn't finish the sentence, but Brognola got the message, loud and clear. It stung, but he couldn't deny its basic truth.

"I gave some thought to that myself. I've got no answer for it."

"Then we shouldn't ask the question."

"I'm sorry that I roped you in on this."

"You made an offer. I accepted. No one got roped into anything."

"I hate it when you make things easy on me."

The warrior chuckled softly. "I'll remember that. And now, I'm out of time."

"You'll keep in touch?"

"If possible." He lingered for a moment on the line, then added, "If we blow it, I expect you'll get the word through channels."

"I'll pretend I didn't hear that, guy."

"Okay. I'll see you."

"Bet your ass."

The line went dead, and Brognola replaced the receiver in its cradle. It was obvious that Bolan was anticipating trouble. Leaks at the DEA would soon confirm that Vos had tagged a decoy, rather than Aguire. Once that information registered, the hunt would be reactivated with a vengeance—hell, it could be underway already, even as he stood there wasting time.

Brognola shrugged his coat off, stripped the cellophane from a cigar and sat down at his desk. A moment earlier he'd been homeward bound, but it would have to wait. There were channels of investigation to be followed, buttons to be pushed and contacts to be made. He needed information on the inner workings of the DEA, and with a bit of luck, a phone call to the Farm should do the trick.

The big Fed punched out a number for the common room at Stony Man Farm, nestled in the scenic Blue Ridge Mountains of Virginia to the south. As always, the phone was answered on the second ring.

"What's shaking, boss?"

"The whole world, Aaron. Can you help me out?"

"We aim to please."

"I need to take a quiet look inside the DEA."

"WE'RE ALMOST THERE. Another six or seven miles."

"Great."

Jason Meyers reached down between his feet and picked an Ingram submachine gun off the Chevy's rubber floor mat. He removed the magazine to verify that it was fully loaded, flicked the safety off and checked the live round in the chamber, then finally returned the stubby weapon to the mat when he was satisfied. Behind him, he could hear the other members of the wrecking crew as they examined their own weapons, preparing for the kill.

He had selected each man personally, these and four more in the trailing car, to guarantee that nothing would go wrong. The dragon had impressed him with the magnitude of the assignment, and as the exalted cyclops of the district, Meyers was determined not to fail.

He had a reputation to protect, and there was heavy money riding on the outcome of the operation. Meyers had spent the past three years convincing brother Klansmen he was fit to lead, and while a few of them still joked about his "Jewish" name when they were liquored up, most of them had the sense to wait until his back was turned.

His last raid had turned his life around, and it was worth the scars he carried from his confrontation with the Muslim, with the hideout razor. Scars were almost mandatory for a self-styled warrior, and his elevation to the post of cyclops was assured when the incumbent started serving eight years federal time for manufacturing explosives. Careless, that, but who would tip the FBI that it should check old Howard's basement for the evidence?

Who else, other than his new replacement on the team?

Meyers felt no guilt about the phone call, knowing in his heart that he'd done the Klan a favor. By the time he went on trial, old Howard had been drinking heavily and topping off his booze supply with money skimmed from dues. Instead of working hard against the blacks and Jews who ran the country, Howard had been working on his liver with a steady stream of sour mash and showing up for Klavern meetings with a load on half the time. It had been damned embarrassing for everyone.

With Jason Meyers in charge, the Klan was moving forward, making progress once again. His raid against the Shreveport Muslims had been small potatoes by comparison with what he had lined up for the congressional elections in the fall. With any luck, he might be putting on the Wizard's purple robe before long.

First things first, however. This night's work was special, on behalf of an important client who supplied the Klan with arms and outside muscle work from time to time. He was a foreigner, of course, but still an anti-Communist, and he was paying cash. A million dollars on the barrel head, of which a solid five percent was earmarked for the leader of the team that made the score.

Meyers had been counting dollar signs all afternoon and waiting for the call from Arnie Norris that would bring him closer to the payoff. He could smell it now, intoxicating him with its nearness. Fifty thousand dollars, paid in cash, untouched by the greedy IRS.

And all he had to do was kill a man, or watch while one was killed.

Correction, three men.

Two were escorts, probably from Washington. They might be U.S. Marshals, FBI—whatever. It was all the same to Meyers, with fifty thousand dollars riding on the line. The Feds had served his purpose once, removing Howard from his post as cyclops, but that didn't mean they were his friends. If anything, the guilty link between them made Meyers hate his benefactors all the more. As stooges of the Zionist Occupational Government, the escorts were fair game for any Klansman with an itchy trigger finger.

"Pull over here," he said impulsively.

"What's wrong?"

"There's nothing wrong. Just stop the car."

He had a sudden inclination to address the troops, and ten more minutes wouldn't matter in the scheme of things. Their pigeons weren't going anywhere tonight.

Except, perhaps, to eternal hell.

"WE NEED TO TALK," Mack Bolan said when he'd closed the motel door behind him.

"Problems?" Johnny said.

"Could be. Vos tagged the decoy."

"Jesus. How?"

"Hal hasn't got a clue. Looks like the same leak at the DEA."

"What's our time frame to exposure?"

"That's another question mark. Pratt means to play it straight, but since we don't know where the leak is, there's a chance we might be blown already."

"So much for security."

"It could be worse. We're better than a hundred miles off-route. If someone pried our schedule out of Pratt, they should be looking south, along the Gulf."

"Good thing we changed the plates."

"It might not be enough," Aguire said, surprising the other two men.

"We're listening," Johnny encouraged.

"I know the way Vos works. He has eyes everywhere. Not only dealers, but police and politicians, judges, 'honest' businessmen. It's impossible to hide forever."

"We don't need forever," Bolan answered. "Just tonight, and two more days."

"A lifetime."

"Giving up already?"

"No." Aguire stiffened. "But I am prepared to die."

"Some other time. We're here to keep you breathing, and I plan to do my job."

The witness flashed a quick, ironic smile. "I wish you luck."

"All this excitement makes me hungry," Johnny quipped. "Who's game? I saw a Colonel Sanders and a Long John Silver's down the road."

"Let's make it chicken," Bolan said. "I've had my quota on the fishy smells for one day."

"Chicken all around," his brother answered. "I'll be back before you know it."

"Keep your eyes peeled, little brother."

"That's affirmative."

The door clicked shut, and the Executioner turned on the television set. He found the evening news in progress, but the program had moved on to sports and weather bulletins, its segment on the national and local news complete. He turned if off and made a mental note to try again around eleven.

"Vos must want you pretty bad."

Aguire smiled. "Enough to make you rich if you deliver me."

"No sale."

"Few men would hesitate to name their price."

"Vos can't afford me."

"He's a very wealthy man."

"He's scum. I make a point to never work for scum."

"A man of principle?"

"They're not extinct."

"It's curious. I've spent the best part of my life corrupting other men, and now I must depend on two who cannot be corrupted. That's ironic, don't you think?"

"Poetic justice."

"I do not believe in justice."

"But you still intend to testify?"

"It is a matter of survival, Mr. Blanski."

"So is justice, in the long run."

"Call it vengeance, then. I know that Vos will kill me, soon. Pratt tells me otherwise, but he is only bribing me with words, pretending he believes I have a chance. If I must die, I mean to take Vos with me."

"He won't burn," the Executioner replied. "The federal government has no death penalty for dealers, and appeals would tie it up for years, regardless."

"He will rot in prison. Lose his palace and his women, cars and money. That is death enough."

"You really hate this guy."

"There was a time," Aguire said, "when I could tell you that I loved him like a father. Now, I do what I must do."

And Bolan followed that just fine.

In fact he knew the tune by heart.

## 8

Christ, it never failed.

The office bell was clanging for attention, interrupting one more rerun of *The Rockford Files*. And just when Jimbo was about to solve the mystery, goddammit.

Justin Harris set his rum and Coke aside, muting the television with his remote control as he rose from his favorite chair. After twenty years in the business, he was still looking forward to getting through one evening—one program—without interruptions. It was half past eight, and anybody looking for a room should have found one by now. But that didn't stop the stragglers from interrupting his evenings. Inconsiderate bastards.

Harris didn't own the Cajun Cottage Motor Inn. That honor was reserved for a consortium of lawyers in New Orleans, but they kept him on to manage things and keep the place in shape. They trusted him to give a square report on revenue, and if the place lost money, no one bitched about it. Justin figured they'd found themselves a tax write-off, but who was he to blow the whistle, when he had himself a goddamned sinecure? As long as things weren't too far in the red, he'd be living free and drawing pay besides.

Still, he would have liked to watch TV in peace, just once.

It was a night for men alone, and Harris wondered if the Cajun Cottage Motor Inn was turning into some damned faggot's rendezvous. First three men checking in to six and thirteen, specifying that they needed space between the rooms. That was fine with Harris, since the place was half-empty. Next two rednecks came along together, and while Justin didn't think they looked like sissies, you could never really tell these days. Some pansies didn't swish the way they used to; they were into chains and leather, all that kind of shit.

Four men were waiting for him, lined up and scowling at the counter. Harris wished that he'd turned on the damned NO VACANCY sign, but it was too late now. He'd be forced to deal with them, and that was the end of it, by God. The sign was going on as soon as Justin had their greenbacks in his hand.

"Good evening, gentlemen. What can I do for you?"

He always asked the same thing, as if it weren't obvious.

"You run this place?"

"That's right." A stupid question, Harris thought, but if you took all four of them and mashed their brains together, you would still be several ounces short of average smarts. "You boys must need a room."

"We need some information," said the tall one in the middle, resting big hands on the countertop.

"Information?"

"On a couple of your customers."

Justin felt a worm of fear begin to wriggle down his spine. "Well, I don't know..."

"We're interested in who checked into number six and number thirteen a while back."

"You guys the police, or what?"

The tall man reached inside his jacket and withdrew an Ingram, sticking the muzzle between Justin's eyes.

"I guess we'd be 'or what,'" he answered. "Now, about that information..."

"Numbers six and thirteen, right. Just tell me what you need to know."

"The names, for starters."

"Let me check the registration card." He bent to reach beneath the desk, and three more guys drew a bead on him. He felt a sheen of perspiration on his brow, despite the air-conditioning. "You want the name, I'll have to check the card," he told them. "I don't pay that much attention to the customers."

"Go on," the tall man said, "but don't start thinking you're a hero."

"No, sir. That ain't likely."

He retrieved the daily registration cards and shuffled through them. "J. B. Green and party's all it says. Sounds colorful." He tried a grin, but the intruders weren't buying it.

"Which room's the doubt?"

"Haven't got a clue," he told them honestly. "I didn't watch them when they stowed their bags. I couldn't tell you who went where."

"If you lie to me, old man, I'll punch your ticket."

"Thought you might. That's why I'm being straight. I told you. I don't pay attention to the customers."

The man studied Justin's face for several seconds, finally making up his mind. "All right. Stay here, Rick. Watch this guy, and waste him if he tries to get away or use the phone."

"You got it, Jase."

Justin Harris knew that he was in deep trouble, then, because they didn't mind him hearing names. That meant they planned to kill him, either way. The old man felt the short hairs rising on his neck. He was about to miss a whole lot more than the last few minutes on *The Rockford Files*.

ARNIE NORRIS WAS PREPARED when Jason Meyers knocked on the door of number nine. He killed the television and slipped his Colt Commander inside its holster. The cyclops stepped inside without a word of invitation, studying the layout of the room as if it held great interest for him.

"You boys ready?"

"As we'll ever be."

Meyers frowned. "Are all these rooms the same inside?"

"I guess so," Arnie replied. "I've only been in this one."

"Mmm." The cyclops didn't seem to like his manner. "Well, we'll have to go in blind. It can't be helped. You're packing?"

"Absolutely."

"Come with me."

He followed Meyers across the parking lot, in the direction of the office, leaving Claude to shut the door and catch up on his own. It suddenly hit Arnie that they hadn't wiped the place for fingerprints. He was about to mention it to Meyers, but kept his mouth shut. He'd been arrested only once—for public drunkenness, in George West, Texas—and he doubted whether anyone would trace his prints from that occasion, some four years ago. In any case, once he got paid, he planned to scrutinize his other options, maybe try a brand-new name on for size.

Six men were waiting at the cars, all armed, and Norris did a little quick arithmetic to figure out how his percentage of the cash would be reduced by splitting it nine ways. If they were even splits, that still left better than a hundred thousand dollars, but he still had one more ace to play.

He started talking fast, before the cyclops had a chance to speak. "We checked things out," he told the other members of the hit team. "I figure we can split it down the middle, and—"

"Who died and made you king?" Meyers snapped.

"I only thought—"

"That was your first mistake," the cyclops growled, and Arnie heard Claude chuckling behind him.

"I didn't mean—"

"We'll split it down the middle," Jason said, ignoring him. "That way we ought to have them covered. We'll synchronize and blow both doors together, go in shooting, wasting anything that moves. The rooms are simple." As he spoke, the cyclops traced a squat rectangle on the Chevy's hood, using his index finger as a pointer. "Main room here, with beds on left or right, depending on the door's location. Bathroom just behind, a straight shot from the door. The only snag's if someone's in the shower. He'll be out of sight at first. We'll have to go inside and check."

"Be funny if we caught one of them on the crapper," someone said, and laughter rippled through the group.

Disgruntled by his own humiliation, Arnie Norris wondered who this "we" that Jason talked about might be. He'd have bet his life that the cyclops planned to hang well back and let his gunners do the fighting for him.

"Everybody set?"

There was a general flourishing of shotguns, carbine and automatic weapons. Arnie drew his .45 and wished that he'd brought the 12-gauge, anything at all to seem a little more impressive. As it was, he had the feeling of a younger sibling who had to stand to the side and watch while the big boys played their games.

Well, he'd have to show them, that was all. If Jason thought that he would dump on Arnie Norris, then he'd have to think again. Yes, sir, he might be in for a surprise at that.

"Let's do it, then," Jason said. "We haven't got all night."

THE COKE AND ICE MACHINE were tucked between rooms ten and eleven, secluded in a special alcove. The overhead lights had burned out long ago, but the vending machine provided sufficient illumination for Johnny to count his pocket change, confirming that he had enough to purchase two Coke Classics and a can of root beer. On top of the ice machine beside him, Johnny's plastic bucket brimmed with half-inch cubes.

He had the Cokes lined up and was about to feed the vendor one more time, when his attention was distracted by the sound of new arrivals in the parking lot. He poked his head around the corner, thankful now for the alcove's darkness, and watched two dark sedans pull up outside the office. Dome lights flared, and Johnny counted eight rough-looking men before the doors were closed. Two passengers got out of each car and headed toward the office, disappearing from his line of vision.

And he had counted more than heads in those brief seconds. Rifles, shotguns—Johnny couldn't tell, but he'd seen two barrels carelessly displayed inside the second car. Knowing that seasoned hunters wouldn't travel with their guns exposed that way, he drew the only logical conclusion. He cursed as he gauged the distance back to room thirteen—no more than fifty feet, but it was lighted all the way. Johnny pocketed his change and palmed his Beretta, thumbing back the hammer as he saw three men emerging from the office. Leaving one behind could only mean that the manager was under guard, and there would be no phone calls to the police before the shooting started.

Seven men were on their feet now, clustering around the cars. One guy detached from the group, approaching Johnny's hideout with determined strides. The younger Bolan ducked back out of sight, prepared to fire if anyone intruded on the alcove. But the new arrival hammered on a door to Johnny's right, not close enough to make it number ten. He made it eight or nine, and listened as the door was opened, closed again. The process was repeated moments later, and he risked another glance around the corner, watching three men join the others near the office.

Cursing underneath his breath, Johnny realized that they had been under surveillance for hours, possibly since moments after they arrived. He had no time for puzzling the mechanics of it all; they had been traced, and "how" would have to wait for later. If there was a later. At the moment he was concentrating on survival, wondering how he could warn his brother and Aguire, short of dying in the process.

Johnny shifted the Beretta to his left hand, wiped a sweaty palm against his jeans and shifted back again. The gunners were discussing strategy. He couldn't overhear their words, but it made little difference. If the manager had spilled his guts—and Johnny took it for granted that he would—the gunners knew their two rooms.

The nine men moved as one, and Johnny watched as four broke off in the direction of room six. As the others drew near his position, he stepped back into the shadows. So far they were following the game plan, but his brother and Aguire had no way of knowing it was almost kickoff time.

Five men trooped past the alcove, weapons at the ready. Johnny glimpsed an Ingram and a pair of stubby shotguns as they passed. They carried ample hardware for the job, and Mack would never know what hit him if they opened up without a warning.

Johnny left the shadows, edging forward, index finger taut on the Beretta's trigger. He risked another glance in each direction, saw the gunmen lining up like firing squads outside each room. He raised his pistol, sighting down the slide, and chose his target, guaranteed of one clean shot before all hell broke loose.

"Show time," he muttered.

And squeezed the trigger twice.

MACK BOLAN FINISHED doling out the chicken onto paper plates and reached for the container of potato salad. Unaware of hunger while they'd driven through Mississippi and Louisiana, he was suddenly ravenous, the aroma of chicken and warm biscuits making his mouth water. Seated on the nearby bed, Aguire also eyed the food with interest, but made no move to serve himself.

"Dig in," the Executioner advised. "It's getting cold. The drinks will be here in a minute."

Carlos chose a drumstick, studied it, then addressed a question to his guardian. "Why are you doing this?"

"I'm hungry," Bolan answered.

"No, I mean the escort. Surely you must recognize the danger."

"We're okay so far."

"I know the government," Aguire pressed. "They can't be paying you enough."

"The fact is," Bolan told him, "they're not paying anything."

"You volunteered for this?"

"Let's say I was available."

"And Mr. Green?"

"Him, too."

"In my world, men who risk their lives expect rewards."

"I get my share. Cash doesn't enter into it."

"You are—how do you say it—an altruist?"

"I wouldn't qualify. A soldier does his duty."

"Some decide to serve themselves."

"Your chicken's getting cold."

Bolan didn't like the conversation's drift and sought to cut if off. Explaining motive to Aguire, things like duty and responsibility, struck the warrior as a waste of time. They came from different worlds, as Carlos had remarked, without a common frame of reference.

In Aguire's world, a man was judged by what he owned, the money in his pocket and the measure of respect he could command through fear. A job well done involved corruption, murder, poisoning the youth of his adopted country, leading them to ruin in the name of profit. To Aguire, his mistake was getting caught by agents of the DEA. The larger issues simply didn't register. He had no more in common with the Executioner than Bolan had in common with the Queen of England.

But at another level, Bolan knew, their worlds were much the same. Both lived with treachery and death from day to day, uncertain whom they could and couldn't trust. In Bolan's case, the list of friends had been dramatically reduced by trial and error, whittled by attrition in the midst of everlasting war. Aguire, for his part, had been completely isolated. At the moment, he could claim no friends at all.

The Executioner was momentarily distracted by a nagging thought. His brother had been gone far longer than he thought a trip for ice and soda should require. The kid was capable of looking out for number one, and there'd been no sounds of struggle, but he heard the first, faint clamor of alarm bells in his mind.

Too long. If anything had happened—

At the sound of pistol shots, he threw himself across the intervening space and caught Aguire in a flying tackle, toppling the witness backward, both men plunging into empty space between the double beds. Aguire spluttered underneath him, cursing, but his voice was drowned by heavy metal thunder as the windows shattered, under a blast of automatic fire.

Aguire fought to catch his breath as bullets raked the walls above his head, dislodging artwork, spewing plaster dust from countless holes. He heard a muffled scream next door, a woman's voice, and tried to wriggle underneath the nearest bed as Bolan rolled away from him, a pistol now filling his hand.

There was no room beneath the bed, although one arm and leg fit well enough before Aguire's chest and rib cage jammed the narrow space. He visualized his death, policemen standing over him in tailored uniforms and inexpensive suits, bland faces creased by gloating smiles. It would be obvious that he had tried to hide like some pathetic gigolo, his death diminished by an act of cowardice. The bastards would be laughing at him when the morgue attendants zipped him up inside a rubber bag and carried him away.

Enough!

He rolled clear of the bed, dust trailing from his sleeve and trouser leg in streamers. Aguire wasn't rash enough to stand, but from his new position he could see his guardian slithering across the floor in the direction of a duffel bag that occupied a nearby chair. He reached it, scuttled backward with his prize and nearly had it open when the door crashed open. Two men surged across the threshold, submachine guns blazing.

Bolan raised his pistol in a single fluid motion, squeezing off a 3-round burst that pinned one gunner to the wall and sent his comrade staggering for cover. Dipping back inside the duffel bag, the warrior hauled an Uzi machine pistol clear and snapped the bolt back, chambering a round as he moved to greet the rest of the attack force.

Outside, the firing faltered for an instant, then resumed, but in the lull Aguire knew he heard more weapons, at a greater distance, firing to the crisp accompaniment of breaking glass. Their other room was under siege as well, and they would doubtless have been killed if all the gunmen had been massed outside their windows, firing simultaneously.

Bolan fired a burst through the shattered window, whipping tattered curtains in a new direction. Fewer weapons answered this time, but one was firing through the open door, a shotgun spraying buckshot into walls and furniture. One blast dispensed with Colonel Saunder's, riddling the cardboard chicken bucket and blowing it away. A ventilation wing glanced off Aguire's shoulder.

He stuck his head above the mattress, spotting movement in the doorway as the gunner made his charge. Bolan met him with a rising burst that ripped the man from crotch to breastbone, punching him into an awkward pirouette of death.

Still firing with the Uzi, Bolan dipped his free hand inside the duffel bag and withdrew a grenade. He pulled the pin and lobbed the orb overhand, retreating toward the cover of the bed as startled cries announced the grenade's arrival on the sidewalk.

Detonation, microseconds later, tore the night apart with sound and fury. Bits of shrapnel whined through the door and windows, peppering the walls and ceiling. As the ringing in Aguire's ears subsided, he could hear a tortured voice begin to call for help. A gunshot was the answer, and the voice fell silent.

Aguire made his move without thought. Gathering his legs beneath him, he lunged for the duffel bag. He wouldn't cower in the shadows while his escort bore the brunt of the fighting. There were weapons in the bag, and—

Bolan intercepted him, resting the smoking muzzle of his Uzi against Aguire's chest.

"Don't even think about it, guy."

"You must allow me—"

"Save it," Bolan snapped. "I don't have time to play the ground rules back for your amusement."

"I am not a child!"

"That's right. You're baggage. And I say again, no guns."

"I won't—"

Aguire saw the blow, but there was nothing he could do to brace himself or pull away. The Uzi clipped him sharply on the left side of his head and drove him backward. Darkness spread its cloak to catch him, and before the world shut down, Aguire heard the sound of distant guns.

**9**

In the wake of the grenade explosion, Bolan heard the crack of pistol shots outside. He thought of Johnny, trapped outside, and realized the kid had more mobility—more combat stretch—than if he had been "safe" inside the room.

Reloading as he moved, the soldier scuttled forward, covering the open doorway and the window frame. Outside, the Cajun Cottage sign provided green and blue illumination for the parking lot, and Bolan felt a little like a deep-sea diver as he cleared the threshold in a combat crouch.

One of his enemies was standing in the open, looking dazed, his eyes shifting back and forth between the door to number thirteen and a station wagon on his left, the windows shot to hell. Four men lay stretched out on the pavement, leaking life.

The gunner spotted Bolan in the doorway and pivoted to bring him under fire with a Heckler & Koch submachine gun. Bolan beat him to it, rattling off a short burst from his Uzi that knocked the man off his feet into an awkward sprawl. His heels drummed briefly on the blacktop, raising dust before the last faint spark of animation flickered out.

Downrange, a burst of fire from secondary forces filled the air with angry hornets, driving Bolan to his knees. He reached the station wagon, heard the body work absorbing hits, and was prepared to answer fire when sudden movement on his left flank demanded full attention. Bolan had his finger on the trigger when recognition flooded him with sweet relief.

"Where's Carlos?" Johnny asked.

"He's napping. You okay?"

"I think the Cokes are getting warm."

The soldier grinned. "How many have we got down there?"

"I counted four outside the room. They left one in the office with the manager."

"Okay, we'll call it five. I don't want any stragglers."

"Right." Johnny nodded in the general direction of their enemies. "They might have other thoughts on that."

"We'll have to be persuasive."

"I heard that. Suggestions?"

"One or two." The warrior laid down his Uzi and freed a pair of fragmentation grenades that he had clipped onto his belt. He handed one to his brother. "I hadn't planned to use these all at once, but what the hell. On three."

They pulled the safety pins together, cocked their arms and Bolan started counting.

"One."

If they succeeded, there would be a period of several seconds while the opposition was disoriented, dazed, and they could take advantage of the lag time for a final rush. If they should fail . . .

"Two."

He tried to calculate the distance in his mind, preparing for the pitch. His only view of their assailants was a fleeting glimpse before he hit the deck and scrambled to the cover of the station wagon. A miscalculation now would make the grenades fall short, their force diffused by distance, the shrapnel less effective.

"Three."

No time for doubts now. Bolan and his brother broke their crouch in unison, arms whipping forward to release their missiles. Thirty yards away, the enemy responded with a concentrated burst of fire that rocked the station wagon on its hinges, stray rounds drilling through both doors and whispering past Bolan's face.

He hugged the pavement, waiting for a thunderclap that would save his world or end it.

THE PUNK CALLED RICK was getting fidgety, and that made Justin Harris wonder how much longer he had to live.

They'd be forced to kill him once the shooting began outside. He knew their faces and a couple of their names—first names, at any rate—and they'd have to be insane to think that he would keep that information to himself, no matter what he promised in a desperate bid to stay alive.

And if they meant to kill him, he didn't have a goddamned thing to lose.

Harris kept an Army-issue .45 out front, concealed where he could reach it as he stood behind the register, to make him feel secure when nights were long and weirdos came in off the highway. He had practiced shooting cans and paper targets with the pistol, knew the moves and combat stance, but he'd never been confronted with a killing situation on the job.

Before tonight.

And now the goddamned gun was twenty feet away, with Rick prepared to blow his ass to kingdom come if a sudden move was made in that direction.

They were seated in Harris's living room behind the office, where he sat and drank and tried to watch TV between the interruptions from his customers. The bedroom and a tiny bathroom lay behind his captor, with the exit to the motel office on his left, the gunner's right.

It might as well have been the frigging moon.

"You want a beer?" He gestured toward the six-pack on the stand beside his easy chair. "It's warm, but it ain't bad."

"No beer."

"You mind if I go on and have one, then?"

Rick thought about it, finally nodded. "Might as well."

"My thoughts, exactly."

Sudden gunfire echoed from the parking lost, two shots in rapid-fire and then all holy hell broke loose. Rick flinched, half rising from his chair, and Harris saw the only opening that he would ever have.

Without a second thought, he pitched the still-unopened beer can, lunging from his chair before the missile struck Rick's forehead with a hollow *thunk*. The gunner toppled backward, squeezing off a reflex shot that gouged the ceiling, missing Harris by a yard or more.

The manager made the office doorway, almost stumbling on the threshold where the carpet changed to vinyl, and dropped to his knees behind the register. His fingers scrabbled for the Colt. He snapped back the hammer as he found his grip and turned to face his enemy.

Sweet Jesus, was it loaded? Had he left a live round in the chamber?

There was no damned time to check it, as Rick lurched through the doorway, blood streaming from a crescent wound above one eye. The gunman fired again, a wild shot that drilled through the register and rung up a void. The cash drawer rattled out to full extension over Justin's head, and he was praying as he squeezed the trigger, startled by the weapon's recoil in his hand.

Rick took the heavy round in his breastbone, and it emptied out his lung. A shocked expression crept over his face as he slumped against the doorjamb. He was sliding toward a crouch, his pistol still at full arm's length when Harris fired again.

The bullet punched a blowhole in Rick's forehead, its explosive exit stenciling a crimson halo on the watt. The gunner dropped his pistol as his buttocks thumped the vinyl floor. His mouth sagged open, drooling blood and spittle down his shirt.

Outside, the battle had been heating up, complete with automatic weapons and explosions, sounding just like reruns of *The Rat Patrol*. It would have been the smart thing, Harris thought, to phone the sheriff right away, let someone else sort out the whole damned mess. But he was angry now, and flying on a rush of pure adrenaline that made him feel like he could lick the world.

"That's one," he said to the lifeless Rick, and hobbled out to join the war.

From where he stood, it seemed to Arnie Norris that the operation had already gone to hell. Meyers had screwed things up beyond redemption with his too-cool attitude and the obnoxious way he had of pushing everybody else aside so he could run things his way.

*His* way sucked.

"You see them, Claude?"

Bodeen stood on tiptoe and craned his neck. "I can't see nothin'. We've got 'em, though."

Like hell.

The fact that they had two men pinned behind the wagon didn't mean anything to Arnie, now. If the truth were told, it felt as if he were in the trap, his opposition holding all the cards. If they could kill five men that quick and easy when they were surprised, who knew what they were capable of doing once they got their act together?

Behind him, Jason shouted, "Blast them out of there!" He fired a burst directly at the car, exploding window glass and puncturing a tire, but he was wasting bullets. Claude joined in, unleashing three quick rounds, but Arnie played it smart and held his fire.

In case.

A nagging premonition of disaster made him turn and glance toward the office—just in time to see the old man waddle out, a pistol in his hand. Arnie faced the new arrival, catching just a flash of Jason from the corner of his eyes, convinced the cyclops thought he was about to break and run.

"Look out!" he bellowed, swinging up his Colt Commander as the old man let loose with what sounded like an Army .45. Before he could return fire, Claude Bodeen was on his knees and groping for a bloody wound above his belt line in the back.

"I'm hit!" he cried. "Aw, Jesus, Arnie..."

"Bastard!" Norris triggered two quick rounds and watched the old man totter, before falling down as if his legs had been yanked out from under him. Blood pooled in Harris's lap, but he still held the automatic leveled straight at Arnie, finger frozen on the trigger as a warning shout distracted Norris from the game.

"Grenade!"

Already moving, Arnie shot the old man once again, indifferent to the outcome as he broke for cover, wondering if he could reach the nearest vehicle in time to make a dive and—

Thunder wrapped itself around Norris, lifted him completely off his feet and hurled him toward the car he had selected as his sanctuary. He hit the fender with his face, and everything shut down.

THEY FOLLOWED THE EXPLOSION in a rush, each circling a different way around the car. As Bolan cleared the grille, he saw one gunner on his feet, another kneeling on the asphalt, wounded. Others had been dropped by the explosions, lying torn and twisted on the ground.

The standing gunner missed the warrior, somehow. He fired off a burst at Johnny, then broke toward a car that had been parked outside the office. Bolan tracked him with the Uzi, lining up his sights too late. His target scrambled behind the wheel before he had a decent shot.

The engine growled to life, and brake lights flared as Johnny started firing his Beretta. Bolan held the Uzi's trigger down and emptied the magazine, two seconds' worth of concentrated firing at a cyclic rate of seven hundred and fifty rounds per minute. Parabellum rounds chewed up the trunk and smashed the vehicle's rear window.

And somewhere in the middle of it all, one round—or several, found a spot in the fuel tank, sparking with sufficient heat to trigger an explosion. Bolan felt the heat wave where he stood, and he watched a fiery mushroom melt the canopy above the car.

In the smoky no-man's land, a lone survivor of the raiding party saw his death approaching as he knelt on the asphalt, pistol in hand. He saw grim death before him, multiplied by two, and the predominant expression on his face appeared to be surprise.

"We should've had you," he announced. "Meyers fucked it up. I knew he would."

"Who are you?" Johnny asked.

"What difference does it make? I'm dead."

"Not necessarily."

"Oh, yeah. I'm checking out, all right." The man was fatalistic in his mortal pain. "The only question left is, who goes with me?"

"Don't be stupid," Johnny cautioned, sighting down the slide of his Beretta.

Bolan was immediately conscious of the fact that he had let the Uzi run dry. Would there be time, he wondered, to draw the 93-R from its shoulder rigging?

And he knew the answer as he met the wounded gunner's eyes. It would be Johnny's play or no one's.

"Eeny meeny," the gunman taunted, managing a grin.

"Don't do it."

"Miny mo." His weak voice faltered, but he dredged enough strength up from somewhere to continue. "Catch—"

Bolan saw the move in progress and faded sideways, digging for his weapon in a hopeless race with time as Johnny fired a single shot that slammed the gunner backward, dead before his shoulders hit the asphalt.

"One more inside the office?" Bolan asked his brother.

Following Johnny's gaze, he saw the structure wrapped in leaping flames.

"I doubt it," Johnny answered, turning back toward room thirteen. "We've got some company."

Aguire stood outside the room, one hand pressed to his aching head, examining the bodies strewn about the sidewalk. Lights were going on in other rooms, but none of the assorted guests showed themselves until the soldier found a fire alarm and rang it in.

"Let's go," he said above the din. "It's checkout time."

**10**

"How the hell did they find us so quickly?"

"Your guess," Bolan answered, "would be as good as mine."

Johnny swiveled in his seat and pinned Aguire with a steady gaze. Their passenger looked sullen. "Man, if you've got anything to tell us, now's the time."

"You think I knew those men? Did they behave as if they hoped to rescue me?" The witness looked disgusted with his escorts. "You told me Pratt has problems with security. A leak, perhaps."

"Pratt doesn't know our route. He can't send shooters somewhere that he's never heard of."

"Then it must be Vos," Aguire countered. "He may have a full description of the car by now...perhaps of you, as well. His eyes are everywhere."

Somehow it didn't play. The pieces wouldn't fit.

"We changed the plates," he said to no one in particular. "There have to be a couple thousand Jimmys in the state at least. What kind of network are we talking about that can pick us up that fast and put a hit team in the field?"

"Whatever," Bolan replied, "it ought to take a while for them to get the word on what went down back there. Add more time while they cast the net again. I'd say we have an hour, anyway."

"We won't make Texas in an hour," Johnny told him.

"I don't plan to. First I'm touching base with Wonderland, and then we burrow in to get some sleep."

Johnny recognized the wisdom of his brother's plan. If someone had them marked—and clearly someone *did*—the highways could be crawling with patrols inside the hour.

Ambush or a running battle through the darkness was a solid possibility, attracting the police and God knows who else in the process. It was safer to find a hole and pull it in behind them.

He missed the chicken. Hunger gnawed around the edges of his stomach, grumbling audibly.

"You guys enjoy your dinner?"

"We were interrupted," Bolan replied.

"I know it's probably a bad idea for us to stop, but still..."

"I need a pay phone," his brother said, "Keep an eye peeled. Maybe we can do both jobs at once."

"I'm on the case."

They found an all-night gas station and convenience store outside of Taylortown, in Bossier Parish. Bolan parked on the side, where they wouldn't be immediately visible to passing traffic. Out front, a pickup and a pair of motorcycles occupied the parking lot.

"The menu's up to you," Bolan announced, already rummaging in the console for a role of quarters. "I'll see if I can find out what we're up against. Ten minutes ought to do it."

"Easy," Johnny replied. He disembarked and pulled the passenger's seat forward for Aguire to exit. "Everybody out."

"My head—"

"You'll live," the younger man cut him off. "And I'm not letting you out of my sight."

They left the Executioner at the outside pay phone and pushed through glass doors. In a corner, Johnny noted the surveillance camera that covered the entrance and the register. Two biker types were paying for an eight-pack, while an older, balding man browsed through the meager fare of skin magazines displayed beside the dairy cooler. Johnny nodded to the night clerk, an imposing slab of muscle sporting tattoos on his arms and pale scars on his knuckles.

"See anything you like?" he asked Aguire.

"I'm not hungry."

"Suit yourself. I think it's safe to say we'll miss the champagne brunch tomorrow."

Grudgingly the man chose a hero sandwich wrapped in cellophane, a bag of corn chips and a soft drink. Johnny added two more sandwiches to the list, more chips and half a dozen candy bars of different types. He kissed the balanced diet off in favor of convenience, knowing it would be a bitch to handle cans. They couldn't afford a fire to heat things up, in any case.

"How long until they find us?" Aguire asked as Johnny stopped to grab a quart of milk.

"You're asking me? I don't know how they found us this time."

"We are as good as dead."

"You might be right, but when we go, it won't be from starvation. Here, my treat."

THE TELEPHONE ROUSED Hal Brognola from the twilight zone of sleep. He checked his watch and snared the receiver as it rang again.

"Hello?"

"I'm on a pay phone," the familiar voice informed him. "Can you talk?"

"We should be clean. I ran a recent sweep."

"Fair enough." The soldier hesitated for a heartbeat, then said. "We've had a problem."

"Oh?" Brognola didn't like the way his flesh had started to crawl, as if the ants were burrowing beneath his skin.

"A welcoming committee. South of Shreveport. Have you got a pencil?"

"Shoot."

"Check out the Cajun Cottage Motor Inn, Red River Parish, down in bayou country. Closest town I saw was Cross Roads."

"That's the name?"

"Affirmative."

"What happened?"

"Uninvited company came knocking. They've been taken care of, but we also had civilian casualties. The place was smoking when we left. It should be on the air by now."

"No line on whose they were?" the big Fed asked.

"I have a surname, probably the crew chief's. Meyers. It isn't much."

"I'll run it down," Brognola told him. "I've got contacts with the state police down there. With any luck, we'll make your playmates and the names will lead us somewhere. Numbers?"

"Nine or ten, from what I saw."

"Survivors?"

"None I know of."

"Jesus."

"Right. I'm interested in learning how they traced us."

"So am I. A little birdy tells me that you changed the route."

"He put out spotters?"

"That's affirmative. Security and so on. Tried to act relieved that you were showing some initiative, but I don't know."

"How goes it with the plumbing?"

"Last I heard, they're leaking right on schedule. I've been trying this and that to run it down, but nothing so far."

They were already running long on time, so Bolan broke it off. "I'll get in touch tomorrow sometime through your office."

"Do that. If your boys have jackets, they'll be on my desk by lunch time. And be careful."

He was talking to a dial tone, and he cut it off, a finger on the plungers. There were calls to make and wheels to set in motion, but he had to put his thoughts in order. Disorganized response was often worse than no response at all, especially when lives were riding on the line.

He hadn't asked about Aguire, for the soldier would have told him if they had a problem there. The witness was alive, so far, but that didn't translate to mean he was secure. If Vos—or someone else—had run him down this soon, they could expect more trouble on the road before their songbird reached Los Angeles.

Assuming that he ever got there.

Brognola reached for a cigar, thought better of it, and began to make a mental list of people he could call. His closest friend on the Louisiana state police was a captain based in Baton Rouge, but he would know the people Hal should contact. Nine or ten dead gunmen at a rural passion pit was bound to raise some eyebrows and the troopers would be out in force.

As would the journalists.

The big Fed lusted for a drink, decided it could be postponed with the cigar. Ten bodies made it headline time, complete with a story on the network news show. How it played would be dependent on the ID's of the casualties. If they were traceable to Vos—a slender possibility, at best—it wouldn't help the dealer's case. Conversely, if the stiffs were independents, mercenaries, there was still a chance to bury the connection while the Bolan brothers brought their package safely home.

Damage control was the first priority, and Pratt would have to deal with fending off the media. Brognola's mind was forced on the more specific problem of Aguire's—and the Bolans'—safety. There was no way he could chart their route, but if he made the shooters who had blown it, there was still a chance that he could mount a swift preemptive strike against the brass.

He lifted the receiver, punching numbers before the dial tone had a chance to register.

It was time to wake some people up.

"WE'RE ON LINE to trace the shooters," Bolan told his companions as he slide behind the wheel. "It'll take a while. They figure noon."

"That leaves us close to thirteen hours in the dark," Johnny said. "I don't like flying blind."

"We've got no options."

"Game plan?"

"Still the same. No point in changing routes again if they can track us down that easily."

"We could call in the cavalry."

"I thought of that. It makes a bigger target, and we don't know who we're dealing with when they arrive."

Aguire cleared this throat. "I want to help. I tried last night before you knocked me out."

Bolan turned to face him. "Nothing personal but we've already had this little chat. No guns."

"I can defend myself."

"No doubt, when you've got warning and it's one-on-one. The plain fact is, we've got the job of making sure you don't get killed by Thursday. In the meantime, I'll feel better if I know where all sniper fire is coming from."

"You think I wish you harm?"

"I think you've got a world-class motive for a disappearing act. Delivery is part of our assignment, and I'm not prepared to lose you, one way or another."

"If I was interested in being a defenseless human target, I'd have done the time Pratt offered as an option. That way, Vos could pick me off in prison when he had the urge."

"I didn't write your contract with the DEA. If you have second thoughts, you're welcome to express them in Los Angeles."

"We'll never make it. Not alive."

"I don't think I can stand this lavish optimism," Johnny remarked.

"I'm being realistic," Aguire answered. "I don't know who tried to take us out tonight, but I can tell you where the orders came from. He won't give up because you dropped the hammer on a couple of his soldiers. They're a dime a dozen. He's got hundreds more where those came from."

"Sounds awesome," Bolan said. "It makes me wonder why you tried to burn Vos in the first place."

"Greed," Aguire told him honestly. "What else? I wasn't in the business for my health, you know. I saw an opportunity to make some easy cash, no kickbacks to the man, and I bought in. I might not do the same again, but what the hell, it's done."

"You couldn't cut a deal with Vos?" Johnny asked.

"He didn't get to be the man by giving second chances. One strike and you're out."

"Unless you've got the balls to walk."

Aguire forced a smile. "I don't intend to rabbit, gentlemen. While Vos is still in charge, there's nowhere I could go. I have to deal with him before I make the break. We'll have a better chance of getting to L.A. with three guns. It was close tonight. They won't take any chances next time."

"We'll get by," Johnny told him.

"But I know these people."

"Then you won't have any trouble prepping us before the action starts."

Aguire raised an eyebrow. "I'm not sure I understand."

"You know the territory and the players," Bolan said. "You should have some idea about their operating methods, contacts, how they'll try to hit us when the time comes."

"I can tell you that, all right," Aguire answered. "After what just happened, they'll use every man and every gun they have. Make no mistake about it. Vos won't rest until I'm dead."

"In that case," Bolan countered, "we intend to see your old amigo lose some sleep."

Johnny flashed a winning smile. "I'd say he's in for some insomnia, and no mistake."

Aguire concentrated on his sandwich, knowing that debate was fruitless. They wouldn't permit him to defend himself, so he'd have to find a way around that obstacle. If Green and Blanski meant to sacrifice themselves in the pursuit of duty, that was one thing. He had no wish to share their martyrdom.

Aguire would survive until he reached Los Angeles, no matter what.

And God help any man who tried to stop him now.

TRASK RAN HIS FINGERTIPS across the bars of tempered steel that formed his cage. They were cold to the touch, chilling him at the juncture of metal and flesh, raising instant goose bumps on his arms and back. Repulsed, he broke the contact, backing up until he stood precisely in the center of the small enclosure.

He couldn't explain his presence in the cage, nor did he recognize the building that surrounded him. A vacant warehouse, possibly, although encroaching shadows barred his view beyond a range of ten or fifteen feet. The sole il-

lumination was a naked bulb inside the cage, itself surrounded by a screen of wire to keep him from removing it.

As if he would have dared.

The darkness frightened Trask, a legacy from childhood
he had never fully overcome. Not any darkness, mind you,
but the kind that brooded, threatening, in strange environ-
ments, hiding enemies and monsters of his own imagination.

He could hear them moving in the shadows now, beyond
the boundaries of the light. Their steps were slow and heavy,
dragging on the concrete floor, and they were closer now
than when he first heard them. The light was keeping them
at bay so far, but if it failed . . .

Another chill. Trask wondered if the predators could see
him trembling, smell the fear that radiated from his body in
sour waves. Some animals—and men—were driven mad by
the smell of fear, choosing victims on the basis of their in-
stantaneous reaction to a threat. The bold and strong survived, while others were devoured.

At the moment, Nathan Trask felt neither bold nor
strong.

What was he doing there? The answer came to him immediately: Vos. Somehow, unwittingly, he had displeased
the dealer, and he'd been taken from his home, confined
inside this cage until a fitting punishment could be decided.
He was marked for death, the only questions being how long
it would take and how much he would suffer in the meantime.

Knowing Vos and the sadistic streak that he concealed
behind a thin veneer of charm, Trask had no hope of mercy.
Had he been a pious man, he might have prayed, but even
that escape hatch lay beyond his grasp.

"Good evening, counselor."

Trask recognized the voice. It was his contact from the
number Vos had given him in jail. The man in charge of
tracking down Aguire.

"What the hell is going on?" he asked, attempting to
present a bold facade.

"You're being phased out, counselor. I thought you
knew."

"This is preposterous."

"We don't reward incompetence. Much less a coward."

"Let me speak . . ." But even as the sentence formed it-self upon his lips, he knew that it was useless.

"Speak to whom?" his captor asked. "To Vos? I'd like to, counselor, but that's impossible, as you well know. He's doing life plus ninety-nine because you fucked things up. I drew the job of passing on his thank-you."

Trask was honestly bewildered. How could Vos be serv-ing life plus ninety-nine without a trial. It made no sense at all, but he wasn't in a position to debate the question.

From the shadows, men dressed in black, with ski masks covering their faces, moved in the direction of his cage. Trask counted six of them, more curious than frightened when he saw the box they carried slung between them. It was made of plywood, painted black, and when they set it on the floor, it blocked the trapdoor that appeared to be the only entrance to his prison.

"Something here to kccp you company," the disembod-ied voice informed him. "Like a house pet, I suppose you'd say."

Trask caught a whiff of something rank in the box, re-coiling as the occupant began to claw against confinement, raking slivers from the walls.

"It's hungry, counselor. We haven't fed it in a while. I thought you might take care of that, okay?"

"You must be crazy."

"Nope. I just love animals."

One of the men in black had bent to unlock the door to Trask's cage, sliding it upward on runners. He then reached down to free a hatch that closed the near end of the snarl-ing box.

"No, wait."

"I think it's waited long enough, don't you?"

"For Christ's sake, don't!"

"A little playmate, counselor."

The hatch was rising, and he cringed against the bars, with no place left to run. The box burst open in front of him, but before he had a chance to glimpse the snarling an-imal, the solitary light went out.

Trask screamed, as an alarm began to clamor in his brain. It rang incessantly and deafened him to every other sound, as if—

The telephone.

He sat bolt upright in the bed and lifted the receiver with a trembling hand.

"Hello?"

"I hate to wake you, counselor."

The voice. And calling him at his hotel.

"What is it?"

"We've got problems. Nothing I can talk about right now. I have to pull some strings, but I'll be calling you again at half past seven. Have you got that?"

"Seven-thirty. Yes."

"Not there."

"I understand."

The voice reeled off a State Street address. Trask repeated it for confirmation, startled when he got it right.

"Check out the first booth on the left, and don't be late. You miss this call, you miss the boat."

The line went dead, and Trask sat holding the receiver for another moment. The dial tone humming in his ear. He replaced it and rose to stand before the window, staring down at Jacksonville by night.

There would be no more sleep, despite the time. He had an unexpected meeting scheduled for the hour when he usually woke, but that was nothing in comparison to the horrific power of his dream.

He dared not face the cage again, to find out what was waiting for him there.

THEY FOUND a narrow access road off Highway 71, south of Taylortown, leaving the blacktop and following a rutted dirt track for three hundred yards through palmetto and scrub. Bolan parked their vehicle inside a stand of willows, and killed the engine, listening to metal ticking in the darkness as it cooled.

"We should be covered here," he said. "They can't get close without a giveaway. I'll take first watch."

"You sure?" his brother asked.

"No sweat. I need the time to sort things out."

"Okay. You'll wake me, what, say two o'clock?"

"Let's make it three. You need the beauty sleep."

"A sit-down comic, yet. Terrific."

In the back, Aguire huddled on the Jimmy's bench seat, breathing deeply. Faking? It would make no difference, either way. He wasn't going anywhere, and if the Executioner was forced to drive that lesson home by deeds instead of words, so be it. They had promised to deliver one live witness in Los Angeles, but no one ever guaranteed that he would arrive untouched by human hands.

With sunrise and a bit of luck, they would be exiting Louisiana, rolling west across the Lone Star State. If any members of the Cajun Cottage raiding party had survived—a scout, for instance—chances were that he'd be tied up with a debriefing from his sponsors. Failure never went down well with men like Vos, and the recent foul-up had been nothing short of monumental. The authorities would have some pointed questions of their own.

Bolan had a witness to deliver, with a two-day deadline still remaining, and his gut was telling him that worse times lay ahead. Aguire might be laying on the doom and gloom a little thick, but he was close to Vos and knew the way the dealer operated.

All or nothing.

Scorched earth.

It was a game the Executioner knew very well, indeed. He'd been playing on the home team all his life.

## 11

Still bleary-eyed from lack of sleep and wired from too much coffee, Trask drove once around the block before he found a parking place convenient to the bank of phone booths. Following directions, he was standing in the proper booth—and feeling damned conspicuous—at seven-thirty. Even so, despite the order and his preparations to obey, Trask jumped when the telephone began to ring.

"Hello?"

"Good morning, counselor."

"What is it?"

"Good news, bad news. Let's dispense with bad news first, okay?"

"I'm listening."

"Good job. Some friends of mine ran down your pigeons in Louisiana, south of Shreveport, but they fucked it up. Aguire and his escort got away."

Trask felt his stomach lurching through a barrel roll, a resurrection of his meager breakfast imminent.

"You said—"

"Don't tell me what I said, okay?" A spark of sudden anger in the voice was both frightening and gratifying. The bastard could be touched, and by extension, wounded. "Seems these boys I fielded didn't come prepared. They got their asses kicked, but there's no way they're talking to police. No way they're talking, period."

"You mean? . . ."

"I mean these baby-sitters got their act together. Next time we'll know who we're dealing with."

Trask didn't like the sound of "we," however distant and abstract its implication.

"Next time?"

"Sure. You think it's finished? Vos wants this Aguire taken care of. I'm the man. One fumble doesn't wrap the game. I've got some other people on it now."

"But if they got away—"

"A temporary setback, counselor. No sweat. We'll pick them up again before you know it. They're not going where I can't follow."

Trask put on his best attorney's voice. "I'm certain Mr. Vos will be disturbed by this report."

"I wouldn't be surprised. Just tell him everything's on track, and that nobody's giving up the ghost. When he gets into court out west, he'll find the prosecution short one major witness."

"I'll relay your message."

"Beautiful."

"And if I need to get in touch again?"

"I've got your private number, counselor."

"I think we'll both agree that isn't wise. You never know who might be listening in."

"Okay, let's say we talk again tomorrow. Same time, same station. Good for you?"

Another anxious night, Trask thought. With any luck, anticipation might produce insomnia and block a repetition on his nightmare.

"Fine."

"All right, then. You hang tough now, you here?"

He hung up on the chuckling voice and stalked back toward his car. It was still two hours before he could see Vos in jail, but he'd need the time to polish up his message, find the perfect turn of phrase to keep the volatile Colombian from going crazy when he heard the news.

A fumble? From the lawyer's viewpoint, it appeared to be a bona fide disaster, but he would confess a limited degree of expertise in the domain of contract murder. Things could still work out, if Vos's soldier made it right the second time around.

And if he blew it?

Trask deliberately made his mind a blank and put the Porsche in gear, unaware of the dark sedan that fell into place behind him as he made his way downtown.

IT HAS BEEN SAID that all of Texas looks the same. By nine o'clock, his second morning on the road, Mack Bolan had seen nothing that would make him call the statement into question. Flat and dry, with distant hills and stands of trees that always seemed remote from Bolan's line of travel, Texas seemed to be a boundless prairie, one mile indistinguishable from the next. And by midmorning, Texas had begun to simmer.

They had followed Highway 71 into Shreveport, alert for tails and roadblocks. They encountered no resistance as they picked up Interstate 20, westbound through the Lone Star State. It took an hour for the Executioner to shake his stiffness from a night of sleeping in the driver's seat, but he felt better as they put the miles behind them. By nine o'clock, the Dallas-Fort Worth sprawl was dwindling in their rearview mirror.

"We're making decent time," Johnny said, a road map open in his hands. "I make it something like two hundred miles before we catch the interchange. Fill us in on Texas, Carlos."

Lounging in the back, Aguire seemed intent upon the landscape rolling past his window. "Biker territory," he finally responded. "The Italians have some action down in Dallas, but it's nothing heavy. Some Vietnamese along the Gulf, in Galveston and Corpus Christi. Bikers handle all the major traffic, serving as liaison with the other syndicates."

"Which club?"

"The Mongols are on top right now. They've had some run-ins with the Angels, and they came out second-best in California, but they've still got Texas by the balls."

"They deal with Vos?" Johnny asked.

"Everybody deals with Vos," Aguire replied. "The Mongols have their labs to manufacture crank—that's speed, to you—but when they want some flake for party time or resale, Vos takes care of all their needs."

"And in return?"

"They pay the same as anybody else, but sometimes Vos will take it out in trade, instead of cash. The Mongols are stone killers, man. They'll hit anybody for a price, and sometimes for fun. New members have to make their bones before they qualify to wear the colors. Some clubs have their private armies—like the Angels with their 'Filthy Few'—but you won't find a single virgin in the Mongols. Every one of them has been bloodied, going in."

"Nice boys."

"They pull their weight. Remember, it's a business. Anybody tries to cut you out, you cut him first. Survival of the fittest."

"So now we're watching out for motorcycles, too?"

"We're watching out for anything and everything," the Executioner put in. "I've got a call to make in Roscoe, but it won't take long, and we can catch a bite there. Anything but plastic heroes."

Johnny grinned. "You should have seen the tuna salad. It was positively gruesome."

VOS READ MISFORTUNE on his lawyer's face. Trask was an open book, his narrow range of moods transparent in their private meetings, though he could approximate a decent poker face in court. It was obvious from the attorney's grim expression that he bore bad news.

"You seem discouraged, Nathan."

"I've been talking to your boy," Trask said, a trace of angry color rising in his cheeks. "He called my goddamned house last night. The private number."

"Ah. A breach of etiquette. I'll speak to him about it when this business is behind us."

"Never mind the etiquette. He muffed it."

Vos was silent for a moment, studying Trask's face and working to control his own emotions. "It" would be the contract on Aguire's life. The dealer managed to suppress a grimace as the thought of failure drove a spike of pain between his eyes.

"Explain," he said, his voice not betraying his inner turmoil.

"I don't have the details. Some bunch of assholes found Aguire and his escort in Louisiana, and they let him get away. I don't know where or how. It hasn't made the news yet, and I'm hoping that it won't. If the courts get hold of this, we will both be in for major heartache."

"Relax," Vos said. "A minor setback. If they found Aguire once, they'll pick him up again. We have two days."

"I don't like working in the dark, Ernesto."

"Understood, but I have taken these precautions for your own protection . . . and for mine. The man you're dealing with has served me well in other matters. I expect him to succeed."

"And if he blows it?"

"Then you'll have a chance to crucify Aguire on the witness stand. The cross-examination of a lifetime. But I don't believe that it will come to that."

"I won't be any good to you if I'm in prison, too," Trask grumbled, sounding petulant.

"You are my eyes and ears outside these walls," Vos told him. "It is known that I have no living relatives, and my associates . . . well, let us say the Yankee prosecutors are reluctant to approve their visits."

"All I'm saying is—"

"You're frightened. It's an understandable reaction for a man whose life has been made up of books. You're in no danger, Nathan, I assure you."

"This man is calling me at *home*, for God's sake. I don't know who's listening these days. The IRS or the DEA—it could be anyone."

"Or no one."

Trask was plainly not convinced.

"It would be foolish for the government to intercept your calls," Vos said. "The conversations of a lawyer and his client are protected under law. Their case would self-destruct if they attempt to use—"

Trask interrupted him. "Your batboy's not my client. Nothing that he says to me is privileged. They can use it all, assuming that they have the proper writs approving wire-taps, and the only case they'll have to make is one for criminal conspiracy. If they accomplish that, you're out one lawyer, and they'll have a long head start on proving any other charges filed against you.''

Vos leaned forward, with his free arm resting on the table, conscious of the deputy outside the conference room.

''Aguire must be dealt with, Nathan. He betrayed me, and he places me in mortal danger every moment that he lives. His depositions will be dealt with in Los Angeles and Washington, but he must not survive to testify. Once he appears in court, we're finished. Both of us.''

The final comment startled Trask, but he requested no interpretation. The attorney had been well rewarded for his service to the syndicate in years gone by, and he would be rewarded on the basis of his success or failure in the present case. Success would leave him rich beyond his wildest dreams. A failure, would, of course, result in punishment.

''I don't respond to threats,'' Trask said when he found his voice.

''And I don't threaten valued friends,'' Vos said. ''A simple statement of the facts for your consideration. Call it an incentive for success.''

Trask folded his hands on his briefcase. ''As you say. If there is nothing further? . . .''

''I look forward to tomorrow's visit, Nathan. Better news, perhaps.''

''I'll be in touch.''

''Of course.''

Trask signaled for the deputies, and Vos sat passively while they released his shackles, lifting him as if he were an invalid. It wouldn't be much longer now, he told himself. A few more days before the government was forced to play an empty hand.

He flashed a parting smile at Nathan Trask and let the men in uniform return him to his cell.

THE FLIGHT to Washington had left Pratt stiff and grumpy, and anxious to complete his business and be gone. A public servant always travelled coach, and Pratt had spent the past two hours sandwiched in a narrow seat, between a catatonic punk and an obese young mother with a squalling newborn in her lap. His ears were ringing with the child's incessant cries.

Brognola had an escort waiting for the ride to Justice. Pratt sat back and made the trip in silence, fending off the first attempt at small talk with a grunt-and-shrug routine that he'd practiced to perfection. He was never comfortable in Washington, where rules and regulations were devised by bloodless pencil pushers, rubber-stamped by winners of last year's chaotic popularity contest. When he thought of Washington—the payoffs and corruption, the confusion and stupidity—he marveled that the country had survived as long as it had.

Some cynics called it Wonderland. No matter what the label, Washington was still the seat of power, where the brass at DEA decided policy and OMB controlled the purse strings. Pratt had always been an agent who preferred the field, where he could use initiative and lay the book aside. It was a damned sight easier to win forgiveness than approval, and he tried to stay away from all the trappings of bureaucracy whenever possible.

Today, Pratt thought, he was distinctly out of luck.

He was welcomed to Brognola's office by a smiling secretary, then ushered to the inner sanctum, where the head Fed sat behind a broad expanse of desk.

"I'm glad that you could make the trip."

"It sounded urgent."

"Please, sit down."

Pratt found himself a chair and settled in. "Is something wrong?"

"You haven't heard?" Brognola seemed surprised.

"Look, if there's something I should know—"

"I'm waiting on a call from Striker. He got jumped last night."

"Say what?"

"Some little burg in Bayouland. They toughed it out. Your package is intact."

"What happened, for God's sake?"

"State police down there are looking at eleven bodies, one of them an innocent civilian. Background on the other ties them in with the Confederate Resistance Movement. That's a tri-K front group, linked with half a dozen shooting incidents and twice that many bombings in the past two years. They popped an armored car outside New Orleans back in '87, killed two guards—both black—and bagged three-quarters of a million for the cause.''

"I knew Vos had political connections, but I never thought they went that way.''

"We need to get our act together, Felix. I don't like surprises.''

Pratt was working on a comeback when the telephone began to ring. Brognola snared it and listened for a moment, frowned, and said, "Hang on a second. I've got someone here. I want to put you on the speaker phone.''

The line picked up the hollow tone when Brognola had made the switch, and Bolan heard an echo of his own voice as he spoke. "I hope you've got some news.''

"A bit. Your party crashers were a delegation from the sheet-and-swastika brigade. Pure corn pone with an Auschwitz flavor.''

"Understood.''

"You don't sound too surprised.''

"Not really.'' Bolan frowned at his reflection in the phone booth's dirty glass. "Our friend already mentioned that his playmate has connections with the good old boys.''

"I took it easy with the state police,'' Brognola said. "They think we're interested in Klan activity, per se. We're letting them believe it was some kind of factional dispute, for now.''

"Seems fair.''

"I asked our friend from citrus country to drop by,'' Brognola said. "I'm hoping he may have some thoughts on what you're up against out there.''

Pratt's voice was small and faraway. "I don't know what to tell you, Striker. From the looks of things, I'd have to say that anything can happen.''

"I'd be interested in knowing how they traced us.''

"So would I, believe me.''

Brognola's voice interrupted the exchange. "I might have something for you there. We put a shadow on the mouthpiece, and he's shown a sudden interest in Ma Bell. Like, overnight the guy's in love with phone booths. So far, traces show three calls originating out of pay phones in Miami."

"Which leads nowhere," Bolan said.

"It isn't quite that bad. We missed the first one, but we're on his phones at home, and someone called him up last night, arranging for a callback in the morning. We had time to find the booth and run a wire. We've got the sleaze on tape, times two."

"I hope it's useful."

"Yes and no. We've nearly got enough for an indictment on obstruction and conspiracy, but that's the limit. Everything's been pretty cryptic, and we haven't got a clue on what they're planning down the road."

"No matter." Bolan played a hunch. "I'm thinking we might try a fast one. Shift back to the first route that we chose."

Brognola cleared his throat. "If you're sure that's what you want to do."

"It couldn't hurt. Hey, I appreciate the tip. We're out of here."

"Stay frosty."

"All day long."

Returning to the Jimmy, Bolan slid into the shotgun seat and Johnny put the rig in motion.

"Call it."

Bolan didn't hesitate. "Take 84 to Lubbock," he responded, "like we planned."

THE VAN FELT STRANGE. Skag was more accustomed to the open air, but he relaxed and held his pace, a safe half mile behind the Jimmy. He dragged on his cigarette and blew a cloud of smoke in the direction of the Wolfman.

"Better raise the prez and tell him we've made contact."

"Right."

The CB crackled for a moment, clearing as a strong, familiar voice came on the air.

"We're reading. What's the rap?"

"A solid contact," Wolfman said. "We're on his tail."

"Where are you?"

"Leaving Roscoe, north on 84. You want to meet us on the road, or what?"

"It's taken care of, brother. All you have to do is keep the mark in sight, and make damned sure he doesn't slip."

"We got it covered like a Trojan, man. This dude ain't going anywhere without a tail."

"Don't let him catch you at it."

"Never fear, the Wolfman's here."

"All right, we're rolling. Call back if there's any change."

"You got it, bro'."

Skag kept his eyes fixed on the target, nearly lost against the background of the desert and the distant hills. The paint job was a natural for camouflage, but it wasn't about to save the runners, now. They had already come too far, and they were in too deep.

It was a shame, Skag thought, that he wasn't allowed to hunt more often. Running crank had its rewards, but everybody needed recreation now and then. A little sport to keep the mind sharp, and if someone should insist on paying Skag for doing what he loved, so much the better. It wasn't every day that you could have your cake and eat it, too.

"I wonder what these fuckers did?"

Skag had been wondering, himself, but it was still bad form to ask.

"Who cares?"

The Wolfman shrugged. "It's no big deal, you know? Just curious."

"The contract came from the Colombian," Skag said. "The way I figure it, somebody must be stepping on his toes."

"Some fucking moron."

"Yeah."

They had to be some kind of idiots to mess the with Colombian and try to hide on Mongol turf.

That went beyond bad form.

In fact, it added up to suicide.

## 12

Despite his words to Brognola and Pratt, the Executioner didn't intend to double back and catch I-10 as scheduled. He'd let them think so for a while, diverting any desperate search that Brognola might launch for friendship's sake, thus drawing more attention to their route. And if the leak was close enough to Pratt himself, the hunters might be drawn away, allowing them some breathing room.

Survival was the game plan and the goal. Progress from A to B and do so with your troops intact. There were no other rules, and if you had to trash a couple dozen—or a couple hundred—savages along the way, hard luck.

"How far?" Aguire asked him.

"To Lubbock?" Bolan calculated from the last sign he'd seen. "I'd say another hundred miles should do it."

"Ah."

The witness never seemed to tear his eyes away from the unfolding desert, cooled and colored like some kind of science fiction moonscape. The view from Bolan's seat, by contrast, was a glimpse of hard reality, the landscape dry and baking underneath a sun that gave no quarter, recognized no truce.

He knew that cotton was still grown along the Gulf, but a glimpse of northern Texas, burned and brown, belied the childhood lessons that described how opening the Lone Star State to great plantations, manned by slaves, had pushed the nation one step closer to a catastrophic civil war. There was no hint of Dixie on the road to Lubbock. They had left mint juleps and gentility behind.

This land had mothered gunmen from the earliest of times, and some of them had gone on to fame or infamy in different generations. Nowadays the Texas gunman drove a sleek Mercedes or a chopped-down Harley-Davidson, and he was less concerned with driving sheepmen off the range or robbing banks than with the sale of speed, cocaine and heroin.

He studied their surroundings, realizing that the wasteland would be perfect for an ambush. Not because of hiding places, which were nonexistent, but because they seemed to be a thousand miles from nowhere. Anything could happen, and the secret would be absolutely safe with prickly cactus, rattlesnakes and shifting sands.

It was the perfect no-man's land, a custom-tailored killing ground.

The warrior settled back to make himself at home.

"WE NEED TO THINK about tonight," Bolan said. Johnny swiveled toward his brother's voice, distracted from a survey of the barren landscape.

"I've been thinking maybe we should drive straight through," he offered. "Sleep in shifts and try to beat our schedule. That might throw them off."

The warrior frowned. "I wouldn't want to be out here at midnight, when it hits the fan."

Another glance across the wasteland made his brother's point. Except for twisting gullies, washed out by erosion, there was nothing in the way of cover, nowhere they could hide themselves or make a stand against concerted opposition. In the open, they'd have two choices: run, or stand and fight, without apparent hope in either case.

"Okay," Bolan said, "we'll pass on Lubbock. Try to find a pit stop closer to the border, off the road."

"It works for me."

"Objections?"

In the back, Aguire shrugged and shook his head. "It does not matter. If they find us, it is all the same."

"I wish you'd try to tone down that optimism a little," Johnny said. "I hate to get my hopes up."

"Are we halfway there?" Aguire asked.

"More like two-thirds," Bolan answered.

Satisfied, the Cuban turned back to his window, lost in thought. Johnny wondered what it must be like to throw your life away by accident, and find yourself caught up inside a living nightmare, trapped, with no place to turn.

His brother's case was different. Mack had made a conscious choice, electing sacrifice as an alternative to standing back and doing nothing while the cannibals devoured his world. Aguire had been grabbing for the tarnished ring and missed it, plunging headlong into circumstances he couldn't control.

It was no better than the guy deserved, all things considered, but the younger Bolan felt a trace of sympathy, regardless. He shrugged it off and concentrated on the highway, heat waves rising from the asphalt to create a shimmering illusion that the lanes were flooded up ahead, the nonexistent tide receding as they chased it over flatlands bleached of promise, void of hope.

From his position at the spearhead of the pack, Chill knew that he'd be the first to spot the target. He was looking forward to it, psyched up for the kill, intent on showing off the guts and other qualities of leadership that marked him as a special member of the Mongols motorcycle gang.

Chill pushed the Harley at a steady sixty-five, its thunder blown away behind him by the desert wind that scorched his cheeks above a ratty beard. Grime and motor oil had smudged the several patches on his vest: the one-percenter badge that signified an outlaw biker; swastikas and SS lightning bolts; a skull and crossbones; the initials FTW—short for Fuck The World.

Chill's favorite patch, worn just above his heart, was red on white and bore a single word: Deguello. Lifted from the title of a song that General Santa Ana played before he massacred defenders at the Alamo, it sent a message of no quarter asked or given in a combat situation, worn by bikers who have violently resisted arrest. The pointman's face and knuckles bore the scars of those encounters with the law: his rap sheet testified to forty-three arrests on charges ranging from possession of narcotics to attempted murder. The successful murders—eight in all—had not been prosecuted, but he was a standout in the gang, regardless. None of his associates could boast of more than twenty-eight arrests.

A dozen other Harleys filled the southbound lane behind Chill. Two of the bikes were big three-wheelers, packing shotgun riders on their buddy seats, and all fifteen of the selected Mongols traveled armed. Chill wore a compact walkie-talkie on his belt, an earplug keeping him in touch with Skag and Wolfman, who were somewhere up ahead. They should be making contact soon, and then it would be show time.

Fucking ay.

There had been nothing from the scouts since they identified their target forty minutes earlier. No news was good news on a deal like that, and in a few more minutes they should have the bastard spotted, heading north. It would be simple, falling in behind him, running up his track to set his ass on fire.

Chill relished the occasions when he was required to mete out punishment for some transgression of the Mongol bylaws. It was even better with civilians, when he wasn't forced to pull his punches, and the damage he inflicted could be permanent. When he was called upon to kill, he could take care of business with the best.

It pleased him that the Mongols had been tapped to make a score for the Colombian. It showed that years of faithful service really did pay off, and once the syndicate was satisfied, the heat relieved, there'd be bigger, sweeter deals in store. Instead of cooking crank all day and pushing it to speed freaks in the barrio, the Mongols could begin to trade in finer merchandise, developing an upscale clientele. Hell's Angels had already cracked the denim barrier in California, moving on to suits and ties like normal businessmen, giving the old-line Italians a run for their money, and Chill envisioned a day when the Mongols would follow the same route, reserving their bikes for ceremonial runs on Labor Day and the Fourth of July.

Moving up in the world, bet your ass.

But first there was a job to do. It lay somewhere out in front of him, along the two-lane blacktop. Chill could feel it coming. He could smell it in the wind.

It smelled like death, and it was damned near sweet enough to get him high.


THERE WERE DAYS when Frank Chaney thought he was getting old. The Sam Browne fit a little tighter than it used to—tighter than it had last month, in fact—and when he hoisted his two hundred and fifty pounds out of the cruiser to write a citation, there was an occasional twinge in his lower back, a faint precursor of advancing age.

Chaney wasn't overly concerned. He had his twenty years in, and he knew that he could pull the plug at any time. But the fact was, he had nothing else to do, without the job life would have been an endless armchair snooze with beer in hand, the boob tube blaring mindless crap all day.

Chaney had been working western Texas in a one-man car since he completed his probationary period in 1967. He believed that he'd seen it all, from hit-and-runs to foxy ladies cruising in their birthday suits to truckers wired so tight on bennies that they couldn't even see the double-nickel signs. In twenty years, he was responsible for more than seven hundred and fifty righteous collars, and he'd been forced to use his blue-steel Smith & Wesson twice.

That afternoon, Frank Chaney had parked his cruiser north of Justiceburg, in Garza County. He was screened on one side by an eight-foot sand dune and by a stand of Joshua trees on the other. He liked to sit and watch the road for speeders sometimes, rather than patroling where his black-and-white was visible a mile away. You couldn't write citations if the jerk-offs saw you coming and had time to brake before you got a solid reading on the radar gun.

Frank heard the choppers coming from a mile away, their engines growling on the flats. He watched them pass and counted heads, unhappy with the odds but knowing he should tag along regardless, just in case the scumbags were up to something. Chaney knew that they were *always* up to something, but the trick was finding evidence, and tackling fifteen bikers was a risky proposition for a SWAT team, let alone one officer.

Deciding he could always call for backup, he gave the Mongols ninety seconds before falling in behind them at a distance. He could close the gap in no time, if he had to, but Chaney wanted ample room between them in case the bikers spotted him and doubled back to have some fun. Before they closed the intervening mile, he could release the 12-gauge pump gun from its dashboard mount or choose his target for a head-on jousting match. But there was no way Chaney meant to let the bastards take him by surprise. No way at all.

THE WEATHERED HIGHWAY SIGN announced that Gas-Food was available in twenty-seven miles.

"What's gas-food?" Johnny asked.

"Never tried it," Bolan answered, "but I think it's long on refried beans."

"Makes sense."

Behind them, glinting in the rearview mirror like a bright, metallic insect was another vehicle. Bolan couldn't make out details yet, and he wasn't prepared to bolt in case it might turn out to be a lawman on his normal rounds. Thus far, they hadn't broken any laws in Texas, and he meant to keep it that way—if he could.

Johnny tracked his brother's gaze and caught the other vehicle's reflection in his own wing mirror. "Company?"

"I wouldn't think so. People must drive through here all the time."

In fact, they hadn't passed a dozen cars within the past two hours. Even snakes and armadillos had retreated from the midday heat, the absence of life increasing Bolan's sense of isolation as he pushed the Jimmy north. If they were being tailed, against all odds, the enemy had found a decent place to make his move.

Ahead of them, as if on cue, another flash of sunlight glinted painfully off polished steel. the haze of heat and distance blurred Bolan's vision, but the new arrival seemed disjointed somehow, oversized and awkward, like a semi with its trailers out of line.

They closed to half a mile before he recognized the fleet of motorcycles roaring south with one man on the point, the others riding two abreast behind him. One glance told the Executioner they were outlaws, their machines stripped clean of fenders, windshields, saddlebags and running lights.

The bearded leader made a point of glancing over at them as he passed, a cool grin etched across his face. Bolan counted thirteen motorcycles—fifteen riders—as the grim parade rolled by.

"Those friends of yours?" Johnny asked Aguire.

The Cuban offered no reply. His face was grim, and Bolan caught a faint, reflected gleam of apprehension in his eyes.

Behind them, the outlaw pointman made a graceful U-turn, doubling back to follow. His companions emulated the maneuver like a sleek precision drill team in a holiday parade.

"Not friends," the Executioner said quietly. "Let's try acquaintances."

"I was afraid of that."

Johnny popped the glove compartment open and removed the mini-Uzi from beneath a pile of road maps. With an easy, practiced move he snapped in a magazine and drew the bolt back.

"I'm getting tired of asking this," John said, "but how the hell? . . ."

"We'll ask them if we get the chance."

But Bolan knew there would be no opportunity for conversation. If he couldn't outrun the Harley hogs—and that was little more than wishful thinking—they'd have to let their weapons do their talking.

Bolan clenched his teeth and pressed the pedal to the floor.

## 13

"That's it." Skag grinned. "They made us."

"So get moving," Wolfman countered. "Don't want Chill and those guys having all the fun."

Skag got it moving, stepping hard on the accelerator as the van dug in for traction. He was too far back to give the Harleys any major competition, but with any luck it ought to take Chill's men a mile or two to run their pigeon off the road. From that point on, Skag thought, things might get interesting.

"Step on it, bro'," the Wolfman urged.

"I've got the fucking pedal on the floor, man."

The bikes had finished cranking through their turn and were homing in on the target now, breaking formation as they filled both lanes, sticking close to the Jimmy. It reminded Skag of a Disney cartoon, where Donald Duck goes looking for some honey in the woods and winds up with a swarm of angry bees chasing his little duck ass into a lake. The image made him smile, and he reflected that the poor dumb shits inside the Jimmy were about to get stung for real.

"Party time," the Wolfman gloated, easing up a sawed-off double-barreled shotgun from its hiding place beneath his seat. He broke the stubby weapon open, checked its load and snapped it shut again.

Skag hoped he wouldn't blow the windshield out, but it was no big deal. The van had been stolen in Lubbock, and the plates went back a month or so to Dallas, where a member of the club had ripped off half a dozen sets as spares. Their fingerprints inside the vehicle could be a problem, but Skag meant to wipe the van—maybe torch it—after they were finished with their little party.

In the meantime, he would be a kind of Welcome Wagon in reverse. Unwelcome Wagon? Yea. He liked the sound of that.

Ahead, the bikes were swarming now, moving up on both sides and crowding their rabbit toward the center stripe. The bastard cut his wheel hard right as they began to crowd him, clipping one hog, spinning it away in an explosive cloud of dust and gravel. As he raced past, Skag thought he recognized a brother called Magoo, dumped on the roadside with his legs twisted under him at awkward angles.

"I want those bastards," Wolfman snarled.

"You'll have to stand in line, bro'."

"I don't mind. There ought to be enough to go around."

Skag hoped so. He'd never been a great fan of Magoo's, but no one took a brother out and lived to tell the tale. It was a law of nature, just like gravity.

Whoever went up in a Mongol's line of fire was surely going down.

BOLAN COULD SEE in the mirror that some of the bikers were holding weapons. The extra riders on the back of the three-wheelers were packing what looked like a shotgun and Mini-14 assault rifle, respectively. The first few shots were wild, aim spoiled by Bolan's weaving, but he knew their luck could never hold.

"These guys are serious," Johnny said.

As if in answer to his comment, several shotgun pellets rattled off the tailgate window, leaving milky scars on the bulletproof glass. Pistol rounds began to pock the Jimmy's flanks, gouging divots in the paint before they were deflected by the armor plating underneath. Where bullets struck the glass, they left dark streaks or smudges that resembled fingerprints.

The soldier thought of slamming on his brakes and letting two or three of the attackers taste his bumper, but a slowdown would allow the bikers to surround them in an instant. Bolan knew the limitations of armor plating and "bulletproof" glass under point-blank fire, and he meant to avoid being in the center of a concentrated barrage if possible. The engine would be vulnerable to head-on fire, and there were still the tires to keep in mind.

"I wish this rig had gun ports," Johnny said. He held the mini-Uzi in his hand, but he'd have to roll a window down to use it, thus exposing everyone inside to hostile fire.

"We need to get off-road," the Executioner replied. "Their bikes aren't built for plowing up the landscape."

In the rearview mirror, Bolan saw a dark van gaining on the bikers, running up behind them. He wasn't expecting help, and any fleeting hopes were dashed when one of the outlaws fell back, out of formation, pacing the van for a quick word with the driver.

"Reinforcements," Bolan told his brother.

John checked it out and scowled. "How many do you figure?"

"Hard to say. We'll have to take them out, whatever."

"Right." If there was any skepticism in the younger Bolan's tone, it didn't show.

The squad car seemed to come out of nowhere, as they topped a rise with bikes strung out behind them like the long tail of a kite. The Executioner had time to recognize a highway patrol insignia on the door, glimpsing a startled face behind the windshield as the officer found himself cruising into a mobile war zone.

One more player in the game of death. Bolan hoped there would be cards enough to go around.

CHILL PULLED LEVEL with the van. "We need you up in front," he shouted, struggling to make his voice heard over wind and engines.

"Where? Up there?"

"We have to ram the bastard."

"Ram?" Skag seemed confused, as if the desert furnace draft was blowing in one ear and out the other, sweeping all coherent thought away.

"He's armor-plated, damn it! Get up there and run him off the road."

The grin spread from ear to ear. "You got it, bro'."

Skag started lying on the horn, and when a couple of Mongols craned their necks to find out what the hell was going on, Chill waved them over, clearing the southbound lane for Skag to pass. The van swung out and started to accelerate, its horn still blaring, but a heartbeat later it veered back across the line, the brake lights flashing like a pair of dragon eyes.

Before Chill had an opportunity to grasp what was happening, the van clipped two brothers, slamming them together in a dead-end slide to nowhere, faces flayed on asphalt in the heartbeat left before their engines detonated, spewing fire and shrapnel.

Chill rode wide around the lake of burning gasoline, and nearly took a header through the windshield of a squad car in the other lane. He saved it, with perhaps three inches breathing room to spare, and noted that a portion of the cruiser's inside fender had been peeled away on impact with some other obstacle.

Chill didn't have to guess what that might be. An instant later he was howling past the twisted hulk of yet another Harley-Davidson, its driver a mangled slab of raw meat on the center stripe.

Behind him, with a squeal of rubber, the patrol car made a sharp U-turn and joined the fool's parade. Chill twisted his accelerator, working hard to put some space between himself and the policeman, thinking fast. He knew the cop would have to die—that was a given in the circumstances—but his crew had already been shaved by twenty-five percent. And they had yet to score a solid hit on their primary target.

Chill decided contracts sucked, but it was too damned late to pull out now. They had a mess to clean up first, and witnesses to silence. After that, there would be fallen brothers to secure.

But first the kill.

And if they did it right, that just might make the game worthwhile.

THE CRUISER STREAKED PAST in a blur, already braking by the time Johnny swiveled in his seat to chart its progress.

The collision was inevitable. Two bikes swung back across the line in time, but a third was too slow to make it and the squad car struck it squarely. Folding in upon itself, the Harley spun and wobbled, fell over with the rag-doll driver trapped beneath its twisted bulk.

"That's two," Johnny said. He'd barely uttered the words when the van veered back from the passing lanes, colliding with another pair of choppers in the process. "Make that four. We ought to sit this out and let them waste each other."

"No such luck. Hang on!"

Bolan took the Jimmy off-road in a cloud of dust and gravel, jolting over ruts and stones before they reached an unpaved access road that seemed to run forever toward the far horizon.

"Where the hell does this go?"

"Does it matter?"

Knowing that his brother had a point, Johnny turned to watch the bikers eat their dust. A couple of the Harleys surged forward, drivers squeezing off a round or two before they fell back, lost to sight, and others took their place. He couldn't tell if they had shaken any of the enemy, but four—at least—were permanently out of action. That would cut the odds a bit when it came time for them to make their stand.

And that moment, he knew, couldn't be too far off.

The Jimmy could outrun their opposition in the rough, but driving overland was a diversionary method, and the bikers would be waiting when, inevitably, they were forced back to the highway. Likewise, the addition of a squad car to the chase meant reinforcements would be on the way, and their itinerary didn't make allowances for killing time in jail.

So they'd have to stand and fight. Soon. Case closed.

"Check this out."

Johnny tore himself away from their backtrack, following his brother's gaze though the windshield. They were closing on a makeshift refuse dump. Piles of garbage, broken furniture and rusting auto bodies had been roughly heaped to form a cul-de-sac. The access road veered left to skirt a central pit that had been excavated by erosion, with a helping hand from man.

"Looks good to me," the younger Bolan said as the warrior applied the brakes and swung the Jimmy's wheel around.

"It's all we've got."

The Jimmy shuddered through a rough one-eighty, throwing up a cloud of dust that momentarily obscured the track, the pit and the surrounding dunes of trash. Aguire popped up from the floor in back, fear draining the color from his face.

"Why are we stopping?" he demanded.

"We've got nowhere else to go."

A pair of outlaw bikers hurtled through the dust cloud, saw the pit too late and soared off into space. The next one through was quicker, laying down his hog and sacrificing skin in time to save himself, his backup closing in and circling like Apache raiders as the dust began to settle.

"Ready?"

John flashed a smile. "Why not?"

The Executioner hauled the CAR-15 from underneath his seat and drew back the cocking lever. It was the last that Johnny saw of his brother before he threw his own door open, leaping clear.

And somewhere in the middle of it all, obscured by engine sounds and gunfire, masked by settling dust, a siren had begun to wail.


"OFFICER NEEDS ASSISTANCE!" Chaney shouted into the radio microphone, spinning the wheel with his free hand and hanging on for dear life. "Highway 84, north of Justiceburg. Shots fired. I'm in pursuit of twelve to fifteen Mongols, plus a dark blue van. Three bikers down...no, make that four. They're firing on another vehicle. Looks like a Blazer or a Jimmy. Get some backup out here, now!"

He dropped the microphone and tuned his mind out to the nasal tones of the dispatcher's voice. No matter how the troops responded to his call, the nearest cars were probably in Lubbock, maybe down in Roscoe, and he'd be lucky if he saw their flashing lights within half an hour. In the meantime, he was on his own, and that meant trouble.

Chaney had nearly lost it after flattening the biker in a head-on crash, and he knew how fortunate he was that hog and rider hadn't wound up in his lap. Collision with a full-sized Harley-Davidson meant damage to the cruiser, and a better hit would certainly have cracked his radiator. As it was, the left-hand fender looked like rumpled tin foil, and he felt a tremor that betrayed a problem with the black-and-white's alignment.

Chaney shrugged it off and concentrated on his driving. He had no idea why fifteen Mongols and the driver of a van had suddenly decided to pursue another vehicle, guns blazing, but the chase had cost four punks their hides already, and he meant to see the rest of them locked up or planted for their trouble. They'd have to be disarmed, of course, before he got around to asking any questions, and the odds were looking grim from where Frank Chaney sat. In fact, it looked like suicide, but he'd taken on the risks when he began to draw his paycheck from the state.

He drew his Smith & Wesson, shifted hands, and held it in his left, extended from his open window. A couple of bikes at the end of the line were weaving back and forth to cut him off, as if running interference, but he had no patience left for fun and games. If they were looking for a new career as road-kill, Chaney would be happy to oblige.

As if on cue, the bikers veered apart, accelerating, and a squat three-wheeler drifted into Chaney's path. The passenger had twisted half around to face the cruiser, and he aimed a shotgun at Chaney. He just had time to duck before a charge of buckshot took out his windshield, the pebbled safety glass cascading over him like marbles. Driving blind, Chaney floored the pedal, holding steady on the wheel. He heard a warning shout before the three-wheel's driver goosed it, staying just a shade ahead.

A second shotgun blast ripped through the headrest on his seat. Then trooper sat up quickly, sighting through the open windshield with his Magnum, and squeezed off two rounds in rapid-fire. One missed, but he was right on target with the second, which drilled through the shotgun rider's chest to score a secondary hit between the driver's shoulder blades.

He saw the bike begin to swerve, and steered his cruiser in the opposite direction, passing close enough to graze the bike's rear end and flip it over like a capsized tortoise on the shoulder of the highway. Up ahead a boiling dust cloud told him that the lead car was attempting to elude pursuit by taking off across the desert, maybe falling back on four-wheel drive.

He wished them luck.

The Mongols weren't riding dirt bikes, but they weren't about to let their quarry slip away because the ground got rocky, either. As for Chaney, he'd hang in to the bitter end, unless his vehicle gave up the ghost.

He saw the last two bikers in the lineup disappear, their figures swallowed in a wall of swirling dust. Chaney followed, choking as the grit billowed at him through the open windshield. Nearly blind now, praying he could hold his breath until it cleared, the trooper kept his foot on the accelerator.

If the Mongols thought that they could shake him off that easy, they could damned well think again.

A BULLET RATTLED OFF the Jimmy's open door as Bolan hit a combat crouch, the carbine set for automatic fire. He loosed a 3-round burst in the direction of the milling bikers. One tumbled from the saddle, and the rest scattered with a roar of engines, churning more dust with their tires as they wheeled off in all directions, seeking cover.

On the far side of the car, he heard the Uzi's rattle of defiance. The bikers were returning fire, still rolling, hot rounds spurting dust around the vehicle or spanging off its armored body. Bolan caught a quick glimpse of Aguire, scrambling for the driver's door. Then the guy was kneeling in the dirt beside the Jimmy, looking for a place to hide.

He broke in the direction of the trash pit, bullets snapping at his heels. Bolan was compelled to follow, after toppling another outlaw with a blitzing figure eight that left his colors spouting crimson through a layer of chalky dust. The punk was dead before he hit the ground, his chopper settling heavily across his legs and pelvis.

Aguire reached the pit, appeared to stumble then disappeared beyond its rim. Hostile fire began to churn the air around the Executioner, forcing him to veer off course and slide across the rusting hood of a '67 Chevrolet. Outlaw bullets drilled its bodywork as if the hulk were made of tin.

The soldier cursed Aguire as he crawled forward and tried to find himself a field of fire. It was a trade-off: meager sanctuary might of saved his life, but it had also pinned him down, while giving Carlos time to slip away.

If he was still alive.

It played the same in either case—a missing witness or a dead one. Vos would walk.

Fat chance.

The game was blown unless he brought Aguire in alive, and there was no way he could do that while he lay there eating dust. Disgusted, Bolan poked his head around the Chevy's tarnished bumper, ducking back again with some idea of how the opposition was arrayed against him. He could see four of them, and two were closing in a pincers movement, while two more served as anchors in the middle, laying down sporadic cover fire.

The others would be going after Johnny, but the kid would have to look out for himself. The Executioner was all tied up at the moment.

It would be timing all the way, he would either pull it off or he wouldn't. Whatever, he was dead already if he didn't make the effort.

Bolan crept backward, shifting from the place where he'd last been seen, already counting down the doomsday numbers in his mind. He came up firing, hitting back with everything he had. And praying it would be enough.

## 14

All things considered, Aguire thought that running from the Jimmy was a bad idea. It seemed essential at the time, with bullets hammering against the body of the vehicle and cracking off the windows, but he found it even worse outside. The Mongols had a clear shot at him, and there was nothing he could do but run for cover, praying that a well-placed bullet didn't find him first.

He'd been huddled in back on the Jimmy's floor when the vehicle had stopped, and rolling clouds of dust had blocked the view before Aguire made his break. He thought the rising mounds of rubbish ought to offer some protection, but he hadn't seen the pit in time to save himself.

Or maybe it was fate.

Whatever, he was sprinting for what seemed to be the closest cover—and not nearly close enough—when suddenly the earth gave way beneath his feet. He felt the ground begin to shift at first, then crumble in an avalanche of cardboard, cans and bottles. When he tried to put the brakes on, things got worse and momentum pitched him forward onto his face.

In retrospect it hadn't been a fall as much as it had been a slide. The near side of the garbage pit was canted at nearly a forty-five degree angle, with refuse heaping outward toward the bottom. After plunging six or seven feet in freefall, Carlos landed on his belly, hands outstretched to catch himself, and slithered downhill like some kind of lizard in a mud slide. He was nicked and gouged along the way, his clothing ripped and fouled, but he'd live.

Perhaps.

Two Mongols had already found the pit before him. Twisted, smoking motorcycles lay within a few yards of each other, mangled in their plunge from the heights. One of the drivers had died with his machine, spine snapped on impact, but the other was up and moving, after a fashion, studying the boundaries of his prison through a veil of blood.

The biker saw Aguire coming, and he responded with a quickness that belied his seemingly dazed state. The Mongol searched desperately for weapons, lost when he'd made the plunge, but there was nothing to be found. Recovering, the nightmare figure drew a sheath knife from his belt and moved to the attack.

Aguire had perhaps ten seconds to prepare himself, and he couldn't afford to quibble in his choice of weapons. Scooping up a rusty shower rod, he gripped it like a fighting staff, two-handed. The far side of the pit was seemingly reserved for odds and ends of lumber, and Aguire thought if he could make it that far, he might find himself a decent club.

The biker read his mind and moved to intercept him, closing swiftly. Carlos batted at him with the rod, and it was slapped aside contemptuously, offering no hindrance to his enemy. The Cuban's rage boiled over, then, erupting in a stream of curses as he charged the startled outlaw, flailing with his makeshift staff and landing several solid blows across the man's back and shoulders.

Fleeting exultation vanished as the shower rod was captured, twisted from his grasp and tossed aside. Aguire stood defenseless as the blood-smeared savage rushed him, feinting with the blade down low and hacking toward his face.

No one was more startled than Aguire when he caught the biker's wrist and held it fast. The other man's momentum drove him backward and swept him off his feet, but the Cuban somehow kept his grip despite the fall. A false move now was death.

A knee slammed into Aguire's groin, retreated, and came back strong. Carlos felt his stomach knotting and opened his lips in time for the remains of lunch to spatter his opponent's face. The biker cursed and tried to wrench himself away, but he couldn't escape Aguire's grip. Lashing out with combat boots, he bruised Aguire's ribs and thighs, but still the Cuban clung to him like death.

Until his fingers slipped.

Aguire stumbled to his knees, the outlaw backing off a pace before he realized that he was free. Recovering from the surprise, he moved in for the kill, and Carlos raised his eyes in time to see the blade descending toward his face.

FOUR GUNNERS OPENED FIRE in unison as Bolan came up shooting, rusty bits and pieces flying from the junked car that provided him with cover. One guy was blasting with a shotgun while the other three fired pistols. He took out the scattergunner first as a precaution, knowing that the outlaw's weapon made him the most lethal close-range adversary.

Bolan had his targets pegged before he made his move, and while the flankers were in motion, circling to close the trap, Mr. 12-gauge and a sidekick held their ground at center stage. They both saw Bolan as he rose from cover, but their weapons had been trained on the wrong end of the vehicle, and it took them nearly a heartbeat to correct the error.

Too long by half.

The shotgunner took four rounds across the upper chest as Bolan's CAR-15 tracked from left to right. The biker triggered a last, reflexive blast in the direction of the clouds. His sidekick bolted for the only cover close at hand—the Jimmy—firing as he ran. A short burst churned the ground behind him, but the flankers weighed in their automatics then, and Bolan had to let the runner go.

He concentrated on the two remaining gunmen, knowing they'd be on him soon. If they were capable of a concerted rush, attaching simultaneously, he'd have to choose between them, offering his back to one man or the other in a suicidal game that he could never hope to win.

The rusty Chevy had no doors on Bolan's side, and its rear seat had been removed. With seconds left to spare, he saw the golden opportunity and seized it, edging forward, careful not to show himself or tip the car as he crept silently inside.

A spider scuttled over Bolan's hand, but he ignored it, huddled in the oven, concentrating on the predators outside. A burst of automatic fire erupted from the general vicinity of the Jimmy, but he put it out of mind, refusing to divide his concentration now.

When the bikers made their move, it was a marvel of precision timing, both men popping into view at once, their weapons primed and ready. Neither came expecting empty air, and they were squeezing off before they recognized each other, stopping lead with flesh before they realized their fatal error.

Bolan burst from cover as the guns fell silent, triggering a burst to starboard. He finished his man on that side, twisting in midair to bring the other under fire. His opposition had collapsed on hands and knees, blood pumping from a shoulder wound. Bolan ended all his earthly worries with a single head shot.

He thought of Johnny first but went to find Aguire, moving in a crouch as he approached the garbage pit. Below him, the Cuban and a wounded biker grappled for a knife, the outlaw kicking at Aguire, finally breaking free of his restraining grasp. Aguire stumbled to his knees, and Bolan set the carbine's fire selector switch on semiautomatic as the biker moved to finish it, the long knife poised to strike.

One shot at thirty yards was all it took. The 5.56 mm round caught his target just below the jawline, nearly taking off that shaggy head before the biker fell. Aguire took a moment to discover he was still alive, and then he picked out Bolan's figure on the west rim of the pit.

The soldier left him there, secure for the moment if he had the sense to hide. There was still a war in progress, and the growl of engines, coupled with the wailing of a siren, told him reinforcements had arrived.

SKAG COULDN'T SEE a goddamned thing with all the dust, but he could hear just fine. The cop was still behind them, eating landscape all the way but hanging in there, with his siren whooping like some kind of frigging jungle bird on speed. His flashing lights were visible from time to time—when he got close enough. Every time that happened Skag poured on the gas, determined to hold their narrow lead.

"We need to shake that bastard, man."

The Wolfman grinned. "It's covered, bro'."

He left his seat and jostled Skag before he cleared the space between them, rocking with the motion of the van. It was a miracle they hadn't cracked an axle yet, and he was sure they couldn't take much more. The van was solid, but a Jeep hadn't been requested when they sent him out to bag civilian wheels. All this off-road shit was getting hairy.

Still, he thought, it could be worse. The brothers on two wheels were getting pounded, sucking sand like there was no tomorrow, and it took some kind of balls to push the chase in those conditions. Payback would be that much sweeter when they caught the assholes they were chasing. In the meantime—

"Jesus, will you slow this fucker down?" The Wolfman was on hands and knees, his shotgun slithering across the floor. "I can't do a damned thing in a fucking roller coaster."

"Yeah, all right. Hang on a second."

"That's all I can fucking do. Hang on to this, bro'."

Skag was shifting to the brake halfheartedly, afraid of being left behind or getting corn-holed by the cruiser on his tail, when suddenly the dust cleared in front of him and he beheld the promised land. The Jimmy they were chasing stood in front of him, nose pointed back in the direction they had come from, and packed with bullet marks. Choppers were mobbed in the foreground, brothers taking off on foot and pegging shots at targets Skag couldn't make out from where he sat.

"We've got 'em bro'!"

"Hold on a sec—"

Skag mashed the brake and held it to the floor as they began to fishtail in the dirt. Wolfman triggered off a shotgun blast before deceleration pitched him backward—that is, forward—toward the driver's seat. The impact drove Skag's face against the steering wheel, a jolting blow that cracked his nose and left him drooling blood across his naked chest.

The Wolfman wasn't moving, but his shotgun lay beneath the dash. Skag retrieved it, feeling dizzy when he moved too quickly, and wondered if something might have snapped besides his nose.

No matter.

He had counted bikes before the roof fell in, and there were only eight in sight, which meant their strike force had been cut by half. His brothers needed him, and pain was nothing in a situation where it all came down to do or die.

Skag worked the shotgun's slide to chamber up a hot one and went out to meet the enemy.

BLINDED BY A ROLLING CLOUD of dust, Frank Chaney never saw the gunner aiming at his cruiser from the van's back door. He *did* see brake lights flaring as the vehicle in front of him began to slide, and then the world blew up in Chaney's face. A blast of buckshot ripped through his radiator, flinging back the hood to cut off any vestige of a forward view.

He jerked the steering wheel hard left, accelerating in a bid to miss the braking van and simultaneously spoil the gunner's aim. There was no second shotgun blast, no impact, and he was preparing to congratulate himself on the evasive move when everything went wrong. The front tires on his cruiser lost their traction, while the rear dug in and punched him through a broadside skid.

Remembering his training, Chaney cut the wheel in that skid's direction, trying to correct, but it was hopeless. When the cruiser rolled, he hung on to the steering wheel, white-knuckled, cursing as the microphone from his dash-mounted radio whipped out to smack him in the face.

The shoulder harness saved his life, though Chaney wasn't sure of it for several moments. Hanging upside down, the vehicle filled with swirling, choking dust, he might have been in hell as easily as Texas. Only pain told Chaney that he was still alive, and at the moment he hurt everywhere.

The cruiser's roof hadn't collapsed, and he attributed that fact to sandy soil as much as any triumph of construction from Detroit. The siren moaned and died, a sweet relief, and only hissing static issued from the radio. He would have lost the whip antenna, surely, but there was a walkie-talkie in the glove compartment. Once he freed himself...

Despite the ringing in his ears and sounds of gunfire in the middle distance, Chaney could hear footsteps crunching on the sand and gravel. He groped for his empty holster, then remembered that the Smith & Wesson had been in his lap before he rolled. There was no sign of it now. For all he knew, it could have been thrown clear of the vehicle.

That left the shotgun. Straining, he could just grasp the barrel, but his fingers wouldn't reach the latch to free the weapon from its dashboard mount. He needed four more inches, and he'd have to lose the shoulder harness first, before he had a prayer.

Too late.

The footsteps halted just outside, and Chaney craned his neck to catch a glimpse of denim cuffs and motorcycle boots. He made another lunge to reach the shotgun latch and missed it, fingers scrabbling for the latch securing his seat belt when the outlaw knelt beside his open window, bending down to show a broken nose and bloodied smile.

"You're hurting, old man." The smile was gloating now, and Chaney wondered if the punk was stoned. "What say I help you out?"

He saw the shotgun then, a sawed-off Remington. Up close it looked like a bazooka, and its blast would have about the same effect on human flesh.

"I'll prob'ly get myself in trouble," the biker said, "shooting piggies out of season."

"Reinforcements coming," Chaney told him, marveling at how calm he sounded. "Don't make it any harder on yourself."

"You got it wrong, pig. I'm about to make it hard on you."

The punk reached through the window, snuggling the shotgun's muzzle against Chaney's forehead. "Pucker up, old man. It's time to kiss your ass goodbye."

HUNCHED DOWN behind the bullet-scarred vehicle, Johnny waited for the jackals to find him. He was fuzzy on the details of the action, but he knew the squad car had arrived. As well as a van that carried reinforcements for the enemy. How many? He didn't have a ghost of an idea, but it would make no difference in the long run. The Bolans had to deal with all the bikers, or they'd be dead.

A bullet cracked against the Jimmy's windshield, followed quickly by another, and he tried to gauge the angle. It was hopeless. He'd have to meet the enemy before he could destroy them, and it galled him, crouching under cover while they stalked him.

It was time to move.

He broke from cover at the Jimmy's tailgate, churning dust with loping strides as two guns started tracking, barking at his heels. He placed them, saw the bikers start to follow, and it was all he needed—something in the way of solid targets, a substantial enemy instead of fleeting shadows in the wasteland.

The nearest cover was an old, cast-off refrigerator. The door had been removed, in deference to safety, and the shelves inside were filthy with a combination of petrified food scraps and accumulated desert soil. He slid behind the reefer, just as bullets started smacking into bleached enamel, but he wasn't going to be pinned this time.

Instead of lying low, Johnny kept on moving, circling around the fridge and emerging into view before his enemies could halt their charge or change direction. The younger Bolan caught them in the open, his mini-Uzi rattling at full throttle. The first rounds nailed the biker on his left, causing the guy to trip over his own feet, and he spun as he fell with arms outflung in death.

The second guy veered sharply off his course and snapped off two pistol rounds that very nearly did the job. Johnny heard them whisper past his face, and then the Uzi answered, chopping down his adversary on the run. The biker stumbled, nearly caught himself, then his brain shut down, his heart pumping blood through holes instead of veins and arteries.

A scarecrow figure was emerging from the outlaw van, and Johnny moved to intercept, alert to any other dangers, but spotting none. The biker seemed to be unarmed, and he looked startled as he noticed Johnny, standing with the Uzi leveled from his waist. "Well, shit," he said, "this ain't my day."

For reasons Johnny would never comprehend, the biker started to run for the Jimmy, his knees and elbows pumping as he made a desperate run to nowhere.

Johnny shot him with reluctance, knowing as he pulled the trigger that the guy would find himself a weapon somehow, somewhere, conscious of the fact that letting him survive would jeopardize their mission and their lives. He made it quick and relatively clean, if such an adjective can be applied to parabellum manglers tearing into flesh at seven hundred and fifty rounds per minute.

Either way, he got it done, and an eerie silence settled on the killing ground. But where was Mack? And where the hell, in all that carnage, was Aguire?

BOLAN CIRCLED toward the capsized squad car, making a half circuit before he spotted the biker, kneeling in dirt beside the inverted driver's door.

"Pucker up, old man," he said. "It's time to kiss your ass goodbye."

"Make sure you really want to pull that trigger," the soldier cautioned, leveling his CAR-15 at the disheveled figure.

Frozen in his place, the outlaw turned his head enough to give himself a view of Bolan and the weapon that was pointed at his face.

"I'm pretty sure," he said, and grinned.

"You're tired of living?"

"Everybody has to go sometime."

"Your choice."

The biker seemed to have a sudden inspiration. "See, thing is, I've got a job to do, you dig?"

"He's not a part of it."

"Pig made himself a part of it. He has to learn you don't go fucking with the Mongols, man."

"And when you pull the trigger, when you're dead, what happens to your job?"

"It's fucked, man. Someone else will have to pick it up from here."

Again, the soldier said, "Your choice."

If there was any thought behind the move, it didn't show. The biker rocked back on his haunches and swung up the sawed-off 12-gauge, triggering a blast as Bolan sidestepped and dropped to a combat crouch. At farther range, the pellets would have nailed him, but he had allowed for distance and the shots skimmed past him, scattering across the wasteland at his back.

A short burst from the CAR-15 punched his adversary backward, leaving crimson traces along the squad car's dusty fender. Kneeling beside the car, he peered inside and saw a middle-aged patrolman hanging in a shoulder harness, bruised and coated with a layer of grit, but otherwise intact.

"Need help there?"

Johnny had approached without a sound, and now he helped his brother pry the driver's door open, and haul the cruiser's single occupant clear of the wreck. When he was on his feet and mobile, Bolan turned to his brother and said, "You'd better get our friend. He's in the pit."

"Can someone tell me what the hell is going on, here?" Even in his shaken state, the officer was working, trying to make sense of what had happened. He was conscious of the gun in Bolan's hands, but he didn't appear intimidated.

"I'd say you deserve some answers," Bolan told him, "but the plain fact is, I haven't got the time to fill you in."

"You won't be going far in that."

The trooper nodded toward the Jimmy, which was scarred by more than a hundred slugs. Bolan saw that it had settled heavily to port and both tires on the driver's side were punctured.

"You've got a point."

He glanced in the direction of the van, which seemed intact, and caught a glimpse of Johnny and their passenger, returning from the pit.

"We're changing cars," he said when they arrived. "Let's shift the gear."

"You mean to leave me out here?" There was apprehension in the trooper's voice.

"You should have company before too long, but just in case, you'll find a CB in the Jimmy."

"What the hell am I supposed to call all this in my report?"

"A moving violation?" Johnny suggested, edging toward the van with heavy duffels from the Jimmy. Aguire had cargo of his own, but Johnny kept a watchful eye on their companion, making sure he didn't help himself to any hardware.

"Why'd you take him out?" the trooper asked. "That punk, I mean. You could have popped him after, and you'd have no witnesses."

"It cost too much," the soldier said. "I'll take the odds the way they are."

The trooper thought about that for a moment, something softening behind his eyes. "I owe you one," he said at last.

"Take care," the Executioner replied and turned away to join his brother and Aguire in the van. He knew they'd be lucky if they made it to the highway and got clear before more cruisers started to arrive. If they could make it into Lubbock, they could think about another change of wheels—or license plates, at least.

But Lubbock lay two hours north, across the killing ground.

## 15

They spent an anxious hour in Lubbock, hosing down the van at a self-serve car wash. They also exchanged their license plates for a new set, which were in the parking lot of a suburban shopping mall. It was the best that they could do, without a whole new paint job or a different set of wheels. Bolan had decided that their risk in sticking with the van would be no worse than that entailed in ripping off another car.

"I still don't like the way these guys keep popping up," Johnny said. "It's like we've got a tail, but we can't see it. Someone's tipping off the opposition everywhere we go."

It hit the soldier all at once, a plausible solution he could never prove, yet it covered all the facts.

"The Jimmy," Bolan said simply.

"How's that?"

"We got our wheels from the DEA. Suppose they came with something extra?"

"Damn! I never thought of that."

"I didn't either, until now."

"You think?"

"Pratt was concerned about a leak. Could be the opposition has a man inside the motor pool."

Aguire poked his head between them. "I don't understand. What do you mean?"

"A homer," Johnny told him. "You can plant it anywhere inside a car—or outside, for that matter—and the signal registers with various audio-visual receivers. With a homer in the car, they could lay back and follow every move we made from something like a mile away."

"It plays," the Executioner agreed. He felt embarrassed that he hadn't checked the vehicle in Jacksonville, but if the homer had been properly concealed, he might have missed it, anyway.

"And now that we have lost the car?" Aguire sounded hopeful, but his face was sculpted in a frown.

"We should be home and dry," Johnny said.

"Not necessarily." The solder felt his brother and Aguire staring at him, waiting for the other shoe to drop. "We can't afford a case of overconfidence," he said. "There *might* have been a homer, but we don't know that for sure. And if there was, we haven't won the war by ditching the vehicle. How many Mongols are there in the state?"

Aguire shrugged. "Perhaps three hundred. I'm not sure."

"That means at least two hundred and eighty still alive, and any one of them might pass along this van's description to the others. Hell, it could be on the air, for all we know. Without the Jimmy's scanner, we can't even check to find out if we're wanted."

Johnny made a sour face and checked his mirror. "Man, you sure know how to rain on a parade."

"Just covering alternatives."

"I hate it when you're right. It always means bad news."

"What can we do?" Aguire asked.

"We're doing it," the Executioner replied. "Keep rolling while we can, and flatten anyone who tries to stop us. It's the only game in town."

"WHAT KIND OF PICKUP did you say it was?"

Frank Chaney made a show of thinking hard, as if the question taxed his brain. A Chevy. Eighty-six or eighty-seven, if I'm not mistaken."

"Black?"

"As coal."

"And you saw . . . what? Three bikers in the cab?"

"Don't quote me. I was kind of busy there, if you recall."

The Texas Ranger stowed his notebook in a pocket, lifting off his Stetson long enough to wipe a handkerchief across his sweaty forehead. He'd heard the story out, doubling back on minor points to keep the details fresh in mind.

"Okay," he said, when he was finished with the hat trick. "Let me see if I've got everything. You saw this pack of Mongols on the highway and you started trailing them to see what they were up to."

"Right."

"You hadn't gone too far when they swung back and started blasting at that Jimmy over there."

"The Jimmy and a pickup."

"Right. I'm not forgetting that. The one that got away."

Frank Chaney forced a smile. It went against his grain to lie that way, but he was paying off a debt the only way he could.

"You couldn't see the number on that Chevy?"

"I was lucky I could see the highway," Chaney countered. "First I crack one bike head-on, and then the bastards blow my windshield out. I couldn't find the rigging dashboard once we left the pavement and I started eating everybody's dust."

"All this—" the Ranger waved an open hand to indicate the scattered dead "—was taken care of by the time you got here?"

"Damned if I know. They were shooting when I got here, then I took another hit and rolled the cruiser. I'll be catching Billy hell for that. I guarantee."

The Ranger nodded sympathetically. "I know exactly what you mean. Once they get over being grateful you're alive, they're bound to chew your ass out."

"My commander likes to do the chewing first, so nobody mistakes him for a bleeding heart."

The Ranger had been mulling something over, and he laid it out for Chaney. "You know," he said, "on deals like this I always figure we've got two clubs fighting over territory, sales—whatever."

"That makes sense."

"But have you noticed anything about the dear departed?"

Chaney glanced around the battleground, where several bodies had been bagged by ambulance attendants, ready for their last run to the morgue. He frowned and shook his head. "Like what?"

"Their colors."

"So?"

"They're all the same. All Mongols. It's a funny thing, I mean. They start the shooting, they do all the chasing, and we haven't got a single body from the other side."

"I hadn't noticed."

"Well, you had your hands full, like you said. It strikes me funny, though. It strike you funny?"

"I'm no expert," Chaney said. "You don't see many gang wars when you're writing out citations all day long."

"I guess that's right."

"The plates might tell me something."

"I've already put them on the wire, but it's a long shot. Chances are they're stolen, or the car is. Maybe both. I wouldn't hold my breath."

"Okay."

"About that peckerhead who tried to waste you in the car..."

"Uh-huh."

"Somebody up and shot him there, before he had a chance to dust you off?"

"I'm standing here."

"You wouldn't have a notion why they did that, would you?"

Chaney shrugged. "I figure he was on the losing side. I just got lucky with the timing."

"Yeah, could be." The Ranger didn't sound convinced. "Things happen like that, sometimes."

Chaney's captain arrived, crawling from his chauffeured cruiser and slapping dust from trousers creased so sharply they could cut your skin. "Goddamm it, Frank," he bawled from fifty feet away, "what happened here?"

"It looks like snack time," Chaney told the Ranger, putting on a weary smile.

"Good luck," the Ranger told him. "I expect we'll be in touch."

"Be looking forward to it," Chaney said, and turned away to face the music.

There were worse things, he supposed, than having someone chew your ass. Like being dead, for instance. Or like running for your life, with every man against you, knowing there was no place you could hide.

Frank Chaney waited for the storm to break and smiled, because he knew damn well that it was good to be alive.

BROGNOLA TOOK THE CALL at home as he was sitting down to eat. His wife knew better than to make an issue of the interruption, and she went ahead without him. Bolan's voice was no surprise at that point, but his message killed the big Fed's appetite.

"We had a little trouble on the road," he said by way of introduction playing safe on what he knew to be an open line.

"Like last time?"

"More or less. No sheets this time. Two-wheelers."

"On the road, you say?"

"Affirmative. They picked us up a couple hours south of Lubbock."

"Just like that?"

"I'm no believer in coincidence," the Executioner replied.

"How's everybody holding up?"

"We're all intact. The package got a little frayed around the edges, but it's functional. We had to get new wheels."

"I don't know what to tell you, Striker. We can still arrange a pickup, independent of our friends, and try to—"

"Negative," the soldier interrupted. "I think we might have solved the problem when we ditched the Jimmy."

Brognola stiffened. "I don't like the sound of that."

"You ought to hear it play from this end."

"I'll be looking into this myself," he promised. "If the problem runs that deep, we could be compromised across the board."

"I'm not in a position to be pointing fingers," Bolan said.

"That's my job. I've been working on some angles here, but I can see we'll have to push a little harder."

"What about delivery?"

"I've been wondering that myself. Our friend might be a little peeved if we preempt him, but I don't see any other way to go."

"I hate to ask..."

Brognola didn't need to hear the question. "I don't know," he said before the Executioner could finish. "I could swear we have no problems at the Farm, but otherwise... well, anything's a possibility."

"Maybe it's time to do some weeding."

"When we get this job behind us, I intend to make it top priority."

*If* they could get the present job behind them. Brognola didn't voice his apprehensions, knowing Bolan would be miles ahead of him in that regard, and pessimism wouldn't serve their cause in any case. They needed action, now, and the big Fed was working on a plan when Bolan made the move to disengage.

"I'll try to keep in touch," the soldier said. "I don't know when."

"No sweat. If you can think of anything you need—"

"I've got your number," Bolan said. "Stay frosty."

"You should feel the chill from there."

Brognola lowered the receiver. He didn't feel like dinner now, but he would eat, because his wife had made the effort and he needed time to think.

They had expected treachery, of course, but if the Executioner's suspicions were correct, Aguire had been marked to die from the beginning, and the Bolan brothers had been nothing more than window dressing, chosen by the enemy within as sacrificial lambs.

Brognola wiped the dark scowl from his face before he reached the table, digging in as if his meal was still hot and appetizing. There would be calls to make when he was finished, cages to be rattled, but he didn't want to rush it in the heat of anger. Any blunder at this point could rebound against his soldiers in the field with grim results.

PRATT KNEW THE CALL could only be bad news, but he answered anyway, hoping that he might be wrong. The sound of Hal Brognola's voice erased all doubt, and Felix felt his acid indigestion kicking in before they had disposed of the amenities.

"My people had another run-in with the opposition."

"Shit."

"In spades. Are you familiar with the Mongols?"

"Badass bikers covering the Texas action, sure. Is it confirmed?"

"I touched a contact in the capital. There's no mistake."

Pratt wished that he could reach the Seagram's bottle on the far side of the room. "How are they playing it?" he asked.

"So far, it's looking like a gang war, but they're not a bunch of idiots down there. In another day or two, they might start talking to Louisiana and comparing notes about that business with the Klan."

"Another day is all we need," Pratt countered.

"Right. Striker had to lose the wheels."

"Say *what*?"

"They took some hits. He couldn't take it on the road looking like something from the last reel of *Bonnie and Clyde*."

"Hell no, I understand. It's just I had to sign the damned thing out."

"No sweat. When they deliver in L.A., you'll be a hero. No one's going to be counting pennies then."

"I hope you're right."

"Believe it. Bureaucrats are all the same. I thought you ought to hear it from a friendly voice before you catch it on the nightly news."

"Hey, I appreciate the call."

"My pleasure."

First thing Pratt did when he was off the telephone was to pour himself a double whiskey, concentrating on the heat that radiated from his throat and stomach as he drank it down. It didn't calm him, so he had another, stopping after two because he had to keep his head clear.

Things were going badly, any way you sliced it, and he knew that distance wouldn't insulate him from the problem. When it blew up in his face, the shock waves would be strong enough to flatten him, no matter where he tried to hide. The only way to slay a dragon was to face the bastard in his lair and fucking do it, one-on-one.

Pratt understood that much, and knew the time had come for him to take things in his own two hands.

If he wasn't too late already.

DESPITE THE URGENT WARNINGS to his unknown contact, Nathan Trask was waiting for the phone call, dreading it. He recognized the voice at once, although it seemed to lack the normal, mocking tone.

"Good evening, counselor. I hope you're dressed."

"Of course."

"Terrific. You're about to take a drive."

The voice delivered clipped directions to another phone booth, at an all-night supermarket half a mile from Trask's address. The lawyer shrugged into a jacket and tucked a licensed .38 inside his belt. A friendly judge had granted him a carry permit on the theory that his clients might have enemies. Tonight would be the first time Trask had packed a weapon in defense against his so-called friends.

The booth was occupied when Trask arrived. A teenaged girl was discussing her complexion problems with a friend and smoking like an amateur, determined to appear sophisticated in her halter top and skintight jeans. Trask waited, rather than attempting to dislodge her from the booth, which would inevitably cause a scene. His contact would be fuming, but it was a risk you took when using public phones to beat the heat.

Five minutes wrapped it up, and Trask was pleasantly surprised to hear the girl say she had to hustle or her parents would be frantic. Trask had never married, never seriously contemplated children, and he watched a perfect argument for birth control strut past his car, all hips and wiggles as she moved across the parking lot. Somebody's daughter, hanging out at night and flaunting it like any other tramp. Her parents would be frantic? Christ, they ought to have their head examined.

The phone was ringing as he reached the booth.

"Hello?"

"The phone was busy, counselor. What's going on?"

"Some kids. You picked the booth, remember?"

"I sincerely hope that you're not jerking me around."

Fatigue and anger met head-on, and Trask couldn't contain himself. "Goddamm it, you're the one who chose the time and place. I didn't leave my home to play some kind of childish guessing game or be insulted. If you have a message, spit it out."

"You sound a little testy, counselor."

"One minute, and I'm leaving."

"Shouldn't take that long," the voice informed him. "We've encountered further difficulties with our interception of the package."

"Christ, I thought you people were supposed to be professionals."

The tone became defensive, granting Trask a minor victory. "I blew a judgement call, okay? It's being taken care of."

"Like the last time?"

"Negative. I'm cutting out the bullshit with the middlemen and sending in the first team. Tell your client not to worry. We've got time."

"And he'll be doing time, if you can't do your job. Can you imagine how he would reward a failure in this case?"

The caller obviously could imagine, but he tried to play it cool. "I've never stiffed a paying customer. You tell the man I'm taking charge of this in person. That should put his mind at ease."

"Somehow, I doubt it."

"Watch the headlines, counselor. You won't be disappointed."

"It's not me you need to be concerned about."

The line went dead, and Trask allowed himself a cautious smile as he retreated to his car. The news was bad, of course, but he had managed to assert himself a bit with the anonymous connection, forcing the other man into a defensive posture. It felt good for a change, after skulking in shadows and following instructions from a stranger he'd never seen before. Their latest terse exchange reminded Trask of court, when he was sniping at a prosecution witness, springing traps his opposition was too clumsy to anticipate.

Trask relished the sensation of control, but it was fleeting. In the morning, he'd have to tell Vos that another plan had failed. Aguire was alive and that much closer to Los Angeles. Trask had a faceless stranger's word that everything would be all right, but it wasn't enough.

It was, he thought, not even close.

His mood was broken, and he concentrated on his driving, unaware of the dark sedan that followed him discreetly. The lawyer's mind was focused on tomorrow, and another trip to jail.

THEY OPTED FOR SECURITY and bypassed several motels. Bolan selected an unmarked side road and followed its serpentine track for five miles, until it terminated at a smallish, man-made reservoir. The brothers scouted out their chosen campsite, found no signs of any recent visitors and decided they should be secure until the morning.

"It's funny, finding this out here," Johnny remarked. "I don't see any signs of irrigation."

Bolan shrugged, examining the reeds and cattails that had overgrown the tall banks of the reservoir.

"I suppose it might have been for stock, at one time," he replied. "I'd say no one's been here for a while."

"It's just as well. I've had enough high times for one day."

Bolan grinned. "Don't count on sleeping through the night. We're still on watch."

"I don't mind watching," his brother replied. "I just don't want to see anything."

Aguire helped them build a smallish fire, collecting dry mesquite and piling it beside the van. Bolan couldn't see the lights of traffic bound for Lubbock, but there was no point in taking chances. They would shield the fire and douse it after heating up the canned food they had purchased at a Kwik-Stop west of town.

"You think they've shot their wad?" Johnny said, while they waited for the pork and beans to simmer.

"Vos has lots of friends," he said. "I wouldn't count them out just yet."

"We should have lost them, if you're right about the homer in the Jimmy."

"Should have. Let's not count our chickens."

"Is all this really worth it?"

Bolan raised an inquiring eyebrow.

"I mean, we're spending three days on the road and killing off a couple dozen guys. We could have saved the time and hassle if we whacked Vos first thing."

"I thought about it," Bolan said, "but part of this I do for Hal, because he asked. The rest of it I'm doing for the system."

Johnny looked as if his ears were suddenly receiving in Chinese.

"The system? Did I hear you right?"

"The prosecution's breaking new ground here, with Vos. If they can pull it off, more power to them."

"And suppose he walks?"

"He won't get far," the Executioner responded, "but that's not the point. I never took this on to scrap the system, or to change it. From the evidence I've seen, it's still the best around, when it's allowed to function. When it works, I like it fine."

"And when it doesn't . . ."

"Then I try to iron the rough spots out, and intercept the players who outgrow the rules."

"Let's hope you're right."

"Let's hope."

The Executioner fell silent as they ate, but he couldn't dismiss his brother's doubts. They were echoes of the questions he'd asked himself a thousand times since kicking off his one-man war against the savages. The final answers had eluded him thus far, and Bolan only knew that he had taken on the war because he could. It was within his power, and the possibility—however marginal—translated into duty recognized.

He thought about the mountaineer who had explained his bids to conquer Everest with the quip "Because it's there." Mack Bolan's war was founded on a similar approach to life. His enemies were there, and someone had to intervene before they swallowed Mother Earth and started looking for dessert. One man might not defeat them, but at least he had a chance to slow them down.

## 16

Leo Turrin hadn't looked at the reports before he laid them on Brognola's desk. He found himself a seat and waited while his friend broke the seal on the manila folder and studied its contents with a scowl that could have curdled milk.

"Here, tell me what you think."

Two sheets of graph paper skimmed across the desk, and Leo caught them short of free-fall. One was labeled Subject A, the other Subject B. Both sheets displayed the zigzag patterns of an automatic stylus, like the readings from a hyperactive polygraph. Technology wasn't his strong suit, but he recognized the voice prints as he viewed them side-by-side, then one above the other, finally superimposing the pages and holding them up to the light.

"I'd say you've got a decent match."

"It's perfect, damn it."

Turrin slipped the pages back across the desk.

"So let me guess—it's not good news?"

"The first sheet is a printout from a call received by Nathan Trask, the night before last. The transcript makes it plain he's running interference on a contract let by Vos."

"Aguire."

"Right. Plus Striker and the kid."

"That's one chart."

"Yeah." Brognola's tone was bitter. "And the second comes from a recording I made on my home phone, just last night."

Turrin felt his stomach knotting. "And the lucky winner is?"

"Our old friend, Felix Pratt."

Leo stiffened. "Are you sure? I mean, there's no mistake?"

"You read the graphs yourself."

"We checked him out."

Brognola shook his head. "We checked him out through channels. Obviously there were one or two things that we didn't catch."

"Like Vos, for instance."

"Who knows how he covered up his tracks? A numbered bank account in the Bahamas. Cans of money buried in his own backyard. Who gives a damn? We missed it, and the bastard's been one step ahead of us since Striker hit the road."

"The homer?"

"We're negotiating with the Rangers for a total shakedown on the Jimmy. It'll be there."

"Pratt?"

"The circuit court in Florida is grinding out a warrant as we speak. There's also one for Trask. We've got his fat ass on obstruction and conspiracy, for sure. I wouldn't be surprised if he rolled over."

More insurance, Leo thought, in case the Bolans lost it on the roads. "It couldn't hurt."

"We're prosecuting Vos, no matter what becomes of the DEA and its indictments. Twenty years won't balance life plus ninety-nine, but I can guarantee the bastard's not about to walk."

"You figure bagging Pratt will take the heat off Striker?"

"It could only help, but Christ, who knows? By now, Godzilla could be waiting for them on the road."

"We don't have any kind of fix?"

"We don't even know what they're driving. They're somewhere between Lubbock and L.A. That tell you anything?"

"It tells me where I'm needed."

"Leo—"

The big Fed thought better of his protest and finally nodded.

"What the hell. You have a starting place in mind?"

He shrugged. "If it was me, I'd want to try the shortest distance possible between points A and B. Let's say they've got a leg up on New Mexico by now. That still leaves Arizona."

Brognola produced a highway atlas from his desk and started thumbing through its pages. "They've had trouble on the interstate," he said.

"And they've had trouble *off* the interstate. I'm betting that they'll try to make up time."

"Okay." Brognola spun the book around and shoved it under Turrin's nose. "Which way? They could go south to catch I-10, or north to I-40."

"Split the difference," Leo said. "I'll land in Phoenix. Either way it breaks, I'll have a chance of picking up their trail."

"Or picking up the pieces."

Turrin kept his face impassive. "I'm not writing Striker off."

"Nobody's writing anybody off. We have to be prepared, that's all. In case they blow it."

"Then we do the next best thing," he said, "and kick some ass."

TRASK WONDERED if it was too late for him to find another line of work. He wasn't ready to forsake the law, but there were other clients, corporations and conglomerates, all begging for the kind of legal talent he possessed. There would be no more need of visiting his clients in a holding cell, no risk of winding up in jail himself.

The deals with Vos and others of his kind had been extremely lucrative, with some excitement thrown into the bargain. Trask had relished traveling in fast company, rubbing shoulders with men whose decisions literally encompassed life and death. But lately the excitement had begun to pall. He understood the risks and knew he'd been lucky, so far, to avoid indictment on his own.

The problem was that Vos wouldn't allow him to resign. It wasn't something they had talked about, but Trask had seen what happened to defectors from the "family." Most often, they'd simply drop from sight, but those who surfaced were reminders of the power wielded by Ernesto Vos. Like a possessive lover, the Colombian reacted violently to any hint of infidelity, and the divorce was always final.

Trask was gloomy as he trailed his escort through the checkpoints leading to the High Power tier of the Jackson lockup. Vos would be flying west that evening to keep his court date in Los Angeles on Thursday, and the lawyer thought a change of scene might lift his spirits. At the very least, he'd be treated to a tour of a different jail.

Trask entered the tiny visiting room, taking his usual seat across the table from Ernesto's empty chair. Five minutes passed before the guards arrived with Vos and shackled him in place, retreating in lockstep like some kind of mutant centipede.

Vos faced him squarely, reading bad news on the lawyer's face. "Again, they fail?"

"Your contact asked me to inform you that he's going out to handle things himself. He guarantees results this time."

"This time? The idiot! He should have dealt with this himself from the beginning."

"I'm surprised you tolerate him."

"He has his uses," Vos replied. "But I confess to second thoughts. When this is finished, I believe he will be, also."

Trask wasn't surprised to hear another death sentence pronounced in such casual terms, nor did he grieve for his anonymous contact. At the moment, his full attention was focused on personal concerns, the risks involved in serving Vos.

"They haven't given me a time for your departure, yet," he said. "I've booked a flight to LAX for six o'clock. I doubt if I'll be able to confer with you this evening—though I'll try, of course."

"Of course." Vos pinned him with electric eyes. "What is it, Nathan?"

"Hmm?"

"Your heart is troubled."

"I'm concerned," Trask countered. "If Aguire testifies, there's nothing I can do to tip the scales. So far, your inside man's been going nowhere fast."

Vos smiled. "Whatever happens, Nathan, you'll be taken care of. I promise you."

Trask didn't like the sound of that. He laced his fingers, clenched them tight to keep his hands from trembling on the tabletop. He caught the deputy's eye over Vos's left shoulder, and nodded to indicate that their visit was finished.

"I'll see you in Los Angeles."

"Perhaps we'll go to dinner afterward," Vos said. "A celebration of your brilliant victory."

The door swung open, and the khaki centipede retrieved its prey, Vos putting on a poker face as he was marched back to his cell. Trask joined his escort on the short walk to the elevator, thinking that discussion of a celebration sounded premature.

It might turn out to be a wake instead.

The suits were waiting for him when he cleared the final checkpoint, just where he would normally begin to relax, shaking off the claustrophobic air of prison.

"Nathan Trask?"

"Who are you?"

"FBI."

He recognized the government credentials, and managed to stand his ground despite the fact that everything around him had begun to spin.

"We have a federal warrant here for your arrest on charges of obstructing justice, and conspiracy. You have the right to remain silent."

He tried to bluff it out. "This is preposterous."

"You have the right to speak with an attorney prior to any questioning."

"I *am* an attorney."

"Yes, sir." The agent smiled, his eyes invisible behind a pair of aviator's shades. "You are."

HIGHWAY 84 TURNED into 60 as they crossed the border into New Mexico. Mack Bolan, riding shotgun, calculated that approximately two-thirds of their journey was behind them. They had crossed five states, or part of some, and they were still alive, their mission still on track.

So far.

And yet he couldn't shake a nagging premonition of disaster. They had lost the homer—if there had been a homer—when they ditched the Jimmy. There had been no further opposition on the highway, and the Rangers at a border checkpoint waved them through without a second glance, confirming Bolan's suspicion that the trooper he'd saved was running interference with a false description of their vehicle.

So far, so good.

Bolan should have been relaxing in the home stretch, but he knew that Vos couldn't afford to let it go. They'd be moving into greater danger as they neared Los Angeles, and the warrior had a hunch that different wheels were not about to save them from the coming storm.

They skirted Albuquerque, stopping off for lunch outside of Gallup, at a drive-in where the fry vats simultaneously canceled flavor and the threat of botulism. Bolan wolfed the meal and washed it down with cola that was watery and bland. The very best of desert haute cuisine. When everyone was done, he took the wheel and let his brother navigate.

"How much to Flagstaff?"

"Right around two hundred miles," Johnny answered. "We should be there around four o'clock."

The soldier flipped a mental coin. They had a choice of stopping for the night or driving straight through to Los Angeles, hoping that the enemy would miss them in the darkness. When he thought about the prospect of a highway ambush after nightfall, Bolan realized there wasn't much choice at all.

"I hope you're up to one more night of sleeping in the car," he said.

"I'm easy."

"Should we not go on?" Aguire suggested. "They'll be searching for us everywhere, by now."

"That's why we're stopping after Flagstaff," Bolan answered. "They'll be searching on the roads. We can't rely on luck to see us through another running skirmish."

Johnny turned to face Aguire. "Have you got a handle on the Arizona action?"

"It's beyond my territory," the Cuban replied. "I know Vos has an understanding with the syndicate in Tucson, but I don't know any of the details."

"That would be Don Cipriano's territory. Maybe we'll get lucky. They could concentrate the search down south."

"It doesn't matter," Bolan told him. "Flagstaff's quicker. Once we go to ground, they'll have all night to run the roads and burn out on the game. Tomorrow, bright and early, we're across the line and home. With any luck we should be in Los Angeles for brunch."

With any luck.

THE VAN WAS FITTED OUT for cargo rather than for comfort, and Aguire was forced to sit on the floor behind the driver's seat. The double doors in back had windows, offering a glimpse of sun-bleached sky. When he rose to kneel between the seats and scan the highway every hour or so, the desert always looked the same. He wondered whether they had entered Arizona yet, but didn't care enough to ask.

The Cuban's body was a patchwork quilt of bruises from the fall he'd taken during the encounter with the Mongols. Band-Aids covered lacerations on his hands where he had slalomed down the heap of cans and bottles toward his confrontation with the biker who had nearly killed him.

Frowning, Aguire studied Blanski's profile as the man drove. The American had saved him twice from death in two days' time. It was the first and only time a stranger had done anything of substance for Aguire, and he wondered at Blanski's motive.

He didn't believe in altruism, having dealt with politicians and policemen, televangelists and big-name entertainers in his time. They all responded to the dollar sign without exception, and Aguire had convinced himself that men were basically commodities, like sheep and cattle, stocks and bonds. You paid your money and collected merchandise or services upon demand.

It troubled him to think that Green and Blanski were exceptions to the rule. His faith was shaken, and it would be that much harder to dispose of them when they had served their purpose.

Settling back against the bulkhead of the van, he felt the pistol pressed into the flesh beside his spine. It was a lightweight automatic, lifted from the mangled biker in the rubbish pit. He hadn't used it yet, because the time had not been ripe. He wasn't inclined to lose his bodyguards before Los Angeles was in sight.

Tomorrow, perhaps, when they were closer to the city. It would be a relatively simple exercise in treachery, and he could disappear before the hunters understood what he had done.

Tomorrow.

It would be his last—and only—chance.

DON CIPRIANO'S PEOPLE met the plane in Phoenix. They helped Pratt collect his luggage then marched him outside, crowding close around him in the waiting Cadillac. The capo hadn't come himself, but he wasn't expected. Everything was understood between them, and arrangements had been made. The underboss, a hulk named Solly, was in charge of operations, and had orders to cooperate with Pratt in any way that wouldn't compromise the Family.

"You got the gear?" Pratt asked.

"Four scanners, yeah." If Solly was impressed by DEA technology, he hid it well.

"I'll give you frequencies before your people hit the road." He pulled a map of Arizona from the flight bag at his feet and spread it out between them. "I'll assume they're in the state already. No point concentrating on the border, and besides, there's too damned many ways across."

"I'm listening."

Pratt stabbed a finger at the map. We'll need a scanner here on Highway 8, near Gila Bend. Another here on Highway 10, near Buckeye. Number three goes up on Highway 40, west of Flagstaff. Any way they try to run, they'll have to pass a checkpoint."

"That leaves number four."

"A mobile unit. Put it in a chopper, ready to respond no matter where they surface. If they go off-road, we've got them covered all the same."

"One chopper for the fucking state?"

"If we have options, I'd suggest we base it in the neighborhood of Prescott. You can jump off either way from there, to cover highways 10 and 40 in a clean half hour. A couple backup cars on Highway 8 can slow things down until the chopper makes it, if they have to go that far."

"Okay. We got some friends in Prescott. I can make a call."

"I'll wait there with the helicopter."

Solly's smile was condescending. "Yeah, I heard you wanted some of this yourself."

"I tried to farm it out," Pratt said. "It's hard to find good help these days."

"Ain't that the truth." The mafioso lit a fat cigar and filled the Cadillac with acrid smoke. "Well, you can put your mind at ease," he said. "You're playing in the big leagues, now. We don't fuck up, like certain yokels I can name."

"I'm sure my client will be most appreciative for all your help."

"We're counting on it, pal. I mean, like, nothing's free. You follow?"

"I believe we understand each other."

"Beautiful. I figure understanding makes the world go 'round, with just a little muscle on the side."

Pratt folded his map and stowed it in the flight bag. He wasn't concerned with Mafia philosophy, but it was Cipriano's ballpark now—and Solly's, by extension. Pratt wasn't a member of the home team anymore.

And where was home? He'd be missed in Florida, inevitably raising questions, and his answers would be weak at best. When he was finished with his job for Vos, once he had claimed his bounty, logic told him he should find a friendly, tropical climate where the heat was less intense. Pratt knew of places where a man could live forever on a million dollars.

And Pratt knew that forever was a long, long time.

"WE MISSED THE BASTARD, Chief. I'm sorry."

Hal Brognola's knuckles whitened as he clenched the telephone receiver, but he kept the burning disappointment from his voice. "What have you got?"

"A neighbor saw him bailing out early this morning with a suitcase. Delta had him booked to Phoenix, via Houston. They confirm he made the flight. With the Texas layover, that put him on the ground at three o'clock our time."

"Did you touch base with Arizona?"

"Right away. They've got a shadow on the Cipriano spread in Tucson, but I doubt he'll be invited down to see the Man."

"Let's cover everything, in case."

"You got it. Phoenix is a problem, with the lag time, but they're checking out hotels, motels—the usual. If someone met his flight and took him on from there, you'll need an APB to pick him up."

"Hold off on that," Brognola said. "Our best hope now is that he might not know he's burned. He might touch base and try to string us out for extra time."

"You really think so?"

It was damned unlikely, but Brognola didn't know what else to hope for. "Let's just say I've got my fingers crossed."

"How's the DEA reacting?"

"Does total panic ring a bell? They're pulling every case he worked on in the past ten years and working on a damage estimate. They don't know when he turned or how he's helped the opposition in the meantime."

"Jesus, what a mess."

"Their problem," Brognola responded gruffly. "Ours is making sure we head him off before he makes the tag."

"That's Phoenix. He'd have to be a total idiot to come back here."

"Nobody ever said he was a genius."

"You've got a point."

"We need to get a look inside his bank account or safe-deposit box."

"I'm already working on it. IRS is helping pull some strings."

"Whatever. Keep me posted, will you?"

"That's affirmative."

He severed the connection and tried to put his thoughts in order as he thought about the call that he'd make to Arizona. Leo would be on the ground, by now, and Brognola saw irony in his proximity to Felix Pratt. The timing was close, and with Pratt's scheduled layover in Texas, Leo must have been hot on his heels.

But where the hell was Felix now?

If he was under Cipriano's wing, the big Fed knew that they might never find him. He could disappear without a trace—alive or dead—and they'd always be in doubt, until some girlfriend got a postcard from Honduras or a troop of Boy Scouts stumbled on his bones some day.

Not good enough.

Brognola wanted Pratt, as much for using Bolan and his brother as for selling out the badge. Corruption in a lawman was despicable, but it was something the man from Justice had learned to live with through the years. Betrayal of a private trust was something else, and if it cost the life of Striker or the young man known as Johnny Gray...

He shook himself to break the morbid train of thought. Anticipating a disaster would accomplish nothing. He had to head the bastards off before they intercepted Mack and Johnny.

Searching for a needle in a haystack would have been a picnic in comparison.

Try searching for a live grenade in quicksand, where you lost no matter how you played the game.

Brognola's face was solemn as he lifted the receiver and began to dial.

## 17

When violet shades of evening overtook them west of Flag-staff, Bolan started to search for a place to spend the night. The highway ran through stunted mountains here, and while they posed no challenge to the Rockies or Sierras, it was still a relief to the eye after nearly a thousand miles of desert flatlands. Pine trees lined the slopes in places, and when Bolan rolled down his window, there was a cool snap in the air.

They were descending on the westward slope when Bolan spotted an access road, its course and terminus concealed by trees. He took it on a whim, deciding they could chase it for a mile or three and still have fuel enough to double back if they were disappointed. Four miles later they found a safe harbor.

The ghost town was of relatively recent vintage, circa 1920, and the scars inflicted on surrounding hillsides told him it had been a mining camp at some point in its history. The "residential section"—tents and clapboard shacks, if it was typical of western mining towns—had long since been dismantled and removed, or else had fallen victim to wind and rain. Commercial buildings at the heart of town had been constructed with a greater permanence in mind, and Bolan picked out the general store, a combination dining hall and tavern, and a small hotel, perhaps intended for the use of company officials and assorted VIPs. The rusted hulk of a refinery dwarfed the other buildings, and a tiny chapel had been thrown up in its shadow, almost as an after-thought.

"We're off the map," Johnny told him. "Welcome to the *Twilight Zone.*"

"Don't tell me you're afraid of ghosts."

"You must be joking. Rattlesnakes and scorpions, okay, but ghosts? No problem."

Bolan parked in front of the refinery and left the engine running with the brake set as he left the driver's seat to check out the building. The giant sliding doors had been designed for ore trucks, and it took some muscle for the Executioner to budge them after sixty years of standing idle, but momentum did the job once they began to roll. Inside, the place was spacious, dark and dusty, with conveyor belts and other old machinery fallen into disrepair, abandoned when the local vein gave out. It sent an eerie chill down Bolan's spine to think those doors had last been closed decades ago, and it was possible that no man had crossed that threshold since.

He backtracked to the van and climbed behind the wheel. "No ghosts," he said, "but from the smell, I think we might have mice the size of German shepherds."

"Great. I saw that on the late show," Johnny said. "Peter Lorre played the cheese."

Bolan drove the van inside and killed the engine, pocketing the keys before he joined his brother to unload the weapons. "I suspect we'll find a better deal on lodgings down the street," he said. "The hotel seems to have a vacancy."

"The question is, do they have beds?"

"Don't get your hopes up."

Johnny shouldered a satchel of grenades and ammo clips, the CAR-15 and full-sized Uzi tucked beneath his arms, while Bolan packed the mini-Uzi and the M-16, with two more ammunition satchels.

"Looks like a clean house to me," the younger Bolan replied.

"Okay. We'll find a place to sleep and rig a few surprises, just in case the local ghosts get restless."

Johnny flashed a grin and said, "They slimed me, Egon."

Bolan grinned back and asked his brother, "Who you gonna call?"

PRATT WAS WORKING on a tepid cup of coffee when Solly barged in on him, smiling like a hungry crocodile. "We just made contact," he announced.

"Where are they?"

"North of here and west of Flagstaff. Off I-40 somewhere, on a little dipshit road to nowhere. I've got people covering the road. There isn't any other exit."

Pratt experienced a sudden rush of pure adrenaline. He'd been worried that their prey might drive straight through and risk another running battle on the interstate, with more police and innocent civilians caught in the cross fire. This was infinitely better, with a stationary target cut off from the highway and escape, compelled to stand and fight on unfamiliar ground.

"The chopper ready?"

"Warming up right now."

"Let's go."

As they were moving toward the heliport, he quizzed the mafioso on logistics, learning that a flying squad of thirty men was on the way from Flagstaff to their destination, packing everything except the kitchen sink.

"Don't let them jump the gun," he cautioned. "I want confirmation before the shooting starts."

"Is there a problem here? You think somebody put a ringer in?"

Pratt shrugged the question off as he prepared to board the helicopter. At the outset, he'd been convinced one homer in the Jimmy should be adequate to meet his needs. The second had been tossed in almost as a whim, but it was paying off in spades.

The chopper had two pilots plus four passengers—a pair of Cipriano's hardmen riding shotgun with Pratt and the syndicate underboss. Felix did the math in his head, coming up with odds of thirteen to one against Blanski and company. If he couldn't do the job with those numbers, it was hopeless, a write-off.

He thought about the hardware Blanski and his backup had been issued back in Jacksonville, the ventilated bodies they'd left in Texas and Louisiana. Were they running short of ammunition yet? How many of the Don's men would make the drive from Flagstaff a one-way trip?

No matter. Pratt had obligations to fulfill, and Vos could deal with Cipriano later, when the smoke cleared. In the meantime, Pratt would have his cash in hand and would get the hell away from there before Brognola or his own damned people started sniffing up his trail.

How long? They might be on his case already, but it would take time to run him down, and time was one thing that Aguire didn't have. The stoolie's life was measured out in minutes now, and Pratt felt tremors of the same excitement that he'd once experienced when wrapping up a major bust. In those days, when he still believed in serving man and fighting for the good guys, there had been a certain kick to laying out a raid and watching all the pieces fall together. It had taken time for Pratt to realize that he was going nowhere, battering his head against a cold brick wall of public apathy, corruption and conspiracy. The kick had vanished swiftly after that, and he'd learned to care for number one above all else.

He turned to Solly, raising his voice to be heard above the engines.

"How long?"

"Thirty, forty minutes. Take it easy. They aren't going anywhere."

He settled back and watched the brilliant desert sunset through his window. By the time they reached their destination, it would be fully dark, and that was fine.

In fact it was ideal.


"THEY MADE YOUR BOYS. It's going down."

The words chilled Leo Turrin's blood, and his knuckles whitened as he clenched the telephone receiver.

"Where?"

"The way I get it, west of Flagstaff, twenty miles or so. Some little, nothing road that doesn't go anywhere. I guess they're camping out."

"Who's rolling?"

"Solly's coming up from Prescott with the guy who let the contract, plus they got some troops from Flagstaff on the road."

"How many, dammit!"

"Twenty, thirty... I don't know. Some troops is all I heard."

"Okay. I owe you one."

"I won't forget that."

The line went dead, and Turrin grabbed his jacket from a hook beside the door, already bellowing for action as he moved along the corridor, a proverbial bull in the FBI china shop.

"It's on," he snapped. "They're rolling. Twenty, maybe thirty guns from Flagstaff, and the crew chief flying up from Prescott."

The Phoenix agent-in-charge kept pace with Turrin easily, his face a study in dejection. "There's no way for us to catch them. They're too damned close already. It'll take an hour just to get there."

"Then we don't have any time to waste."

The tip had come from an informant in the Cipriano Family, a convicted dealer who had bargained down a twelve-year sentence to thirteen months by rolling over on his capo, feeding back selective information to the FBI. Initially reluctant to involve himself in Turrin's effort, he'd undergone a change of heart when Leo mentioned certain files that might be dusted off for reevaluation if Aguire died in Arizona.

Now they had at least a rough location, and a pair of Bureau agents would be working Highway 40 west of Flagstaff by the time their troops were in the air. If they could eyeball Cipriano's gunners, it would be a lock, and only time would stand against them.

So much time.

He calculated Pratt would need a good half hour, maybe more, to fly from Prescott to the kill zone. On arrival, he'd have to stroke the troops a bit and chart some basic strategy—ten minutes, give or take. Perhaps the same to get his people in position for the kill. That put his rescue force a quarter hour later, more likely thirty minutes, and he wondered if the Bolan brothers could hold out that long.

A quarter hour under fire could be a lifetime, Turrin knew. Beyond that point the nerves were frayed, and physical reactions lagged, became disjointed. Any cop would tell you that the "normal" confrontation with an armed assailant lasted maybe ten or fifteen *seconds*, start to finish, and beyond that time, you either had a siege or bloody chaos on your hands.

He prayed that Bolan would be able to delay the end, hold off his enemies until the cavalry arrived. It didn't matter now how Pratt had found Aguire and his escort. They were dead if Turrin and his backup didn't reach the scene in time.

Three choppers waited on the pad, with six armed agents boarding each as they arrived. He found a seat in number one, buckling in beside the agent-in-charge, and nodded the signal for takeoff. In another moment they were airborne, speeding north, the desert underneath them painted crimson by the setting sun.

From where he sat, the landscape seemed to be awash in blood.

WORKING WITH A FLASHLIGHT tucked beneath his arm, Johnny stood in gritty dust and finished rigging up a final booby trap. The frag grenade, its pin removed, fit loosely in a rusty can that he'd salvaged from a dump behind the dining hall. The can had been secured with nails, chest-high, inside the entrance to the general store, a simple tug line fastened to the door itself and looped around the neck of the grenade. If anyone should push the door back, they'd have two seconds to regret it as the lethal egg swung free and detonated on a level with their waist.

Around him he could hear the small, nocturnal sounds of rodents stirring, rummaging for food among the ruins of a dream gone sour. Predators might stalk them in the shadows, all a part of nature's food chain, but the only hunters plaguing Johnny's mind were human with a taste for blood and easy money.

He had rigged the back door first, and now he made his exit through a nearby window, taking care to check his pockets for the safety pins before he closed it down behind him. He'd have to pull the traps again before they left, and in the meantime he was counting on the moonless night to cover evidence of traffic through the window.

As he moved along the sagging wooden sidewalk, Johnny wondered what missing residents had called their camp, and what it had been like to mine for gold or silver in another, simpler time. Hard work and little else, he finally decided, glancing at the midnight shadows of the nearest ravaged mountainside. He knew the "romance of the West" was largely Hollywood's invention, with a boost from fiction writers, but there was a certain air about the camp, diminished though it was by passing time, that he couldn't deny.

At one time this had been the cutting edge of the frontier. The veins of precious ore that petered out in 1920—something that had ignited range wars, genocidal conflict with the native Indians, seducing men and women from the East to leave their homes and their established lives behind, risk everything with pick and shovel underneath a broiling sun. It was the story of America in microcosm: people taking reckless chances—sometimes paying with their lives—in the pursuit of El Dorado.

Johnny shook himself back to the present. If anyone came looking for them here, it wouldn't be the Wild Bunch or the Younger gang, and Wyatt Earp wouldn't be waiting in the wings to save them by the time the credits rolled. You could save your high-noon showdowns for the late show on nostalgia night. In the real world, the dead didn't get up and stroll away to a director's cry of "Cut!"

He made a small adjustment to the Uzi's shoulder strap and turned his back on dreams. The darkness swallowed him as he moved off to find his brother.

AGUIRE KNEW that he'd have to time his move precisely, or he'd be sure to fail. His escorts were professionals, and they had proved themselves repeatedly since Jacksonville. It wouldn't be a simple task to take them by surprise, but he was running out of time.

He'd been left alone while Green and Blanski set their troops, and Carlos used the time to make a fresh examination of his captured pistol. It was a 9 mm automatic, with four of the original eight rounds still in place.

Aguire hoped he wouldn't have to kill the men responsible for keeping him alive the past two days. If he was forced to do so, he'd feel a measure of regret. But he had learned to set his principles aside and act on instinct, looking out for number one at any cost. Self-preservation had compelled Aguire to accept the deal Pratt offered him, exchanging testimony for his freedom, and survival likewise forced him to abandon that agreement now.

Aguire realized the DEA couldn't protect him through the weeks or months that would precede a trial in federal court, much less the years tied up in various appeals if Vos should be convicted on his testimony. There would be no testimony now, because Aguire had decided to remove himself from the arena. He was bailing out.

He couldn't go on foot, however. He'd need the van, and that meant a confrontation with his escorts. In the worst scenario, he was prepared to shoot them in the back, or while they slept, but he'd much prefer to take their vehicle, their weapons, and allow them both to live. Aguire hoped they would be reasonable.

Where would he go? Mexico, for starters, which was so close he could almost taste the enchiladas.

If he set off by midnight in the van, Carlos thought that he could be across the border by the time dawn broke. Vos had many friends in Mexico, but it wouldn't be Aguire's final destination. Once he managed to collect some cash, the world would be at his command.

How long could he survive before Vos found him? Months? A year or two? Indefinitely? Anything was better than the certain death that waited for him in Los Angeles. If he continued westward with his escorts, then his life was measured out in days, perhaps in hours.

Breathing deeply to control the nervousness he felt inside, Aguire tucked the pistol inside his belt, the handle pressing tight against his spine. When they were finished with their games, and he had both of the men together, he would make his move. There was no point in waiting until midnight: it was dark enough for him to begin his journey.

Outside he heard the sound of footsteps on the wooden sidewalk, drawing nearer. One man, Carlos thought, and cursed at the delay. With the decision made, he felt his own anxiety increasing, raising beads of perspiration on his forehead, even though the night was cool. He held both hands in front of him, relieved to find that they weren't trembling.

They would be steady when he held the gun. They would do what must be done if he had to kill his escorts.

A GROWLING IN HIS STOMACH reminded the Executioner that he needed to eat. They had purchased cans of food, along with bread and beverages, in Flagstaff, but he'd forgotten about the provisions and the hour in his haste to make their sanctuary more or less secure. He couldn't stop a hostile force from rolling down the dusty street, but he could damn well treat the enemy to a surprise or two before the fight was joined.

It bothered Bolan that the day had passed without some sign of their pursuers. Could they have shaken off the hounds that easily?

He would accomplish nothing, Bolan thought, through idle speculation. Whatever happened, he'd done his best to square the odds, and they'd have to play the rest of it by ear. If they were able to avoid detection through the night, they had a straight run into California come the morning, and their passenger would be delivered to the waiting arms of Justice and the DEA.

It ran against the grain for Bolan to conduct defensive operations. He preferred a swift offense, with the advantage of surprise, but playing escort stacked the odds against him, giving his opponents the edge. In any combat situation, the defender was essentially a passive target, marking time until the enemy revealed himself and praying that the first shot was a good, clean miss. Defenders chose the killing ground, where possible, but their opponents chose the time, the method of attack.

His stomach growled again, and Bolan turned away from the refinery, where he'd done his best to secure their van. They wouldn't travel far on foot, and Bolan had debated staying with the van all night, deciding it would be a grave mistake to split their tiny force. If trouble came, he wanted Johnny by his side, and they could figure out the rules together.

Bats wheeled above his head in search of insects as he started down the street. The town was barely two blocks long, by modern standards, with the dining hall-saloon on one side, sandwiched between the general store and the hotel. Across the street, the empty hull of a machine shop and garage stood close beside a vacant office structure, where the company had doubtless kept its books and doled out pay on Friday afternoons. The rocky hills surrounded them on three sides, and the narrow, unpaved road would be their only exit from the box.

As it would be the only angle of attack.

## 18

The helicopter circled once before it landed so that Solly and the pilots could check out the reception committee on the ground, confirming identities before they committed themselves to the descent. Pratt counted one scout car and four of the big Caddy crew wagons lined up on the shoulder of the highway, looking for all the world like a stalled diplomatic parade or a funeral procession. He didn't like either analogy, and tuned the thoughts out as the pilot took them down to a perfect landing.

By the time Pratt had his feet on the ground, the gunners were emerging from their cars. He didn't bother counting, trusting Solly's word that there were thirty men, knowing that a gun or two should make no difference, either way. Pratt felt conspicuous, and he was anxious to be out of there before another motorist—or, worse, a cop—rolled by and caught their little huddle on the roadside.

"Listen up, you fellas," Solly ordered, silencing the group. "You got some idea of why you're here. Tonight, I'm speaking for your don, and this man—" a big hand settling on Pratt's shoulder "speaks for me...unless I tell you different. Pay attention to him, now. We haven't got all fucking night."

Their rendezvous coordinates had been confirmed by radio, and their pilot—something of an amateur historian, as it turned out—had briefed Pratt on the layout of their target. He had hoped to catch Aguire and his escorts in the open, but the ghost town sounded small enough for thirty men to cover easily. If necessary, they could burn it down around Aguire's ears.

"You may or may not know about our target," Pratt began, immediately lowering his voice when he detected signs of nervous strain. "A few miles off the highway, there's a ghost town, mining camp... whatever. Half a dozen buildings still intact, for what it's worth. You'll have to cover all of them at once. We're hunting three men. Two of them have automatic weapons and they know their business. I won't try to snow you. They've been wasting people for the past two days and skating clear. I need them dead, but more that than, I need to *see* them dead. Is everybody square on that?"

There was a general murmur of assent, and Pratt turned back to Solly with a shrug. "That's it," he said.

"Okay," the underboss announced, "before we roll, I want the lead car using parking lights, and everybody else blacked out. I hate to use the lights at all, but what the hell, it's gonna be too fucking dark without them, and I don't want anybody driving off the mountain. Hang in close behind the lead car, then fan out and cover all the angles once you get there. We'll be tracking you upstairs and coming in to close the back door when you bust the joint. No questions?"

There were none, and Solly cracked a smile. "All right," he said, "let's do it."

They were back inside the chopper and lifting off as the procession began to move. The driver of the lead car kept his headlights on until he reached the entrance to the access road, then switched them off in favor of his parking lights, as ordered. Pratt was thankful that he didn't have to drive the narrow, winding road in almost total darkness.

"Circle wide," Solly told the pilot. "Give them time to get there, and then come in from the rear. We don't want anybody slipping out on foot."

"Yes, sir."

Pratt slipped a hand inside his jacket and removed the automatic pistol he had carried since the DEA went "modern" two years earlier. Before that, it had been a standard Smith & Wesson .28, and while he had been called upon to draw both weapons frequently, he hadn't fired a shot from either one outside the target range.

He wondered what it felt like to eclipse a human life, and knew that he might soon find out. It had to beat the grim alternative, and Pratt reflected that a million dollars could relieve the wildest nightmares. He would never have to sleep alone, and he could leave the night-light on, if necessary.

Still, before he started spending the reward, Pratt had to earn it. There were three men to be killed, and if he had to do the job himself, he would. No pain, no gain.

Tonight, he was expecting some of each.

"WE'VE GOT A FIX on their location."

Leo Turrin faced the Phoenix SAC, leaning closer to hear him over the sound of throbbing engines. "Where?"

"Due west of Flagstaff, twenty-seven miles, a little access road cuts off I-40 to the south. It winds around a couple miles, then dead-ends at a burned-out mining village. Not your classic ghost town but it'll do. They used to call it Oresville. Wishful thinking, I suppose."

"We're clear on this?" he asked.

The SAC allowed himself a frown. "You mean, am I convinced your boys are in there? I have no idea. Don Cipriano's people think so, or they wouldn't waste their time. I don't know what they're going by, or where they get their information."

Turrin pondered those unanswered questions. How the hell could Pratt and Cipriano's people still keep track of their intended prey, despite the change in cars? Unless...

He leaned back toward the SAC and asked, "What kind of receivers have we got on board?"

"The basics—CB, shortwave, cellular. You need to call somebody?"

Turrin shook his head. "Have you got anything for picking up a homing signal?"

"Trackers? Sure, but you don't think—"

"I can't supply a frequency."

"It doesn't matter. Once we're in range we can start to sweep and lock on any signal in the neighborhood."

"What range?"

"Depending on the homer, two, three miles."

"Let's do it."

"Are you working on a hunch?"

"What else?"

The G-man frowned. "Suppose we're right on top of them, and still no signal?"

"Then we do our thing, regardless," Leo answered. "Nothing ventured—"

"Nothing gained, I know. Okay." He gave instructions to the pilot and received a clipped affirmative. "We can't begin the sweep for ten or fifteen minutes. Still not close enough."

"I'll take what I can get," the man from Justice replied, and hoped that it would come to more than bodies on slab.

CARLOS AGUIRE KNEW it was time to make his move when the three men sat down to eat their simple evening meal. His escorts still wore pistols, but their automatic weapons had been laid aside to free their hands for paper plates and plastic forks. It would be relatively simple, he decided, and if either man tried to reach a gun...

They wouldn't try to kill him instantly. Their job was to deliver a living witness, more or less intact, to federal officers in California. He was certain they would fire in self-defense, but first would come negotiations, an attempt to reason with him and persuade him to surrender. By the time they realized that it was hopeless he'd have their guns and car keys...or he would have killed them where they sat.

Pretending he'd bitten into something hard, Aguire set his plate down on the floor, cursing and probing his back teeth with the index finger of his left hand, using the diversion to slide the right behind his back. He had the pistol now, and raised it with a flourish, thumbing back the hammer.

"Please don't make me kill you," he said.

After an initial flicker, neither man displayed surprise.

"You're making a mistake." Bolan told him.

"Going to Los Angeles would be a worse mistake, I think. The car keys."

"Think about it," Johnny advised. "Alone, you've got no cover whatsoever."

"I am touched by your concern. Unfortunately it does not extend beyond your mission. If we live to reach Los Angeles, what do you think will happen to me then?"

"You'll be protected," Bolan replied. "by the DEA. I won't pretend they love you, but they need your testimony for a lock on Vos. They're not about to let his people reach you."

"And when I am finished? When the trial is done?"

"The federal witness program, I imagine. They can build a new identity—new face, if necessary—and install you in a brand-new life."

Aguire laughed out loud. "Your faith is touching. Do you trust the DEA so much? Are you prepared to place your whole life in their hands?"

"I'd say we've done exactly that."

"And what happened? Is it still not clear to you that you have been betrayed?"

"We're coping," Bolan said. "And I can guarantee a shake-up when we hit Los Angeles."

"Too late," Aguire snapped. "I was a fool to deal with Pratt, from the beginning. It is clear, now. All his promises are hollow, meaningless. The government he serves has no intention of destroying Vos."

"So why arrest him in the first place?" Johnny inquired.

"A sideshow. After all the talk about 'war on drugs,' the government must seem to move against its 'enemies.' In fact, if Vos and others like him were eliminated, your police would have to manufacture their replacements. Who will pay the graft, if they are gone? How will appropriations be secured without a 'menace' lurking in the shadows?"

"I won't try to tell you that we haven't got some problems," Bolan admitted. "We have a line on links inside the Administration. That's why we were selected as your escorts, to provide some distance."

"No," Aguire said, "you were selected as a human sacrifice. When I am killed, it must be said that agents tried to save me, gave their lives in the line of duty. You are both courageous men, *muy macho*, but you never really had a chance. And I must leave you now."

"Then, I suppose," the Executioner growled, "you'd better use that gun."

It was a gamble, but Aguire hesitated, glancing back and forth from one man to the other, aiming at a point between them. He rose without removing his attention from the two of them, and Bolan concentrated on finding the kind of a diversion it would take for one of them to reach him, twist the automatic from his grasp. The risks were great. At point-blank range, a man-sized target was difficult to miss.

Aguire seemed reluctant to shoot them—otherwise he would have fired at once, without a warning—but reluctance didn't translate into inability. If pressed, he'd respond like any other cornered animal. It was impossible for Bolan to predict which way the gun might turn. He hated gambling with his brother's life, but neither could he simply let Aguire walk. His duty made the easy route impassable, and left him with a narrow range of options.

"What about the booby traps?" he asked. "You don't know where they are. If you go blundering around outside, you'll kill yourself before Vos has the chance."

Aguire pondered that and swiftly came to a decision. "You will lead the way," he said, a waggle of the automatic indicating both of them at once. "But first, the car keys."

Had Aguire seen him drop them into his outside pocket? Bolan wondered. Could he reach the 93-R in its shoulder rigging, draw and fire before the nervous Cuban shot them both? At such a range, and under pressure, could he wing Aguire, make him drop his gun without inflicting major damage?

Bolan wasted no time wondering about the pistol. Obviously Carlos had retrieved it from a member of the biker hit team, at some point.

The warrior had no method of communicating with his brother, but he knew that Johnny would back his play, however it went down. They stood together, and he only hoped they wouldn't die that way.

"The keys," Aguire repeated, his tone insistent.

Bolan set his paper plate on the floor. His hand was sliding toward his shoulder harness, eyes locked on Aguire's gun, when suddenly he froze—a sound outside, from somewhere overhead.

In spite of distance and the intervening floors above them, Bolan recognized the chopping noise of a helicopter's engine. At a glance, he saw that Johnny heard it, too.

"Sounds like company," Bolan said. Regardless of the threat—or lack of one—he could make use of the diversion.

Aguire became aware of the sound, as well. His pistol wavered slightly, and he cast a quick glance toward the ceiling.

"It's a helicopter," Bolan told him. "Circling, by the sound. I'm not expecting visitors. Are you?"

Aguire glared at him but didn't answer.

"Did you want to shoot us now," the soldier asked, "or shall we wait to see who's dropping in?"

A new sound was recognizable as traffic on the road outside, a blend of tires on gravel and familiar engine noise.

"You're out of time," he said. "Which is it?"

"I will keep the gun," Aguire snapped.

"You'll need it," Bolan told him, reaching out to heft his M-16.

THE DRIVER OF THE LEAD CAR killed his lights as the caravan approached the mining town, and for a heartbeat Pratt lost sight of his support troops in the darkness. They were circling wide, perhaps two hundred feet above the small, deserted settlement, but Felix knew their engine noise might have warned Aguire's escorts. If they hadn't, the arrival of four limousines would do the trick, and he imagined Hal Brognola's soldiers, crouching in the darkness with their weapons, waiting for the enemy to show himself.

The square receiver mounted in the cockpit was emitting steady signals, telling him that they were right on target, but the bleeping sound wouldn't pinpoint his prey. They could be homing on the vehicle, for all Pratt knew. Aguire and his escorts could have scattered, into the shadows, digging in to make their final stand.

And this would be the end of it. It had to be. Pratt's life and all his future hopes were riding on the line with this one play. A fumble now would finish him.

The pilot took them down, extinguishing his running lights for safety's sake, before they touched down in the shadow of an ancient ore refinery. The place was small by modern standards, but it offered countless hiding places for Aguire and the others, not to mention the array of other buildings that stood on both sides of the street.

All remained silent as the gunners left their vehicles and fanned out. Pratt's palms were sweaty, and he wiped them on his trousers, fishing one hand underneath his jacket to retrieve his weapon. He felt better with the gun in his fist, more able to defend himself, but they were still exposed on every side, like targets in a shooting gallery.

"Where are they, dammit?"

Solly's smile carved deeper shadows in his craggy face. "Relax. We'll find them."

"Right."

He watched as Cipriano's strike force broke up into flying squads, the gunners communicating by means of hand signals. Several jogged toward the refinery, the rest splitting up with four men dispatched to cover each of the town's half dozen buildings, three guns playing center field, remaining with the cars. The gunners who had flown with Pratt and Solly stayed beside them now, quite comfortable in their role as bodyguards.

Pratt watched the flying squads begin to subdivide again, two soldiers peeling off from each quartet and circling to watch their target buildings from the rear. It spread their forces thin, but Pratt remembered that his targets were outnumbered more than twelve to one. No matter how you sliced it, those were winning odds.

The first explosion, when it came, took Felix Pratt completely by surprise. A pair of Cipriano's men were entering a combination bar and mess hall, one man pushing through the door while his companion covered, and the blast enveloped both of them. The pointman simply disappeared, a stage magician vanishing in smoke and thunder, while his backup took their shrapnel at a range of less that fifteen feet. His tattered body sailed backward and landed in the middle of the dusty street.

A second blast erupted so close behind the first that Pratt initially mistook it for an echo. Cries of agony destroyed that futile hope—the first two gunners had gone down without a whimper—and he realized that there had been another booby trap in back of the saloon.

Time froze, with Cipriano's gunmen rooted in their places, torn between their orders to advance and knowledge that they might be blown to pieces if they moved. Before their crew chief had an opportunity to win back the initiative, the first car in their lineup suddenly erupted into rolling flames, another thunderclap reverberating from the hills around them.

"Hit the bastards!" Solly bawled. "What are you waiting for?"

They were breaking for the cover of the old refinery, Pratt pacing Solly, when the gunners opened up and hell broke loose in Oresville.

BOLAN WAS IN PLACE and waiting when the first grenade exploded, somewhere to his right. It sounded like the dining hall, but he was only interested in the body count. They were confronting lethal odds, and every hostile gunner they eliminated was another step toward survival.

At the second blast, somewhere behind the line of buildings, Bolan raised his weapon, and knocked out a milky windowpane. Before the nearest shooters could react, he pumped a 40 mm high-explosive round into the nearest limousine, its detonation spewing arcs of burning fuel in all directions, spreading incandescent puddles in the middle of the street.

The blast had knocked two gunners off their feet, though neither man was badly injured. Bolan caught one as the guy staggered to his feet, a short burst from the M-16 reducing him to so much wasted flesh and rumpled clothing in the shadow of the leaping bonfire. Number two had spotted the warrior, and the guy was quick enough to trigger off a probing burst as he retreated, scrambling backward for the cover of the cars.

The gunners were unloading on him now from every direction, their bullets gnawing through the woodwork, driving Bolan back. He crawled on his belly through the dust and broken glass, retreating as a steady stream of fire reduced the hotel lobby to a shambles.

They had scored first blood, at least, and Johnny should be in position now, prepared to lead the hounds away. It was a risky game, this desperate version of divide and conquer, but they had been stripped of options. Any gains from that point on would be a victory of sorts, but he was interested in coming out the other side alive, together with his brother and their charge.

The Executioner was up and running as he cleared the lobby, moving toward the exit they had left unlocked in the event of an emergency. Behind him, concentrated fire was riddling the hotel lobby, chewing up the stairs and etching abstract patterns on the walls.

He was a dozen paces from the door when it swung open and a pair of gunners crossed the threshold in a rush, two automatic weapons blazing as they came. Instinctively the Executioner squeezed off a 40 mm HE round at point-blank range, its detonation striking like a fist that hurled him backward into a clapboard wall.

## 19

Johnny was already in position when the first explosion rocked the street. A small head start was all he needed as he broke from the rear of the hotel and headed north toward the general store. There hadn't been enough grenades to booby-trap each building in the town, so the store had been unprotected until Johnny settled in.

He had a clear shot at the gunners moving toward the store, and saw two of them peel off to watch the rear, while others fanned out to cover every building on the street. He'd have only moments, from the time he dropped the two in front, until their seconds crashed the back door, but there should be enough, if he—

The ripping sound of the grenade was shocking in the silence of the ghost town, and was followed instantly by another as gunners at the back door got an unexpected bonus for their efforts. His chosen targets crouched, then backed away, exchanging glances as they eyed the door. He almost heard the cogwheels turning in their minds. Were all the buildings wired? If not, which ones?

Downrange one of the limos tore apart in fire and thunder, bouncing on its springs as an explosion turned it into a heap of twisted junk. Johnny took it as his cue and triggered two short bursts. The front-door gunners folded like a pair of straw men as the 5.56 mm tumblers crackled in on target. They were down and out before the Executioner started firing up the street, and general chaos suddenly erupted.

Orders were forgotten as the gunners broke for cover, pumping lead at shadows in a bid to save themselves.

Johnny loosed a burst at random, then heard the missing second-stringers crashing in behind him, homing on the sound of gunfire inside the store.

They came in like commandos, shooting from the hip and ventilating everything except their target. Johnny rose to meet them from behind the protection of the heavy wooden checkout counter, pumping three rounds through a stocky gunner's chest before the guy had time to get to cover.

Number two was quicker off the mark, but still not quick enough to save himself. He had an Ingram submachine gun up and tracking when the younger Bolan caught him with a rising burst and zippered him from crotch to throat. The impact hurled him backward, and his body raised a dust cloud as it hit the floor with a resounding thud.

Outside, a couple of the gunners had begun to fire in Johnny's general direction, blasting through the door and windows. He kept his head down as he raced from the store, feeding the carbine a new magazine on the run.

The war was waiting for him, and he didn't intend to be pinned down, immobilized while his brother was out there fighting for his life.

THE SHOCK WAVE EMPTIED Bolan's lungs, but he was on his feet again in a second. One of the hardmen had absorbed the blast full-force, and he was obviously dead, his flesh and clothing torn by shrapnel, smoking from the heat of the explosion. His partner lay twenty feet away, battered, dazed, and bleeding, but alive.

The Executioner swept past him, squeezing off a round between the glassy eyes to guarantee that the guy wouldn't be a hostile gun at his back. How many left? The warrior had no clear idea, but realized he, Aguire and Johnny were heavily outnumbered.

The night welcomed Bolan like a kindred spirit. He'd taken time to buckle on the Desert Eagle .44, and with the mini-Uzi slung across one shoulder, extra magazines and charges for the launcher worn in bandoliers across his chest, he felt prepared to meet the enemy.

A bitter haze of smoke still marked the spot where gunmen had attempted to invade the dining hall, caught short by Johnny's booby trap. One of the bodies lay spread-eagled in the ally, but Bolan couldn't see the other, and he wondered if the guy had managed to escape somehow or simply dragged himself away to lick his wounds.

It made no difference at the moment, as he moved in the direction of the ore refinery, where he'd seen the helicopter land. The airborne brains behind the raid would be there, or close by, and Bolan hoped that he might take the man alive for quick interrogation. Failing that, the leader's death might have some effect on his opponents. At the very least it had to hurt morale, and he would take whatever he could get, with raw survival riding on the line.

The chopper was a dark, insectile silhouette beside the ore refinery, its engine silent now, the rotors dropping slightly. Bolan couldn't tell if anyone was inside, but he was banking on the strike force leader being smart enough to realize the helicopter made a tempting target.

Bolan closed the gap with a 40 mm round, his aim dead-on at thirty yards. The high explosive impacted on the chopper's windshield, punching through before it detonated and granting him a microsecond's view of startled faces in the cockpit.

The helicopter rocked and listed, bright flames leaping from its shattered insect head, the long antennae of its rotors drooping farther, one sheared off completely by the blast. The fuel tanks blew a moment later, finishing the job, but Bolan didn't wait around to watch the barbecue. A squad of five or six gunmen had begun to pepper his position, firing from the shadow of the old refinery, and he was forced back under cover by the storm of lead.

How many? Did it matter? He was more concerned about the van, and wondered whether the invaders had breached the building yet. The sliding doors were booby-trapped with Bolan's final frag grenade, but there were other ways inside. It suddenly occurred to the warrior that a victory—however long the odds against its happening—would leave them helpless if the van was damaged or destroyed. They couldn't walk Aguire to Los Angeles, and if the hostile rolling stock was also put out of commission . . .

Bolan shrugged the problem off and concentrated on a more immediate concern: survival. Several of his enemies were shifting position, angling for a better shot. Retreat seemed futile, even suicidal, and he seized the only option left.

He would attack with everything he had.

PRATT SAW THE HELICOPTER explode and the two-man crew incinerated where they sat. The goons were losing it before his very eyes, and there was nothing he could do to stem the tide.

"For Christ's sake, can't your people shoot?"

The side of beef named Solly pinned him with a baleful eye, then turned away to watch the action. To be fair, his men *were* shooting, demolishing the ancient storefronts with a hail of automatic fire, but Pratt could only wonder if they had a target.

Solly's team had been about to breach the refinery when the helicopter blew, and one of them had spotted something in the shadows. All five men were blasting at the darkness, now, and while it sounded awesome, Pratt wasn't impressed. It didn't matter if they fired a million rounds, unless one scored.

He felt a sudden, near-compulsive urge to move, do anything except stand idly by while everything went down the tubes around him. Pratt had wondered, from a distance, how the other teams had missed Aguire. Now he knew, and he could see it happening again if some decisive action wasn't taken.

"Help me find their car," he snapped at Solly.

"Screw it. I got business here."

Pratt saw no point in arguing. He turned away and circled through the shadows, moving toward the flank of the refinery. He deliberately ignored the giant sliding doors in front, his instinct telling him that if the place was wired to blow, the loading bays would certainly be covered. He'd have a better chance with windows, or prying back a sheet of corrugated metal from the walls.

Why risk it?

The refinery appeared to be the only building where Brognola's soldiers could have stashed a car, and Pratt knew he'd have to neutralize their wheels to guarantee a kill. On foot, Aguire and his escorts weren't going anywhere.

Pratt worked his way along the building's long west flank, the sounds of automatic fire diminished as he turned the corner. Solly's gunners might get lucky, and his gesture might be totally unnecessary, but the man from the DEA had given up on leaving things to chance. If he was wasting time, so be it; but if Cipriano's hardmen blew it, Pratt would have a cool ace up his sleeve.

He found a window and tried it, straining as it trembled. It finally gave, deluging him in flakes of rust and the accumulated grit of decades. Swiping at his eyes, Pratt palmed a penlight, and angled its narrow beam inside, playing it across the tattered fabric of conveyor belts and the Quasimodo hulks of old machinery. He nearly missed the van, but swung the penlight back to double-check by the fleeting glint of chrome.

He had it!

Satisfied that any lookouts would have wasted him by now, Pratt pocketed his flashlight, stowed the automatic in his belt and wriggled through the window. Cobwebs tangled in his hair, and more grit trickled down his collar, but he let it go, refusing to consider the assorted vermin that would surely find the place a happy hunting ground. It didn't matter if an army of tarantulas was waiting for him in the dark. He had the van, by God, and that could only mean he had Aguire by the balls.

UPSTAIRS IN THE HOTEL, Aguire crouched beside a window and peered at the street below. He watched the gunmen scuttle back and forth along the lines of limousines, illuminated by the burning point car, pumping wild, impulsive shots through every storefront on the street. They wasted no rounds on the hotel's upper stories, since no hostile fire had come from that direction. Carlos wondered briefly if he might ride out the storm by simply staying put.

In answer to his silent question, three men broke away from the concealment of the nearest limo, charging over open ground to storm the front of the hotel. He heard the lobby doors burst open, automatic weapons raking woodwork, falling silent as the gunners realized they had no living targets.

Blanski had already gone, the thunder of his exit followed shortly by the destruction of the helicopter, beside the old refinery. A skirmish had erupted there, and Carlos wished the big man well.

The sound of angry voices carried up the stairs. Aguire cocked his automatic pistol, turned from the window and headed toward the open door. He prayed that they would pass by him, and fleetingly considered places of concealment, but realized there was nowhere he could hide in safety if the hunters came upstairs.

At first the silence made him think they had retreated, but he dared not check the window, frightened that his footsteps would be audible to anyone inside the lobby. Long moments passed before he heard the telltale creaking of a stair below, and realized that one of them at least was on the way.

Initial fear gave way to grim determination. Carlos had been faced with other killing situations in the past, and he had never flinched from shedding blood in settlement of arguments or business deals. Tonight, with his survival threatened, he would do his best with what he had.

Four rounds, three targets. He wasn't an expert marksman, but it could be done.

His enemy had reached the landing, hesitating there before continuing his climb. Another moment, and Aguire heard the risers groan beneath the gunner's weight, remembering each sound the stairs emitted during his ascent. He placed the man halfway down the second flight and closing. In another moment, he would clear the landing on Aguire's floor.

No time to waste. The Cuban crossed the landing in a rush, forsaking silence in his bid for speed. The gunman heard him coming, fired a burst to clear the stairs of opposition, but Aguire caught him by surprise, his pistol thrust between the balusters to drill the startled profile with a shot at point-blank range.

The impact drove his target sideways, before he tumbled backward in a boneless somersault. Momentum carried him across the landing and through the flimsy rail.

Aguire spotted the dead man's submachine gun—a compact Heckler & Koch—lying halfway down the stairs, where he had dropped it as he fell. The weapon might be empty, but with only three rounds in his pistol, Carlos knew it would be worth the risk.

He lunged around the newel post, rushed down the stairs and was bending to retrieve the weapon when a bullet sliced the air beside his face. Recoiling, he beheld a second gunman lurching up the lower flight of stairs, an Ingram in his hands. Raw survival instinct took control. Aguire triggered off a double punch in rapid-fire, one round wasted, the other drilling through his target's shoulder and throwing him off balance.

It wasn't enough. The mafioso snarled and raised his weapon, grinning through his pain as he prepared to make the kill. Aguire spent an endless microsecond aiming, then fired his final round. The gunner's head snapped back on impact, his dead eyes rolling back and crossing as if trying to glimpse the empty socket in his forehead.

Aguire scooped up the submachine gun before his lone surviving adversary could recover his composure. He pointed it, and, uttering a silent prayer, depressed the trigger. If the piece was jammed or empty, the Cuban was dead, and it would all have been in vain.

A dozen rounds exploded from the H&K's muzzle, nearly blinding him with the flash before the magazine ran dry. Downrange his target did a jerky little dance of death, held upright by the bullets ripping through his torso. It suddenly collapsed when the puppet strings were clipped by silence.

Slouched against the banister, Aguire drew a grateful, ragged breath and nearly gagged on smoke. The lobby was in flames. The stove had been toppled from its moorings, spilling red coals and ash across the ancient wooden floor.

Flames were already licking up one wall and blackening the ceiling with their touch.

He ditched the submachine gun's empty magazine and circled wide around the spreading fire to reach the body of his first successful kill. Aguire rummaged through the dead man's pockets, breathing through his mouth to counteract the stench of scorching flesh, and found three extra magazines before he backed away.

Two gunmen lay crumpled near the open back door. Aguire raced passed them and made his way outside, escaping from the flames.

"TEN MINUTES, Max," the G-man said.

Beside him, Leo Turrin pressed his face against the nearest window, wishing for a moon to light the rugged landscape. They were apparently on course, but he couldn't have proved it either way. The land below seemed featureless, unchanging, swaddled in a cloak of midnight shadow. On a bet, Turrin couldn't have proved that they were still in Arizona, much less closing on their target.

Too damned late, he thought. The bastards would have made their kill by now. It might be possible to catch them on the road, exact a measure of revenge, but he remembered he was riding with the FBI. Unless the mobsters tried to waste a Fed, their capture would be handled strictly by the book, complete with courteous Miranda warnings, everything all nice and tidy for the courts.

And how else could it play?

The only men with guts enough to go that extra mile were down there somewhere, in the darkness, being used for target practice while the Bureau flew in circles. Helpless anger made him clench his fists so hard his knuckles cracked.

"We've got a visual," the pilot announced. "Some kind of fire, down there."

Perhaps two miles ahead of them he saw a glowing ember in the darkness. As they closed the gap, they picked out the outline of a building totally engulfed by fire, two stories, maybe three, and burning like a tinderbox.

At a quarter mile out they saw the winking muzzle-flashes of weapons in the street.

"Take it down!" he shouted to the pilot.

"Cancel that," the Phoenix agent snapped. "We're not about to set down in the middle of a firefight, mister." Turning to the men at the controls, he ordered, "Put it on the road, a hundred yards this side of town."

Disgusted, Leo found he couldn't argue with the logic. It would be suicidal to land in the middle of hostile guns without cover. By landing on the road, they had a chance—however slim—of taking Cipriano's gunmen by surprise. If nothing else, they would have sealed the only exit from the town, ensuring that their enemies would have to stand and fight or scatter through the hills on foot.

He eased the four-inch Python from its armpit holster, swinging out the cylinder to double-check the load. Six live ones. He patted down his pockets, drawing meager reassurance from the bulk of half a dozen speed-loaders. If he needed more, he'd just have to pick something up along the way.

One chance was all he asked, for Striker and the kid. One chance to bring them out of it alive.

And failing that, one chance to even up the score.

BOLAN'S ENEMIES WERE COUNTING on a concentrated barrage of fire to drive him back, but the warrior caught them by surprise. He fired a 40 mm fragmentation round, reloading while the explosive was airborne, and rode out the shock wave while advancing under cover of the shrapnel swarm.

They saw him coming and opened up with automatic weapons and a scattergun. But they were dazed and shaken by the grenades, and their aim wasn't as accurate as it should have been. They raised a cloud of dust and filled the air with angry, zinging hornets, two of which grazed Bolan, but he answered their fire before they had a chance to score a killing shot.

The launcher belched again. A high-explosive round impacted on a wall of the refinery, spewing flame and twisted shards of corrugated metal. Bolan saw one gunner decapitated by a flying sheet of steel, his headless body lurching through a drunken semblance of the limbo before it finally collapsed.

Another knelt in dust turned muddy with his comrade's blood, an Uzi spitting in his hands. The Executioner was forced to veer hard left, a stream of parabellum manglers knifing through the air and tracking him before he fired a burst in reply, toppling his adversary in an awkward sprawl of death.

At twenty yards, the three survivors lost their nerve and scattered, one man limping on a leg already torn by shrapnel. Bolan cut both legs from under him and dropped him in his tracks, another short burst marching spurts of dust across his prostrate body.

And that left two.

He switched the M-16 to semiautomatic, brought it to his shoulder and sighted on the nearest runner in a world of dappled firelight. Bolan stroked the trigger once and saw fabric of the gunner's jacket pop on impact, dropping him with the concussion of a solid blow between the shoulder blades.

One left. He was ready when the final shooter turned to make his stand. Bolan triggered two quick rounds, the tumblers drilling flesh and fabric at a range of fifty feet. His target vaulted backward, arms outflung as if awaiting crucifixion.

Then Bolan was up and moving, sprinting past the giant sliding doors of the refinery and homing on a smaller access door around one side. Other than some superficial damage from his high-explosive round, the building was intact—and so should be their van. Once inside, he'd be able to disarm the booby trap and throw the great doors wide, prepare to make a break while there was time. If they were in their places, he'd pick up his brother and Aguire along the way.

If they weren't . . .

The soldier closed his mind to the unthinkable alternatives. The door swung open at his touch, and he stepped through into darkness, briefly framed in silhouette by fire-light from outside.

He barely heard the pistol shot that slammed him to the ground.

## 20

The darkness saved his life. Bolan spent a moment lying on the floor of the refinery, exploring the sensations of his body, working on a damage estimate. His knees and palms were scuffed and raw where he had fallen, and there was a distant pounding in his skull, his pulse reverberating, swelling as if someone had applied a tourniquet around his neck. He felt a sudden rush of nausea and rode it out in silence, keeping both eyes open, studying the darkness. After-images of the explosive muzzle-flash were printed on his corneas in multicolored specks of light.

His left shoulder was numb from the impact of a high-velocity projectile, but Bolan could feel warm blood inside his shirt, the fabric sticking to his ribs. The sticky mess had reached his waist already, so the wound was fairly large and bleeding freely. Spreading dampness on his back told Bolan that the wound was through and through.

How badly was he injured? Rolling slightly to his right, he found that he could move his arm, though with difficulty. Nothing broken, then, and no damage to the major ligaments or tendons. He'd have to stanch the flow of blood, and soon, but there was nothing he could do until he found out who had shot him, where they were and how many of them had him covered in the darkness.

As if in answer to his thoughts, a disembodied voice called out "Blanski? Green? Sing out if you can hear me, man."

Bolan recognized the voice as Felix Pratt's, and sudden anger gave him strength to shift positions, crawl on his belly through the dust until he found substantial cover at the base of a conveyor belt. The M-16 went with him, balanced on his shoulders like a blade of grass across a creeping beetle's back.

"We need to have a pow-wow, man," the agent called. "Let's work this out."

"I hear you, Pratt."

He half expected gunfire, but the outlaw Fed responded verbally, apparently conserving ammunition.

"Blanski. Yeah, I figured it was you. Hey, listen, man . . . you have to understand about just now. I've been a little wired, you know?"

"They tell me selling out can do that to you."

"I don't blame you being pissed, okay? My fault, no question. I just figured you'd be shooting first, and asking questions later. I had to get your attention, understand? So we could talk."

Bolan used the momentary lull to wedge a handkerchief inside his shirt, against the bleeding entrance wound. His face contorted in a grimace as the pain began to show its ugly face.

"That's a hell of an icebreaker, Pratt."

"I got carried away, all right? So, sue me."

"I'd prefer to kill you."

"That's your first reaction, sure. But think about it, Blanski. We can help each other out, here."

"How?"

He needed time to gauge the distance and the angles of the shot, and Pratt would give it to him if they bargained long enough.

"You let me have Aguire, and I call the bad boys off. How's that? You get your life, and what the hell, I'll see what I can do for Green, if Cipriano's people haven't nailed him yet."

"Has anybody ever told you you're a sweetheart?"

"This is strictly business, Blanski. I don't have a thing against you guys. Hell, I don't have a thing against Aguire, but I've got to shut him up. There's too much riding on the line. We're talking major bucks, here. Fucking governments are tied up in this thing."

"You're just a patriot at heart, is that it?"

"Let's just say I'm looking out for number one this time around."

The warrior propped his back against the base of the conveyor belt and fed another round into the launcher, double-checking to be certain that the action on his M-16 hadn't been damaged by his recent fall.

"You're asking me to sell out everything that I believe in, Pratt."

"I'm asking you to live. What's wrong with that? You got some kind of death wish?"

Bolan had begun to work his way along the flank of the machine that gave him cover, careful not to drag himself along and thereby give the move away. He thought he had a fix on Felix, now. A few more yards and he'd let his weapons do the talking.

AGUIRE SAW TWO FIGURES running toward him, moving shadows in the firelight, and he hesitated, wanting to be sure before he opened fire. The clincher was an overcoat the taller man wore, selected more to hide illegal hardware than to offer warmth. He didn't need to see their faces after that. They were the enemy.

He let them close the gap to twenty feet before he squeezed the trigger on his captured submachine gun, ripping the gunners from left to right and back again. The men dropped to the ground, unmoving, lifeless faces turned in silent supplication to the stars.

How many left?

Aguire didn't care. Explosions and a steady stream of automatic fire around the old refinery had changed his plans. The van was out. He had decided it was time to go first-class, and one of the surviving limousines would do just fine... providing he could reach one, slip behind the steering wheel and get the hell away from there before somebody blew his freaking head off.

Nothing to it.

From his shelter, he could see that most of the attacking gunners—those still on their feet—had gathered on the far side of the street. The burned-out point car was a smoking hulk, and three other limos and the tail, a standard four-door, were more or less unscathed by the explosions. For safety's sake, Aguire concentrated on the two cars at the rear of the procession. They were closer than the rest, and neither vehicle showed even superficial damage from the fire.

The doors wouldn't be locked, but getting in was only half the battle. He'd have to count on finding keys in the ignition, since the hostile troops wouldn't allow him time for any fancy work beneath the dashboard. If he blew it, he was dead. Case closed.

And if he made it, then what? He would shake this fucking ghost town for a start, and keep on rolling south until he crossed the border onto friendly soil. From there, he thought, life just might take care of itself.

Aguire chose a moment when the gunners he could see were shifting, turning their attention in the general direction of the old refinery. They hardly concentrated on the east-side buildings, now that most of them were flaming hulks. There could be no threat from that direction, now.

He crossed the deadly open space in one concerted rush, pulse hammering against his eardrums as he slithered to the four-door that was last in line. He grasped the handle on the driver's door, then thought about the dome light and decided not to risk it. He would have to get inside, if there were keys, but opening the door to check each car in line was bound to give him away.

He poked his head above the windowsill, but harsh, reflected flames prevented him from seeing anything inside. Aguire pressed his face against the glass and cupped his hand to serve as blinders, cutting out the glare. He shifted his position twice, to guarantee that he saw everything there was to see.

No keys.

The image of an old TV commercial flashed across his racing mind. A public service spot designed to cut the risk of car theft. Close-up on an average citizen removing his ignition keys while an announcer cautioned. "Don't help a good boy go bad."

But what about the bad boy who was bound to get his ass shot off unless he found himself a ride?

He wormed his way along the line until he reached the nearest limousine. If he could get it started, he'd have to back the monster up a yard or two before he could complete the necessary U-turn. That increased exposure time, but he suspected that the limo would be armored, and he only needed ten or fifteen seconds, after all. No sweat.

Aguire made the stretch again. At first he thought the keys were an illusion, but he closed his eyes for several seconds, opened them again, and felt himself relax inside. In his imagination he could hear flamenco music, taste the enchiladas and frijoles, with a cold *cerveza* on the side.

If only no one saw the dome light . . .

Carlos opened the door and tossed his gun inside. He slid across the driver's seat like he was sneaking up on some sweet thing to cop a feel, then tucked his legs in hastily and eased the door shut behind him. So far, so good. He dared not risk a glance to see if anyone had noticed him. Instead he groped around until he found the pedals with his feet and prodded the accelerator, making sure the engine had sufficient juice to start first time around. He gave the key a twist, and was rewarded by a rumble as the engine came to life, responding instantly. He hauled himself erect and put it in reverse.

All hell broke loose. A dozen guns unloaded on the limousine, flaying paint along the right-hand side. The shockproof glass became milky, veined with tiny cracks like ancient porcelain. He floored the pedal, rammed the four-door back a good six feet and slammed the gear shift into *D*—for "Dead," unless he made his turn tight and clean the first time.

The gunfire seemed to die away as Carlos swung the tank around. A few stray bullets rattled off the trunk, and he was ready to congratulate himself on making good his getaway when volley number two came in on target, plastering the driver's side. Involuntarily, he threw both hands up to protect his face, and in the microsecond of forgetfulness he lost it and felt the limo drift, a front tire rolling up across the wooden sidewalk.

Crushing impact snapped a rotting four-by-four in half and dropped the flaming hotel awning on his windshield, blinding Carlos as he grappled with the steering wheel. He smashed a second upright and a third, two wheels up on the sidewalk. Then the limo's weight broke through the woodwork. He could hear the engine screaming as he pressed the pedal to the floor, but he was going nowhere.

Automatic fire was drumming all along the driver's side, and Aguire had to move before the leaping flames made a connection with the limo's fuel line. There was one way open, and he took it. Pushing through the limo's right-hand door, he stepped out into hell.

JOHNNY MISSED Aguire by perhaps ten seconds as the Cuban made his run to reach the cars. He watched Aguire check the four-door, moving on to try the limousine, and he could feel the mission going up in smoke as Carlos placed his hand upon the door latch. Johnny could have dropped him then, but killing their witness wasn't in the game plan. He'd have to find another way.

The hostile gunners found it for him, laying down such concentrated fire that Carlos lost it on the turn and drove up on the smoking sidewalk, literally bringing down the house, and then some. Johnny had an anxious moment when the tank bogged down, but then he caught a brief glimpse of Aguire wriggling across the seat. A door sprang open, and the Cuban made his break, high-stepping through the flames like something from an old Three Stooges comedy.

The gunners had him spotted, tracking with their weapons, waiting for a clean shot if Aguire managed to escape the furnace. Johnny came up firing, the carbine in his right hand and the mini-Uzi in his left. Two hardmen dropped, then three, and their companions scattered in a search for cover. Johnny chased them with a parting burst and turned in time to see Aguire clear the Oresville funeral pyre.

His hair was smoldering, and there were blisters on his face, but otherwise he seemed remarkably unscathed. Aguire stumbled into Johnny, almost losing his balance, and the younger man hauled him back around the corner, out of sight, as probing rounds began arriving from across the street.

Aguire was unarmed, but Johnny kept him covered all the same. "You had me worried, there," he said, and smiled. "I thought you were about to leave without me."

FROM A HUNDRED YARDS, it sounded like the Battle of the Bulge. Leo Turrin cocked his Colt revolver, making members of the Bureau SWAT team jog to match his pace. He envied them their Kevlar vests and M-16s, but there had been no time for suiting up when they received the hurry call, and he wasn't prepared to sit the action out while strangers did his fighting for him.

If there was any consolation, he derived it from the fact that Bolan and the kid—or one of them, at least—must be alive. The streets of Oresville had become a shooting gallery, and Cipriano's men were pros enough to hold their fire unless they had a target . . . or unless someone was shooting back. If Bolan and his brother had enough fight left to draw that kind of mass response, there still might be a chance to bring them out alive.

They reached the outskirts of the mining camp five minutes after touchdown, their arrival noted by a pair of Cipriano stragglers who had taken up positions in the middle of the street. One guy packed a stubby shotgun, and the other held an Ingram pressed against his chest. They could have saved it with a simple hands-up gesture, but the smoke and fire were in their blood, and they were feeling more or less invincible.

With emphasis on less.

The bozo with the Ingram stopped a round from Leo's Colt and collapsed, dead before he hit the ground. His partner tried to use the shotgun, but a storm of fire from half a dozen automatic rifles lifted him completely off his feet and hurled him ten feet backward, like a scarecrow in a hurricane.

They passed by the bodies, and Turrin scooped up the 12-gauge without a break in stride. Across the street, on Leo's left, a limousine was pulled up on the sidewalk, nearly buried in a pile of flaming rubble. The wooden structures on his right were burning now, disgorging hardmen who had gone to ground inside. The Bureau SWAT team forged ahead, accepting the occasional surrender, shooting fast and accurately in the face of armed resistance.

Turrin didn't bother counting bodies as they made the sweep. His eyes were drawn by movement in the shadows to his left, and he veered off in that direction, leveling his captured shotgun as he closed the gap.

"Okay, you got me," Johnny said, emerging from the smoky shadows with Aguire at his side.

There was a lump in Leo's throat that made his voice sound small and faraway. "Are you all right? Where's Striker?"

"Yes, and I don't know." The kid looked worried. "I haven't seen him since the shooting started. If I had to guess, I'd say he went to get the van."

"Where's that?"

"Down there." He glanced along the crumbing row of structures toward a hulk that stood alone, impervious to heat. "In the refinery."

THE SILENCE WORRIED Pratt. He pictured Blanski creeping through the darkness like some kind of jungle cat, prepared to spring if Felix let his guard down for a fraction of a second. He was wounded—Christ, he had to be—but was it bad enough to kill him? Would it even slow him down?

Pratt cursed the darkness, wishing he could catch a glimpse of Blanski's blood trail. It was possible the guy might be unconscious, even dead by now, but there was too much risk involved for Pratt to leave his precious cover yet, before he knew.

How many men had Blanski killed this week? One more would make no difference to him in the long run, but it would make all the difference in the world to Felix Pratt.

"I can't believe you're taking this so personal," he called to Blanski, buying time and hoping he could make the bastard answer him. "I'm sorry you got suckered into this, believe me. I had orders. If I didn't follow through and ask for help from Justice, someone would've pegged me, sure as shit."

No reply.

Pratt shifted to his left, keeping the van in plain sight, covering the direct approach. Whatever happened, Blanski wasn't driving out of there without a fight.

"You're worried that I'm jerking you around," he said. "Okay, I understand. No problem. Give the word, and I can whistle Cipriano's crew chief in here. He can guarantee safe passage. What the hell, I'll let you hold him while I take Aguire off your hands. You clear on out of here and drop him somewhere when you're feeling safe. How's that?"

The silence was oppressive, stifling. Pratt imagined sounds of movement on his flank and spun in that direction, nearly squeezing off a shot before he caught himself. The bastard couldn't be behind him. He was hit for Christ's sake. Blanski was a soldier with his tit caught in a wringer, not some kind of fucking superman.

"I'm getting tired of talking to myself," Pratt complained.

"So talk to this."

The voice was dangerously close, but Pratt reacted smoothly, pivoting to raise his pistol, sighting down the slide at something that appeared to be a human silhouette. Dead meat, he thought.

And then the world exploded in his face.

THE EXECUTIONER DUCKED BACK and down before the 40 mm round exploded its concussion battering his eardrums. Twisted chunks of steel flew through the air, and he heard a crack of glass that told him some had reached the van. No problem. They could roll without a windshield if they had to. Anything to see the last of Arizona and a town reserved for ghosts.

Was that a scream inside the thunder of the blast? He rose, shook off the transient dizziness produced by blood loss and held the rifle steady as he left his cover, stalking Pratt.

The Fed was slouched against a crusher used in bygone days to pulverize uncounted tons of rock. His scalp was split and streaming blood, hair matted to his forehead. He was dust and grit from head to foot, but there was a fanatical determination in his eyes. An automatic pistol, braced in a two-handed grip, was aimed at Bolan's chest.

"I didn't want to kill you, man," he said.

"You haven't yet."

"That's right." Pratt grinned. "An oversight. I'm playing catch-up."

"Want to tell me why?"

"You've heard the song, man. It's the lure of easy money. What's so hard to understand?"

"Betrayal."

"Right. The fucking Administration betrayed me when they pinned the badge on. I've been scrubbing out their toilet bowl for fifteen years, and I've got squat to show for it. The guys I pop are out in twenty minutes, and they're driving Jaguars, Porsches, limos. I want a taste, that's all."

"Somebody tell you it would be a glamour job?"

"Not even close," Pratt snarled. "I bought the Stars and Stripes routine, right down the line. No fucking lie. I meant to turn these bastards every way but loose, and clean this country up. Can you believe that?"

"So? What happened?"

"It was like a miracle. I looked around one day and found out I'd been blind for thirty years. How's that for a discovery? I found out right and wrong is in the eye of the beholder, and I wanted to be holding money for a change."

"You have to know it's over," Bolan told him.

"Yeah, you got that right . . . but not for me."

A new voice joined the dialogue. "I'd guess again, if I were you."

Pratt fired a shot at Bolan, nearly scoring. The Executioner fell back, his balance failing in a sudden rush of dizziness. He triggered off a burst that missed Pratt cleanly, saw the Fed recoiling and squeezing off two rounds in rapid-fire toward Leo Turrin.

Pratt dodged behind the van and out of sight, heels crunching on the gravel as he ran. Pain lanced through Bolan's shoulder as he struggled to his feet, but in his heart he knew that he could never catch his man before Pratt reached—

The sliding doors.

"Pratt, wait!"

A creak of rusty metal was swallowed by the detonation of a last grenade. Bolan stood his ground while Turrin made a brief inspection of the mess, then moved to join him.

"Sucker makes a flash exit. Can I offer you a lift?"

"Aguire?"

"He's a little singed around the edges, but his vocal cords work fine. He's with the kid."

"Okay."

"Okay? That's it? I bring the cavalry to save Will Kane and tame the West, and this is what I get? I don't suppose that you could spare a 'Howdy, pardner'?"

Bolan smiled and slipped an arm around his good friend's shoulders.

"Nope."

# EPILOGUE

"Officially the deal's not set, but I suspect that Vos will cop a plea." Brognola's voice was heavy with disgust, its flavor undiminished by their poor connection. "It's a coup, of sorts, I guess. The cost of trial was estimated at eleven million dollars. That's conservative, without appeals."

"Will he do time?" Mack Bolan asked.

"Hell, yes. I wouldn't want to guess how much, but twenty-five is probably the average on a deal like this."

"Which puts him out in ten or so with good behavior. Then what?"

"Deportation, just like any other undesirable."

"And then he's back in business."

"It's a possibility," Brognola granted, "but I'm not convinced his heir apparent will be glad to have Vos back. Nobody likes to be the king pro tem, and there's the other thing..."

"What other thing?"

"Well, jeez, it's really an embarrassment, but it turns out we've got this leak in Wonderland, ourselves."

"I'm listening."

"The damndest thing," the big Fed continued. "Somehow the word got out that Vos was singing for his supper. Not just cutting deals, you understand, but giving up his home boys."

"That's a funny kind of leak," the soldier said.

"I thought so, at the time." Brognola hesitated. "Listen, I assume you'll need some R and R?"

"A few days, anyway."

"I've got the perfect place."

"That so?"

"Believe it. I was thinking you might bring the kid along, rest up awhile and put the pieces back together."

"Let me think about it."

"Sure, no hurry. Take your time."

"What happens with Aguire?"

"They released him, four o'clock this morning. Last I heard, he was en route to parts unknown."

"So, tell me, was it all a waste?"

"No way. You took some heavies off the street and closed Pratt's show at the DEA. That has to count for something."

"I suppose."

Fatigue was setting in, and Bolan found that he was losing interest in the conversation. "Can I call you back about that R and R?"

"My time is yours."

"Okay."

And no, he thought it hadn't been a waste. No victory was permanent in everlasting war. You faced the enemy and met the challenges as they arrived, aware that you might have to do it all again tomorrow. And the next day. And the next.

It was the life that Bolan had selected for himself, and he had no illusions left, no dreams of saving mankind from itself. He was assigned to fight a holding action, and if that resulted in some minor victories along the way, so be it. He would have to fight again tomorrow. Or the next day.

In the meantime, though, it might be nice to try some R and R.

U.S. Army Special Forces battle the Viet Cong in a bloody fight for stolen territory.

# VIETNAM: GROUND ZERO™

# *EMPIRE*

# ERIC HELM

U.S. Army Special Forces Captain Mack Gerber and his team drive the NVA troops out of Binh Long Province and determine to push their advantage by taking the war to the enemy's doorstep. That's where they teach the VC the first lesson in how to win a war... move in, take ground and when you can, hit the enemy. Hit them hard.

---

# You don't know what
# NONSTOP
# HIGH-VOLTAGE
# ACTION
## is until
## you've read your
# 4 FREE
# GOLD EAGLE®
# NOVELS

# DON PENDLETON's
# MACK BOLAN®

**The line between good and evil is a tightrope no man should walk. Unless that man is the Executioner.**